Nathaniel viewed Betsy Thompson through narrowed lids. 'You have not been a paid employee for very long, have you?'

A delicate blush coloured those ivory cheeks. 'What makes you say that, my lord?'

The mere fact that she was daring to question him like this was reason enough! 'You do not appear to know your place.'

Those blue eyes sparkled with what he knew without doubt to be a fierce temper. 'My place, my lord?'

Had he ever had another conversation like this one? Nathaniel mused ruefully. Somehow he doubted it. 'I believe it is the usual practice to show a little more respect when addressing one's elders and betters,' he drawled with deliberate provocation; after all, the blue of her eyes did look particularly fine when she was in a temper!

Elizabeth fumed silently. As she was really Lady Elizabeth Copeland, the daughter of an earl, he certainly was not her 'better'. Except she was not Lady Elizabeth Copeland at this moment, was she? And she had no idea if she ever would be again…

Carole Mortimer was born in England, the youngest of three children. She began writing in 1978, and has now written over one hundred and fifty books for Harlequin Mills & Boon®. Carole has six sons: Matthew, Joshua, Timothy, Michael, David and Peter. She says, 'I'm happily married to Peter senior; we're best friends as well as lovers, which is probably the best recipe for a successful relationship. We live in a lovely part of England.'

Previous novels by the same author:

In Mills & Boon® Historical Romance:

THE DUKE'S CINDERELLA BRIDE*
THE RAKE'S INDECENT PROPOSAL*
THE ROGUE'S DISGRACED LADY*
LADY ARABELLA'S SCANDALOUS MARRIAGE*
THE LADY GAMBLES**
THE LADY FORFEITS**

The Notorious St Claires
**The Copeland Sisters*

You've read about *The Notorious St Claires* in Regency times. Now you can read about the new generation in Mills & Boon® Modern™ Romance:

The Scandalous St Claires: Three arrogant aristocrats—ready to be tamed!
JORDAN ST CLAIRE: DARK AND DANGEROUS
THE RELUCTANT DUKE
TAMING THE LAST ST CLAIRE

Carole Mortimer has written a further 150 novels for Modern™ Romance, and in Mills & Boon® Historical *Undone!* eBooks:

AT THE DUKE'S SERVICE
CONVENIENT WIFE, PLEASURED LADY

THE LADY CONFESSES

Carole Mortimer

First published in Great Britain 2011
by Mills & Boon, an imprint of Harlequin (UK) Limited.
Large Print edition 2012
Harlequin (UK) Limited, Eton House, 18-24 Paradise Road, Richmond, Surrey TW9 1SR

© Carole Mortimer 2011

ISBN: 978 0 263 22510 5

Harlequin (UK) policy is to use papers that are natural, renewable and recyclable products and made from wood grown in sustainable forests. The logging and manufacturing process conform to the legal environmental regulations of the country of origin.

Printed and bound in Great Britain
by CPI Antony Rowe, Chippenham, Wiltshire

THE LADY
CONFESSES

To my wonderful parents, with much love.

Chapter One

May, 1817—Hepworth Manor, Devon

'How dare you? Lord Thorne, I insist you release me at once!'

Lord Nathaniel Thorne, Earl of Osbourne, laughed huskily, his lips moving to the ebony-haired beauty's throat. She avoided his kiss by struggling in the confines of his arms, the squirming of those slender curves as she lay across him only succeeding in increasing Nathaniel's pleasure. 'You know you do not mean that, my dear Betsy…'

'I most certainly do mean it!' She raised her head to glare down at him with eyes of an indignant and deep blue surrounded by long dark lashes, her dark curls smelling of lemon and jasmine.

Nathaniel smiled confidently. 'A kiss, Betsy, that is all I ask.'

Her mouth tightened determinedly. 'Very well—you asked for this!'

Nathaniel drew in a swift hissing breath as the woman in his arms deliberately pushed against his chest in an attempt to wrench herself free, a painful reminder that he had broken several of his ribs only nine days previously, which had resulted in his being confined to this bed or another ever since.

A fact this little minx was well aware of!

'And you have been asking for this for days!' Nathaniel's arms tightened instead of releasing her as his teeth nibbled at one delicately scented earlobe.

Her struggles ceased, her expression one of blank bewilderment as she looked down at him. 'I have?'

Well…perhaps he exaggerated the situation slightly. But after four days spent in London being confined to his bed and fussed over by his closest relative—his widowed and childless Aunt Gertrude—followed by another four days of discomfort inside his coach as they'd travelled to his aunt's home on the rugged Devonshire coast, Nathaniel had felt in need of some feminine diversion.

Waking from an afternoon nap to find this delicious morsel tidying his bedchamber, also aware that no matter how painful his injuries were they had also allowed him to escape the tedium of a London Season and his aunt's intention of finding him a wife, Nathaniel had decided to reward himself for that lucky escape by indulging in a little sport with his aunt's young companion.

He grinned up at her unabashedly now. 'You have been fussing about my bedchamber, and latterly myself, for this past half an hour: tidying the room, straightening my bedclothes, plumping my pillows.' During which time he had been gifted with a tempting view of the fullness of her breasts as she leant across him and a tantalising glimpse of the plump, rosy-hued nipples that tipped those delicious breasts!

'It was on your aunt's instruction that I sat with you this afternoon.' The ebony-haired beauty looked down the length of her little nose at him.

'And where is my dear aunt this afternoon?' he enquired.

'She felt rested enough from the journey here to be able to go out in the carriage to reacquaint herself with friends in the area— You are deliberately changing the subject, my lord!' She glared her indignation at him once again.

'Am I?' Nathaniel drawled in amusement.

'Yes,' she maintained firmly. 'And I fail to see any encouragement on my part of this—this attack upon my person, in the mundane actions you have just described.'

Which was not to say that Elizabeth had found those attentions completely disagreeable, if she was being totally honest with herself.

Her last kiss—in fact, her only kiss—had been taken—stolen—from her several months ago by the local vicar's precocious fifteen-year-old son, who unfortunately had a propensity for sweetmeats, cakes, spots and an unbecoming plumpness.

It had only been that expression of lazy satisfaction upon Lord Nathaniel Thorne's handsome face, as he'd pulled her effortlessly into his arms, which had prevented Elizabeth from enjoying the sensation of allowing those sensually sculptured—and no doubt much more experienced—lips to possess her own.

The same satisfaction the earl displayed now as he looked down at the plump swell of her breasts made visible by the low neckline of her blue gown. 'A man can only stand so much temptation, my dear Betsy.'

Elizabeth gave an inner wince at Lord Thorne's continued use of the name bestowed upon her by Mrs Wilson almost two weeks ago, after that lady had declared 'Elizabeth' was far too refined a name for the young lady she intended to employ as a companion.

Nor did Elizabeth appreciate the way in which Lord Thorne continued to ogle her breasts; she had no doubts Mrs Wilson would dismiss 'Betsy' without a single reference if she were to enter the bedchamber and witness this damning scene! 'I am sure I offered you no such temptation, sir,' Elizabeth argued.

He eyed her with amusement. 'Then perhaps it was just wishful thinking on my part?'

'And no doubt I should have expected such be-haviour from someone who is obviously so well acquainted with a man such as Lord Gabriel Faulkner!' she came back tartly.

The challenging insult had the desired effect of obtaining Elizabeth's sudden release as she felt his lordship's arms instantly fall back to his sides, which allowed her to struggle back onto her slippered feet. She pulled her crumpled gown into some semblance of order and tidied the disarray of her hair before venturing a glance at him once again.

The icy haughtiness of the earl's expression and the dangerous glitter in the narrowed brown eyes that looked up at her so coldly warned her instantly that she had said something heinous. She sighed inwardly. Despite his suddenly cold demeanour, Lord Nathaniel Thorne, Earl of Osbourne, had to be one of the handsomest men in England—he was certainly one of the most handsome males Elizabeth had ever set eyes upon. His fashionably styled hair was the colour of ripe corn, those brown eyes a rich mahogany. His face was stunningly masculine, with high cheekbones, a long aristocratic nose and sculpted lips above a square and determined jaw.

As the earl had spent the majority of the last

nine days wearing very little other than a shirt, and occasionally pantaloons, for the comfort of his injuries, Elizabeth could also vouch for the fact that he had very wide shoulders, a muscled chest and stomach sprinkled with a fine dusting of golden hair, lean and powerful hips, and long masculine legs perfectly suited to those thigh-hugging pantaloons and the highly polished Hessians he had worn for their journey into Devonshire.

Until this moment, from the occasions she had witnessed him in conversation with his overly affectionate aunt, she would also have said he was in possession of a tolerably pleasant, if slightly haughty, nature to go along with those rakish good looks.

The dangerous glitter that now lit those dark, almost black, eyes showed another side of him completely. No doubt it was that same ruthlessness of nature that had stood the earl in such good stead during his five years of fighting as an officer in Wellington's army.

'You will explain that last remark, if you please.'

The even pleasantness of Lord Thorne's tone did nothing to soothe Elizabeth's feelings of unease— the sort of unease one might feel, she imagined, as if the good-natured cat sleeping peacefully upon one's hearth suddenly turned feral!

Her chin rose. 'I noted Lord Faulkner's visit to you five days ago.'

'On the day of his return to England after an absence of eight years, yes.' The earl's manner remained frosty.

'I—well—his scandalous past is well-known, surely, my lord?'

'Is it?'

Elizabeth's throat moved convulsively at the dangerous edge she now heard beneath the mildness of the earl's tone. 'The servants were all agog following his visit to you and I couldn't help but overhear what they were saying about him, about the scandal that marred his past.'

'Indeed?' Those blond brows rose. 'And am I to take it you are the type of young lady who enjoys listening to such malicious gossip?'

Elizabeth felt her cheeks flush at this deliberate set-down. 'It can hardly be termed as *malicious* when it also happens to be the truth.'

Nathaniel's previous arousal had completely dissipated during the latter part of this conversation.

'How old would you have been eight years ago?' he asked.

'I do not see—'

'I asked how old?' he demanded harshly.

She blinked. 'I believe I would have been but eleven years old, sir.'

Nathaniel nodded. 'And no doubt you resided in Cambridgeshire at that time?'

A perplexed frown marred her creamy brow. 'I have never resided in Cambridgeshire, my lord.'

'Then how can you, a mere child of eleven years, who did not even reside in Cambridgeshire at the time of this supposed scandal, possibly speak with any authority as to what is or is not true with regard to Lord Faulkner's past?' Nathaniel looked at her implacably as he sat up against the pillows she had recently plumped.

A delicate blush darkened her creamy cheeks, although that stubborn little chin remained high. 'It appears to be public knowledge that Lord Faulkner was once involved in the seduction of an innocent young girl.'

Nathaniel was well aware of the gossip that had circulated amongst the *ton* eight years ago with regard to Gabriel Faulkner, one of his two closest friends. He had not, however, been aware that very same gossip was once again in circulation upon Gabriel's return from the Continent to take up his duties as the new Earl of Westbourne. Duties which Gabriel had calmly stated would include making an offer of marriage to one or other of his wards, the three young Lady Copelands, who were the previous earl's daughters. Never having met any of the sisters, Gabriel had apparently not stated a preference as to which of them it should be.

Damn it, Nathaniel should have been in London to at least stand at his friend's side when Gabriel announced his presence back in society, and not languishing in Devon nursing broken ribs. Not that Nathaniel believed Gabriel would need, or indeed appreciate, anyone's support, tacit or otherwise; during his eight long years of exile Gabriel Faulkner had become one of the proudest and most arrogant men the English *ton* was ever likely to meet!

Still, if nothing else, he would have liked to have been present to see some of those well-bred faces when Gabriel took up his rightful place in society. Instead of which Nathaniel had left London for

Devon almost immediately upon Gabriel's arrival back in town, his only means of entertainment being this outspoken young lady who was his aunt's companion.

'Indeed?' he drawled icily.

Elizabeth pursed her delectable mouth. 'You are aware of a different version of events, perhaps?'

Nathaniel's gaze swept over her contemptuously before he replied in a disdainful voice. 'If I am, then I assure you I am not inclined to share it with you.'

He meant to be insulting, and he had succeeded, causing the colour to drain from her cheeks as she felt herself suitably chastened for having seriously overstepped the bounds of her current role of companion.

For it was a role. And one which did not sit altogether comfortably upon the slender shoulders of a young woman who, until two and a half weeks ago, had enjoyed the title of Lady Elizabeth Copeland, the youngest daughter of the previous, and now deceased, Earl of Westbourne.

It was the very reason Elizabeth had taken such an interest in acquainting herself with the gossip concerning Lord Gabriel Faulkner, the man who had not only become the new Earl of Westbourne on the death of Elizabeth's own father almost seven months ago, but also guardian to Elizabeth and her two sisters.

All three of the Copeland sisters had been badly shaken by their father's sudden demise and equally alarmed on learning that, their two cousins having died at the Battle of Waterloo, the title of earl had now passed to a man who was a second or third cousin of their father's. That man was Gabriel Faulkner. A man none of the sisters had ever met. A man, moreover, who was rumoured to have behaved so disgracefully eight years ago that society had chosen to banish him, and his own family had disowned him.

Having lived all of their lives at their father's country estate, Diana, Caroline and Elizabeth had never been made privy to the details of that scandal and, despite having made discreet enquiries upon learning he was now their guardian, none of them had been able to ascertain the exact nature of that disgrace. The only information any of them had been able to garner on the man at the time—it had been left to the recent gossip below stairs at Mrs Wilson's home to fill in the exact nature of that scandal—was his banishment to the Continent eight years ago, and that he had been an officer in Wellington's army for five years, before residing in Venice these past two years.

Lord Faulkner, it seemed, had not been in any hurry to return to England and take up his duties as the Earl of Westbourne, or his guardianship of the Copeland sisters, none of them having so much as set eyes upon him when they had received a letter from that so-called gentleman some months after their father's death, in which he had made an offer of marriage to whichever of the three Copeland sisters would have him!

No doubt, with the scandal of their own mother having abandoned her husband and three young daughters ten years ago—Harriet Copeland had fled Shoreley Park for London and the arms of her young lover, then been shot by that young lover only months later before he had then turned the pistol upon himself—Lord Faulkner had perhaps believed that one of the Copeland sisters would be so desperate for marriage they would be happy to accept an offer from a man equally as shrouded in scandal.

He had been wrong.

Her sister Caroline's answer to that offer had been to run away from her home and sisters three weeks ago. Equally as horrified at the prospect of such a marriage, Elizabeth had followed her sister's example only days later.

Having made her escape from the possibility of that unwanted marriage, and subsequently managing to find employment in London with Mrs Wilson, Elizabeth had then been shocked to her core when Gabriel Faulkner had arrived at that lady's house only days ago to visit Mrs Wilson's injured nephew, Lord Nathaniel Thorne, the two men having apparently been best friends for some years!

Admittedly the new Earl of Westbourne had proved to be exceedingly handsome, more so than Elizabeth or her two sisters could ever have guessed. But those arrogantly dark and fashionable good looks did nothing to lessen the shock she had felt upon hearing the details of that gentleman's past scandal as the servants gossiped below stairs whilst he visited with Lord Thorne upstairs…

Only the fact that the whole of Mrs Wilson's household was to be immediately removed to

Devonshire, well away from London—and Lord Faulkner!—had prevented Elizabeth from fleeing into the night for the second time in as many weeks.

'It was not my intention to insult Lord Faulkner,' she dismissed coolly now, knowing from Mrs Wilson that Lord Faulkner and that lady's nephew had been friends from their school-days; a fact Elizabeth should perhaps have realised sooner, considering that Mrs Wilson had also informed her shortly after she had taken employment with that lady of her nephew's recent return from visiting with a friend in Venice!

'Then perhaps the insult was directed at me?' Nathaniel drawled softly.

She had meant to insult him, Elizabeth acknowledged ruefully. She could not imagine why any gentleman of the *ton* would wish to remain friends with a man as dissolute and rakish as Gabriel Faulkner was reputed to be. Unless that gentleman was equally as disreputable himself?

A fact perhaps borne out by Lord Thorne having received his present injuries in what sounded distinctly like a drunken brawl, as well as his recent unwanted advances towards her? 'I apologise if that was your impression, my lord,' she said stiffly. 'Although, in my defence, I do believe you offered me just provocation,' she could not resist adding.

Nathaniel regarded her beneath hooded lids. At a little over five feet tall, her slender figure shown to advantage in the plain blue gown, with her ebony curls arranged in a simple if fashionable style, and her face one of delicate beauty—fine dark brows, deep blue eyes, a tiny nose above a perfect bow of a mouth—Miss Betsy Thompson somehow did not have the looks, or indeed the voice, of a paid companion to a lady of wealth and quality.

And how would he know what one of those should look like? Nathaniel mused self-derisively.

Yes, Miss Betsy Thompson was in possession of a rare and tempting beauty, and the refinement of her voice spoke of an education, but for all Nathaniel knew of such things that could merely be because she was the daughter of an impoverished gentleman or clergyman, in need of employment to support herself until some equally impoverished young gentleman took her as his wife, before then producing a houseful of even more impoverished children to continue the cycle!

Incarcerated in Devon, and so robbed of rakish entertainment as well as all news of London society—his aunt had refused to even allow Nathaniel to read the newspapers this past eight days in case he 'became overset' by anything printed in them!—Nathaniel had only thought to provide himself with a diversion from his increasing boredom when he'd attempted to kiss his aunt's young companion. Certainly he had not intended engaging in a verbal exchange during which this outspoken young woman had dared to insult one of his closest and dearest friends.

He had no doubts that Gabriel would have simply laughed off such an insult, used as he was to the sideways glances of the gentlemen of the *ton* and the gossip behind the raised fans of their wives and daughters—along with their surreptitious and hypocritical lust for his dark and dangerous good looks. Nathaniel had never been able to dismiss those slights to his friend so easily, and never ceased to feel enraged by them.

Especially as he knew that gossip to be wholly untrue.

His mouth thinned now as he looked at Betsy Thompson beneath hooded lids. 'The apology alone would have sufficed,' he rasped. 'Now, is there not some other service which you need to be busy performing for my aunt? Surely you have completed this one to the best of your ability.'

And been found wanting, Elizabeth acknowledged irritably, very aware that the laughingly flirtatious man who had tried to kiss her a few minutes ago had completely disappeared to be replaced by a gentleman who was now every inch the wealthy and powerful Earl of Osbourne, with vast estates in Kent and Suffolk, as well as a beautiful town house in London.

She gave a brief inclination of her head. 'I believe it is time for Hector's afternoon walk.'

'Ah, yes.' The earl gave a hard, mocking smile. 'I have noticed, with my aunt's cousin Letitia already in residence, you are more companion to my aunt's dog than to my aunt herself.'

Yet another insult, no matter how smoothly it was delivered, Elizabeth recognised with a frown. Unfortunately, experience had shown her that with no references it was almost impossible to find employment in London. Indeed, Elizabeth had only succeeded in securing her present position in Mrs Wilson's household because of her heroic rescue of that lady's pampered and much-loved Scottish Terrier, after he had slipped his lead in a London park one afternoon and run amok.

As such, Elizabeth needed to maintain her employment with Mrs Wilson if she did not wish to return to Shoreley Park and that dubious offer of marriage from Lord Faulkner. A fate Elizabeth still considered—despite now knowing of that gentleman's roguish good looks—to be more painful than death itself.

Lord Faulkner could not know it, but Elizabeth was actually doing him a great service by not accepting his proposal; she was the daughter most likened to her mother in looks, and as such had always been viewed with suspicion by neighbouring matrons of sons of marriageable age, in the fear, no doubt, that she might be like her mother in other ways…

Her chin rose proudly. 'I really do sincerely apologise for any offence I may have given, my lord.'

Somehow Nathaniel doubted that very much. He had easily seen the battle taking place within

Miss Betsy Thompson's beautiful head as she wrestled with the knowledge that she considered herself to be in the right of it, whilst at the same time totally aware that she was speaking to the favourite nephew—in fact, the only nephew—of her employer.

Indeed, that inner battle had been so transparent he might have laughed aloud if he were not still feeling so disgruntled with her on Gabriel's behalf.

After all, he had earlier attempted to steal a kiss from this young woman for his own enjoyment. And the fact that Nathaniel had received his injuries from paid thugs as he'd left a gambling club owned by yet another of his disreputable friends was not in the least flattering to his own reputation…

He viewed Betsy Thompson through narrowed lids. 'You have not been a paid employee for very long, have you?'

A delicate blush coloured those ivory cheeks. 'What makes you say that, my lord?'

The mere fact that she was daring to question him like this, an earl and the nephew of her employer, was reason enough! 'You do not appear to know your place.'

Those blue eyes sparkled with what he knew without doubt to be a fierce temper. 'My place, my lord?'

Had he ever had another conversation like this one? Nathaniel mused ruefully. Somehow he doubted it. 'I believe it is the usual practice to show a little more…respect, when addressing one's elders and betters,' he drawled with deliberate provocation; after all, the blue of this young lady's eyes did look particularly fine when she was in a temper!

Considering Nathaniel Thorne was a mere eight, or possibly nine years, her senior, Elizabeth did not consider him in the least 'her elder'. And as Lady Elizabeth Copeland, the daughter of an earl, neither was he 'her better'.

Except she was not Lady Elizabeth Copeland at this moment in time, was she? And she had no idea when she would become so again. Or, indeed, if she ever would…

Leaving her home had been a purely impulsive act on her part, a response to Caroline's identical response to Lord Faulkner's proposal two days earlier. Those two days had been spent in a fruitless search of the local area for the missing Caroline and had resulted in the other two sisters assuming that she had likely fled all the way to London.

London…

All three of the Copeland girls had always wished for, and repeatedly been denied by their father, so much as a single visit to England's capital, let alone the Season that might have secured a marriage for any or all of them, on the basis, no doubt, that Marcus Copeland had considered the temptations to be found there to be responsible for his wife's abandonment of her family.

Whatever his rationale for the decision, Caroline and Elizabeth especially had longed to experience some of those 'temptations' for themselves; Diana, the eldest sister at one and twenty, had always been the more reserved of the three, taking her responsibilities as mistress of Shoreley Park and surrogate mother to her two younger sisters very seriously indeed.

And so first Caroline, and then Elizabeth, had left the only home they had ever known for the excitement that London represented. Elizabeth could not speak for Caroline, of course, having had neither sight nor word of her sister's whereabouts since reaching the city, but she had quickly realised that the excitements of town only applied to the wealthy and titled members of London society, and that the paid companion she had been forced by circumstances to become was merely a lowly employee at the mercy of the whims and fancies of her employer, with very few glimpses of the world she had so longed to inhabit.

Elizabeth had also had plenty of time in which to realise how much she missed her sisters, how alone she felt without the two of them to laugh and gossip with. To realise how, being the youngest sister, Caroline and Diana had been her companions for all of her nineteen years.

Indeed, Elizabeth had missed them so much that, on the day she had effected the recapture of Hector after he had made his escape from Mrs Wilson in the park, she had briefly, foolishly, thought she had seen Caroline seated as a passenger of the most fashionable coach travelling in the park that day.

It was nonsense, of course, a ridiculous notion only confirmed by Elizabeth's glimpse of the gentleman easily controlling the pair of perfect but highly strung greys in front of that gleaming carriage. An aristocratic gentleman whose arrogant good looks were made to look dangerous by the scar that ran down the left side of his face. The rakish sort of gentleman none of the Copeland sisters had ever, or would ever, be acquainted with.

Nevertheless, that brief encounter had served to emphasise how deeply she wished to be with her sisters again. Unfortunately, Elizabeth—and no doubt Caroline, too—had realised since arriving in London that, when she'd left Hampshire so suddenly she had given no consideration as to how she was ever to learn when or if Lord Faulkner had quit Shoreley Park, thereby making it safe for her to return to her home.

Until a remedy to that situation occurred to her, it was very necessary that she retain her current position in Mrs Wilson's household—something she would not be able to do if she ran foul of that lady's much-loved nephew. 'I apologise again, my lord, for any—any misunderstandings,' she said stiffly, 'but I am sure that your aunt will be pleased to hear how much better you are feeling this afternoon.'

'Indeed?' Nathaniel eyed her closely. 'And what else do you intend telling my dear aunt about this afternoon?'

She looked pained at the accusation in his tone. 'Why, nothing else, my lord.'

'You do not consider I owe you an apology for my own behaviour just now?' He looked across at her shrewdly.

Delicate colour warmed her cheeks as she avoided meeting his gaze. 'I would much rather forget the incident ever happened, my lord.' She looked slightly flustered. 'Now, if you will excuse me, Hector will be waiting for his walk.' She swept him a polite curtsy.

Nathaniel watched beneath hooded lids as Betsy left his bedchamber, knowing a slight disappointment in her response to his deliberate challenge; instead of a return of that temper he had been expecting—hoping for—the light of battle had seemed to fade from those clear blue eyes as she once again assumed the mantle of the young and demure companion of his aunt's dog.

Assumed, because Nathaniel had serious doubts that Miss Betsy Thompson had ever been born to such a subservient role...

Chapter Two

'I have decided, as you are obviously feeling so much better—' Mrs Wilson bestowed a warm smile of approval upon her nephew as he stood somewhat stiffly beside the fireplace in the drawing room prior to dinner '—to arrange a small dinner party. For…three days hence, I believe,' she announced with satisfaction.

'Aunt—'

'As I said, it will be but a small group. Only twenty or so of my closest neighbours,' she added persuasively.

Elizabeth, having entered the drawing room in time to hear this announcement, looked at Nathaniel beneath lowered lashes as she curtsied before moving to the back of the room to sit demurely on the chaise beside Letitia Grant, feeling slightly breathless at how handsome the earl looked in his black evening clothes and snowy white linen, the candlelight casting a golden sheen over his fashionably styled hair and lightly tanned features.

She had instantly seen how his warm mahogany eyes had briefly flared with alarm at his aunt's announcement, before that emotion was as quickly masked by a look of cool uninterest. Elizabeth easily guessed the reason for that mask!

Mrs Wilson, a widowed and still attractive lady in her early-forties, had made it clear she had no interest in remarrying herself, instead preferring to turn her considerable attention to finding her nephew a countess. Indeed, she had already been full of the news, when she'd returned in her carriage earlier, that there were at least three young and attractive ladies in the neighbourhood who were up to the task and might meet her nephew's critical approval.

She considered, she had stated firmly, that at the age of eight and twenty it was past time that her nephew gave up his bachelor life and produced an heir; as he had no mother to guide him, it was her duty to see the woman he chose as his countess and mother of his children was entirely suitable for that role, whether or not the earl had any inclinations in that direction himself.

Nathaniel Thorne's now guarded expression would seem to indicate that he most certainly did not!

After their earlier altercation, Elizabeth could not help but feel a little inward pleasure at the earl's obvious discomfort; Mrs Wilson, once set on a course of action, was rarely, if ever, thwarted. Elizabeth's own presence here was proof of that!

Having secured Hector in the park that day, it had been a simple enough task for Elizabeth to then locate his mistress; she had so obviously been the lady remonstrating most passionately with one of her coachmen as she strode determinedly across the park towards where Elizabeth held the runaway dog in her arms.

The reunion between dog and mistress had brought an emotional tear to Elizabeth's eyes— for a completely different reason than that of the poor coachman, who stood beside his mistress rubbing his ringing ears!

Once reassured of her 'darling Hector's' well-being, Mrs Wilson had turned her narrow-eyed attention to his rescuer, insisting that Elizabeth must return home in her carriage with her and receive more thanks over a cup of tea. Once inside the opulence of that comfortable house, Mrs Wilson had demanded to know what a young lady such as Elizabeth had been doing walking alone in the park at all. Upon hearing that she was merely crossing the park to cheer herself after failing to secure a position in a haberdashery, that lady had insisted that she must come and work for her, that her 'darling Hector' had obviously taken such a liking to her there could be no other course of action.

Before Elizabeth had been able to draw a breath, it seemed, she had found herself, and the few belongings she had brought to London with her, moved into Mrs Wilson's home and herself charged with the care of the mischievous and totally lovable Hector.

If Mrs Wilson had now decided to turn that considerable attention to finding her nephew a suitable wife, then she had no doubts that lady would succeed—whether the Earl of Osbourne wished it or not!

'—it is fortuitous that the Millers have not gone up to town for the Season this year, as they are still in mourning following Lord Miller's demise,' Elizabeth heard Mrs Wilson state with satisfaction as her attention returned to that lady's conversation with her nephew.

'I doubt that Lord Miller sees it as being in the least fortuitous!' the earl drawled drily.

Elizabeth repressed another smile, only for the humour on her face to fade completely as she looked up and found herself the focus of Lord Thorne's intent gaze.

She looked quickly away again to engage the elderly Letitia Grant in conversation, all the time aware that the rakishly handsome earl continued to observe her broodingly...

Nathaniel was only half listening to the twittering of his aunt as she continued to list the guests she proposed inviting to her dinner party on Saturday evening, having absolutely no interest in any of his aunt's guests, least of all the two Miss Millers and their mother, or Miss Penelope Rutledge, the equally eligible daughter of the local magistrate, Viscount Rutledge.

His aunt would no doubt be outraged to learn the only female that in the least piqued Nathaniel's interest at this moment in time was now seated on the chaise at the back of the drawing room and engaged in muted conversation with Letitia Grant—and that his intentions towards Betsy earlier this afternoon had been entirely dishonourable!

Nathaniel had been aware of that young woman's presence the moment she slipped quietly into the room to curtsy politely before joining Letitia on the chaise, the simply styled cream gown she wore a perfect foil for those ebony curls that clustered at her crown and framed the ivory oval of her face, its high waist and low neckline leaving bare her throat and the tops of the breasts Nathaniel had so admired earlier this afternoon.

Miss Betsy Thompson, Nathaniel had decided after she'd left his bedchamber earlier, was a contradiction that warranted further investigation. Discreet enquiries from Letitia Grant earlier had revealed that as far as she was aware his aunt knew absolutely nothing about the young lady she had so recently employed, other than that Hector obviously adored her—which in Aunt Gertrude's eyes appeared to be reference enough!

Nathaniel had a far different opinion—for all any of them knew Betsy could be a runaway wife avoiding detection by her aggrieved husband, or, worse, she might be a felon hiding from justice!

At least, those were the excuses Nathaniel had given himself for his lingering interest in that young lady…

'—are you even listening to me, Osbourne?' his aunt now snapped as she obviously became aware of his inattentiveness.

Nathaniel turned his lazy gaze onto his slightly irate aunt. 'You were extolling the virtues of Miss Rutledge, I believe,' he drawled uninterestedly. 'How accomplished she is upon the piano. That you and others consider her needlework and painting to be of a particularly high standard. That she has acted as competent and gracious mistress of the Viscount's home since her mother's death three years ago. How—'

'I trust you are not mocking me, Osbourne?' His prettily plump, and totally well-meaning, aunt prompted severely.

'I assure you, Aunt Gertrude, that a man as in need of his dinner as I rarely feels the inclination to mock.' Nathaniel presented his arm to his aunt as the butler appeared in the doorway and announced that dinner was now ready to be served.

Elizabeth could not help but appreciate how smoothly the earl had extricated himself from the awkwardness of that conversation as she fell into step beside Letitia to follow Nathaniel Thorne and his aunt through to the small family dining room. Many fashionable young gentlemen—in need of their dinner or otherwise!—would have dealt most severely with Mrs Wilson for being so blatant in their matchmaking. It was a testament of the genuine affection in which Lord Thorne held his aunt that he had chosen not to do so.

Although this did not in any way excuse the set-down he had given Elizabeth earlier in regard to what she considered her perfectly justified outspokenness concerning the scandalous behaviour of his friend, Lord Faulkner.

Or the over-familiar behaviour she had suffered at his hands prior to that…

Which was perhaps not the memory Elizabeth should have been dwelling upon as the earl, having seen to the seating of his aunt and Letitia Grant, now loomed over her attentively as he stood behind her own chair.

'Dare I hope that blush is on my behalf, Betsy?' he murmured, the warmth of his breath caressing the dark curls at Elizabeth's nape as he bent forwards to place her chair beneath her.

Elizabeth tensed briefly before continuing to sit, presenting her stiffly disapproving back and shoulders to the earl as she did so. She couldn't help feeling a little chagrined that he had been correct in his assumption as to the direction of her wayward thoughts! She had been too shocked earlier by the suddenness of this man's advances to completely gauge her own reaction to being held in his arms as he had attempted to kiss her.

Unfortunately, that had not proved to be the case as Elizabeth had later walked Hector in the peace and quiet of the woods adjoining Hepworth Manor... Her thoughts had then returned again and again to the hard warmth of Nathaniel Thorne's body as he'd held her against his muscled chest, the thrill of briefly feeling his lips against hers and the shiver of pleasure that had coursed through her as those same lips travelled the length of her throat. As to the lascivious way in which he had eyed the swell of her breasts, she tingled all over just thinking about it.

The life Elizabeth had led at Shoreley Park had

been a sheltered one, with very few young men living in the area, and hardly any of those considered by Marcus Copeland to be suitable company for his three young daughters. The exception to that rule had been Malcolm Castle, the son of the local squire, but as he had always shown a preference for her sister Diana's company from childhood, that particular avenue of flirtation had been closed to Elizabeth and Caroline.

Even if it had not, Nathaniel Thorne's earlier familiarity could not possibly be called merely flirtatious! The liberties he had attempted to take had implied that he considered Elizabeth as being no more respectable than a—than a woman with whom he had paid to spend the night! No doubt her lowly position in his aunt's household was responsible for that familiarity, but even so...

'I would be as inclined to blush at thoughts of a viper as you, my lord.' Elizabeth muttered back as she turned to smile up at him for the benefit of the watching Mrs Wilson and Letitia, as if she were thanking the earl for his attentiveness rather than insulting him.

Nathaniel's own smile was one of wolfish appreciation for her spirited reply as he slowly straightened before taking his own seat at the head of the table, a tacit signal for the first course to be served and his aunt to begin another diatribe as to the virtues of the local gentry and their marriageable daughters who were to be invited to her forthcoming dinner party.

It was a monologue that Nathaniel again listened to with only half an ear as he instead observed both the refinement of Betsy's table manners and the way in which she graciously engaged the less-than-vivacious Letitia in conversation as the two women sat facing each other across the dinner table. Letitia was, of course, the perfect companion for his Aunt Gertrude, being of too agreeable and insubstantial a disposition to ever oppose her more forceful cousin. But being neither of those things, it was to Betsy's credit that she troubled herself to engage the older woman in conversation.

Nathaniel was so entertained by her efforts to avoid so much as a glance in his direction—and, of course, by the excellence of the dinner provided by his aunt's cook—that he even managed to forget the discomfort of his broken ribs for several hours.

* * *

'I believe it is time for Hector's last walk before bedtime, Betsy,' his aunt finally announced with an affectionate glance across the room to the fire-place beside which that much-loved pet lay in his basket in both warmth and resplendent comfort.

The ladies were about to go to the drawing room in order to drink tea together before retiring for the night, leaving Nathaniel at the table to enjoy the after-dinner cigar and brandy that had been denied him this past week and a half, his aunt having an aversion to anyone smoking cigars in her bedchambers. Reason enough, indeed, for Nathaniel to hasten his recovery!

He had risen politely to his feet as the ladies stood up to leave, but now gave a frowning glance out of the dining-room window. 'Is that altogether safe for Miss Thompson, Aunt Gertrude?' The moonlit darkness on the other side of that window testified as to the lateness of the hour.

'I have never been afraid of venturing out into the dark, my lord,' Elizabeth assured him sharply.

He ignored her protest to continue his conversation with his aunt. 'Perhaps it would be better if one of the footmen attended to Hector's needs last thing at night, Aunt?'

Mrs Wilson looked momentarily disconcerted. 'Betsy has not complained…'

Deep brown eyes swept fleetingly over Elizabeth before Nathaniel Thorne's addressed his aunt a third time. 'Miss Thompson does not appear to me to be the type of young lady to make complaints, my dear aunt,' he pointed out with a wicked little smile.

Elizabeth felt the warmth of the blush that coloured her cheeks at his obvious reference to the fact that she had so far kept her word to make no complaint to his aunt concerning his own forward behaviour earlier today. Nor did she have any intention of breaking that word; given the lowliness of her position in Mrs Wilson's household, the older woman was as likely to blame Elizabeth for the earl's forwardness as she was her much-loved nephew!

'Miss Thompson might encounter any number of…dangerous individuals, roaming about the Devonshire countryside at this time of the night,' the earl added drily.

As far as Elizabeth was concerned the only

'dangerous individual' she might encounter here at night—or any other time—was standing in this very room with her! Nor did she appreciate the earl's interference in a matter that was none of his business; Elizabeth had so far enjoyed the solitude of her late-night walks with Hector, both in London and here. Moreover, she resented any implication from Lord Thorne that she was some lily-livered miss too afraid to go out into the dark of the night.

'This is Devonshire, Osbourne, not London.' Mrs Wilson obviously shared her scepticism.

'Even so…'

'I am sure I shall be perfectly safe, Lord Thorne.' Elizabeth managed to keep her tone suitably demure—at the same time glaring her displeasure at him from beneath lowered lashes.

A glare he met by raising one mocking brow. 'Perhaps I should stroll outside with Miss Thompson, Aunt?' he suggested mildly. 'I can as easily smoke my cigar out there as in here.'

'I could always accompany Betsy,' Letitia offered with obvious nervousness.

'I fear that would only place you both in danger, dear Letitia,' the earl dismissed kindly.

Mrs Wilson frowned her concern. 'You seriously think there is danger in Betsy going outside alone at night here?'

Lord Thorne shrugged those broad shoulders. 'I doubt the smuggling in the area is any less rife now than it has been for several years past.'

Elizabeth had been rendered uncharacteristically dumbstruck by the earl's suggestion that he accompany her on her walk outside, but now she gaped at him. 'Smuggling?'

Deep brown eyes regarded her with mocking amusement as he gave an inclination of his head. 'Still a very lucrative, though totally illegal trade in Devonshire, I believe. One that I am sure the gentlemen involved would prefer not to be interrupted by a young woman walking her dog.'

'I had not thought of that.' Mrs Wilson nodded briskly. 'Perhaps you should accompany Betsy, Osbourne…'

'Betsy' could have screamed with the frustration of being discussed as if she had no will or mind of her own. Which, of course, as Betsy Thompson, companion to Mrs Wilson's pampered and much-loved dog, she did not…

'Unless Betsy believes it improper to venture outside alone with me?' the earl asked huskily.

Elizabeth's mouth tightened as she looked up into his rakishly handsome face, knowing that he was certainly not above mocking her now that his appetite for his dinner had been satisfied. 'You—'

'That is as ridiculous as the suggestion that the maid should not tidy your bedchamber, Osbourne,' Mrs Wilson dismissed impatiently.

Placing Elizabeth firmly in the position of lowly servant, a role she was finding it increasingly difficult to maintain when in the company of the rapidly recovering Nathaniel Thorne...

'How long has it been since you acquired the name of Betsy?'

The young lady striding determinedly at Nathaniel's side on the moonlit pathway that ran along the cliff-top now stumbled slightly at the unexpectedness of his question.

That she was furious at his intervention earlier was obvious, considering the frosty silence with which she had treated him since her return from collecting her black-velvet pelisse from her bedchamber. She had taken Hector's leash from the waiting footman and stalked outside without so much as a glance in Nathaniel's direction.

He had followed at a more leisurely pace, enjoying his cigar at least as he did so, his much longer strides enabling him to reach her side within seconds. From her continued silence, and the subsequent glance down at her resolutely averted features as they walked along side by side, he realised she had no intention of even acknowledging his presence unless provoked into doing so.

Which, unless Nathaniel was mistaken, he had effectively just done…

She looked up at him sharply in the moonlight. 'What do you mean?'

It was a clear spring evening, warm enough that Nathaniel had no need of an outer coat, with not a cloud to mask the brightness of the stars shining in the velvet-black sky overhead. Probably not the ideal night for smugglers to be abroad; Nathaniel believed they usually preferred a few clouds to cover the light of the moon and so mask their movements.

In which case, it should have been pleasant to walk in the moonlight with a young and desirable woman and the happy little white dog trotting ahead of them. Instead it had so far been a silent battle of wills between them.

He sighed. 'I have noticed that you seem to flinch whenever my aunt—or indeed, anyone else—addresses you as such.'

'You are mistaken, my lord—'

'I think not,' he interrupted firmly; his patience with this young woman was not limitless.

Elizabeth glanced up at him warily, knowing that she had seriously underestimated him, that his insight now showed that there was far more to this gentleman than the affectionate nephew he was to Mrs Wilson, or the flirtatious friend of the scandalous Lord Faulkner who had attempted to make love to her this afternoon.

'Your lengthy silence betrays your need to think of a suitable explanation for your behaviour,' Nathaniel said quietly.

She drew in a determined breath. 'You need only question your aunt to receive that explanation, my lord,' she replied lightly as she continued to walk along the narrow path.

'Which, for obvious reasons, I am not about to do!'

No, it really would not do for the Earl of Osbourne to show such an interest in the young lady who was companion to his aunt's dog! 'I assure you there is no mystery to the explanation, my lord; Mrs Wilson did not consider my full name of Elizabeth to be suitable for a servant in her household,' she explained airily.

So her name was really Elizabeth, Nathaniel mused as he continued to stroll along at her side. Yes, he believed the elegance of that name suited this contradictory young woman far better than Betsy. 'Then in future I shall call you Elizabeth—'

'I wish you would not!' She had come to another halt in her agitation. 'I—your aunt would not like it,' she added with far less vehemence.

'I do not recall saying that I intended asking my aunt's permission,' Nathaniel said drily.

Elizabeth frowned her displeasure. 'You have not asked my permission, either, my lord—for if you had I should certainly have refused it.'

'Perhaps when we are alone together like this—'

'No, my lord!'

He shrugged. 'I call Letitia by her given name.'

'Because the two of you are related by marriage,' she reasoned primly. 'Whereas I am merely—'

'—the young lady I kissed earlier today,' Nathaniel completed her sentence huskily.

Deep blue eyes flashed up at him in the moonlight as she came to another halt on the pathway. 'That you attempted to kiss, Lord Thorne! An attempt I believe I successfully routed,' she added with smug satisfaction.

Her satisfaction alone would have been enough to prick Nathaniel's masculine pride; that obvious air of smugness was taking things altogether too far!

Something that Elizabeth also became aware of as she began to back away from him warily. 'You really cannot go around taking advantage of the young ladies who work in your aunt's household, sir.'

'There is only one young lady in my aunt's household in whom I have the least interest in taking advantage of, my dear Elizabeth,' Nathaniel murmured as he threw away the remains of his cigar to slowly follow her.

'I am not your dear anything!' she protested with righteous indignation.

'Not yet, no,' he acknowledged throatily.

'Not ever!' Her dark curls bounced in the moonlight. 'My lord, you really cannot—'

'Oh, but I really can.' Nathaniel nodded with certainty.

'You—oh!' This second protest came to an abrupt halt as he pulled her effortlessly into his arms to hold her tightly against him.

'And, my dear Elizabeth, this time we will have no unfair advantage taken of my bruised ribs.' He grinned down at her wolfishly before his head lowered and he claimed her lips with his own.

Elizabeth had not been mistaken earlier; it was both enthralment and pleasure she felt at having Nathaniel Thorne's experienced lips upon her own. A warm, tingling pleasure began at her breasts, causing them to swell and those tiny swollen buds at the tips to press sensitively against the bodice of her gown, before it surged through the rest of her body and ended between her thighs.

Oh, my!

Elizabeth had never experienced anything like this particular heat before; it felt as if she were swelling there, too, and there was also a dampness that, although slightly uncomfortable, nevertheless made her legs tremble and her knees feel decidedly weak…

Her hands moved to the front of Nathaniel's silk waistcoat, fingers curling into that material in an effort to steady herself, instantly becoming aware of the heated hardness of his muscled body beneath that waistcoat and shirt—firm, ridged muscle that quivered in response to her touch as his mouth continued to devour her own.

It was, Elizabeth decided completely breathlessly, the most thrilling experience of her life. Unlike anything she had ever known or felt before. The heat that coursed through her body increased tenfold as one of his hands moved to capture the swell of her breast—

Elizabeth felt bereft as he suddenly ended that kiss, blinking up at him as he scowled off into the darkness.

'What have you done, you silly girl!' he exclaimed.

What had she—?

'Hector…?' Too late Elizabeth realised she must have let loose the little dog's lead as they kissed, and that Hector, barking somewhere far in the distance, had not only wandered off, but already been swallowed up into the darkness.

Chapter Three

'You are to blame for this!' she gasped furiously.

'I was not the one so taken up with our kisses that I allowed my charge to wander off,' Nathaniel reminded her grimly as the two of them hurried along the darkened cliff path in pursuit of the mischievous little dog. Or, at least, Elizabeth hurried; Nathaniel's normal strides were still more than a match for hers.

'I was not—Hector! Hector!—so taken up with them, either!' She glared up at him accusingly as she continued to call for her charge. 'If you had not—Hector! Hector!—taken liberties—Hector!—'

'A word of caution, Elizabeth—' Nathaniel decided to interrupt what appeared to be warming up to a tirade worthy of his aunt when she had worked herself into an indignant lather '—the smugglers in this area are very real. And if some of them should be abroad at this time…'

'I believe you are merely trying to frighten me, my lord.'

'And why on earth should I wish to do that?' he enquired mildly.

'No doubt because you take some sort of dubious pleasure in doing so,' Elizabeth retorted, having had more than enough of this man's nonsense for one evening, of one type or another… 'And I have no intention of being frightened by myth and legend—' She broke off abruptly as she once again heard Hector barking in the distance.

A bark that was accompanied by a sharp command closely followed by the snorting and whinnying of an obviously disturbed and unsettled horse!

'Hector!' Elizabeth gasped before running forwards into the darkness.

Nathaniel hurried after her, his heart seeming to stop beating in his chest as he saw Elizabeth hurtling headlong towards where Hector could be seen barking up at a huge and ghostly pale horse that snorted and showed the whites of its eyes as it danced precariously close to the edge of the cliff, resisting all of its rider's efforts to regain control as it reared up on its back legs.

'Quiet, Hector!' Nathaniel rasped at the same time as Elizabeth grasped hold of the horse's reins, talking soothingly as it came down on all four dancing—and lethally dangerous—hooves in front of her, eyes wild, nostrils flaring as it continued to snort and prance despite the dog having now been rendered silent. 'Get control, man!' Nathaniel instructed the black-clad rider harshly, ignoring the pain in his ribs as he stepped forwards to take a firm grasp of the horse's bridle.

Held captive on both sides, the grey finally began to calm. 'There's a good lad,' Elizabeth crooned soothingly as she stroked and petted the horse's silky neck. 'Good boy. Good lad,' she continued admiringly as the hose became calmer by the second. 'There's a fine fellow.'

Nathaniel decided he would deal with Miss Elizabeth Thompson's recklessness in approaching a rearing horse later, instead concentrating his not inconsiderable wrath upon the rider of the horse as the man slid smoothly down from the saddle to stand beside him on the pathway. 'What did you think you were doing, man?' he demanded forcefully as he maintained a hold upon the bridle of the still-skittish horse.

'What did I—?' That gentleman seemed momentarily at a loss for words. 'If you had not allowed your wretched dog loose to startle Starlight, then none of this would have happened!'

Elizabeth was very aware—the slight upon Hector aside—that the gentleman's accusation was a merited one. 'I am afraid that was my fault, sir.' The pale oval of the man's face turned sharply in her direction. 'I inadvertently allowed Hector's leash to slip through my fingers, and in doing so obviously caused—'

'Who are you?' the man demanded sharply, his black cloak billowing gently about him in the darkness, his tall hat having also somehow remained secure upon his head. Elizabeth was startled by the intensity of the question. 'I am Eliza—Betsy Thompson, sir. And I sincerely apologise if I have caused you and your horse any distress. I am afraid I was momentarily—distracted, and allowed Hector to escape.' She scowled at the reason for that distraction.

'Eliza Thompson, you say?' that gentleman prompted tersely.

'Elizabeth. But I am called Betsy,' she said. 'I trust you and Starlight have suffered no harm, sir?'

'I cannot vouch for that until I have Starlight back in his stable and a lantern to see by,' the man growled.

'Is that you, Tennant?' Nathaniel asked suddenly.

'My name is Sir Rufus Tennant, yes.' The other man eyed him down the length of his nose. 'And you are…?'

'Osbourne.'

That single name had the desired effect as some of the tension appeared to leave the other gentleman's broad shoulders. 'Nathaniel Thorne?'

'Just so,' the earl confirmed tersely.

'You are staying at Hepworth Manor with your aunt?'

'Obviously,' Nathaniel said drily. 'What on earth are you about riding the cliff-top in the dark, Tennant?'

'A gentleman does not discuss his night-time pursuits in front of a lady, Osbourne.' Sir Rufus Tennant sounded ruefully amused.

And so leaving Elizabeth, as she knelt on the

ground stroking the heavily panting Hector, in some doubts as to whether he was involved in smuggling, after all, or was simply a gentlemen returning from a lovers' tryst.

'You surprise me, Tennant…' Nathaniel murmured slowly, obviously believing it to be the latter.

'Indeed?' the other man came back coolly.

'I believe it is time we were returning to Hepworth Manor, my lord.' Elizabeth straightened, Hector's leash once more safely secure in her hand.

'Introduce the two of us, Osbourne,' the other man instructed curtly.

'Betsy Thompson. Sir Rufus Tennant.' The earl's terseness was evidence of his irritation at the other man's high-handedness.

'Miss Thompson.' Sir Rufus Tennant sketched her a bow. 'Do I have your permission to call upon you tomorrow?'

Elizabeth was rendered momentarily speechless for the second time in the past few minutes. That Sir Rufus believed her to be a guest at Mrs Wilson's home was obvious. That she was not was made glaringly obvious to Elizabeth as Nathaniel answered the other man.

'Miss Thompson is my aunt's companion, and will no doubt be busy about her duties if you should decide to call tomorrow,' he bit out harshly. 'But I am sure Mrs Wilson will be only too pleased to receive you.'

Elizabeth, although aware that Sir Rufus's searching gaze was still fixed firmly upon her, remained stoically and uncomfortably silent, having been reminded all too forcibly that companions to wealthy ladies did not receive visits from titled gentlemen.

'Are you going to remain silent for the whole of our walk back to Hepworth Manor, too?' Nathaniel snapped, his ribs now aching abominably from the force necessary to quieten Tennant's mount, an ache not helped in the least by the quickness of the pace Elizabeth had set for the both of them. No doubt in her hurry to be free of his company!

'I had thought you would prefer it, my lord,' she responded. 'I am sure that the tedious chattering of a mere lady's companion would grate upon a gentleman's nerves!' she obviously could not resist adding waspishly.

Once again Nathaniel was alerted to the contradictions that surrounded this young woman. That Tennant had also believed her to be a lady of quality from the mere sound of her voice had been obvious from his request to call upon her tomorrow—a request Nathaniel had found not in the least pleasing! Any more than Elizabeth had obviously found the sharpness of his reply to Tennant to her liking.

'I do not find the chattering of this particular lady's companion in the least tedious,' Nathaniel admitted.

Glittering blue eyes were turned to him in the darkness. 'I find that very hard to believe, my lord!'

'Why is that, Elizabeth?'

'I have told you not to—'

'And I have told you that when we are alone I have every intention of addressing you as Elizabeth.'

She gave him an exasperated glance. 'And as I am employed by your aunt I am to have no say in the matter?'

He gave a shrug. 'Do you prefer the name of Betsy?'

She gave an inelegant snort. 'Of course I do not.'

'Then why object to my calling you Elizabeth?'

'Because you did not ask, my lord, you told.' There was the heat of anger in her voice.

'Very well.' Nathaniel gave a slight inclination of his head. 'May I address you as Elizabeth when we are alone?'

'No!' she obviously took great delight in denying him.

'Now you are just being deliberately difficult,' he rasped impatiently. 'Is all this indignation because I told Tennant that you are employed by my aunt?'

Elizabeth stiffened. 'Why should I be in the least concerned at your having stated the truth?'

'I have no idea, I only know that—damn it to hell!' Nathaniel had turned to take a firm grasp of Elizabeth's arms, only to then draw his breath in sharply as the agony in his chest caused him to abruptly release her and fight back the urge to double over with the pain.

'My lord?' Elizabeth was full of concern as she turned to him in the darkness.

'I apologise for my language,' Nathaniel grated through clenched teeth as he slowly straightened.

'Never mind that now.' She gave an agitated shake of her head, dark curls bouncing beneath her bonnet. 'You have hurt yourself again—'

'I have merely exacerbated the original injury,' he corrected, jaw tightly clamped to ward off the pain. 'Owing, no doubt, to the fact that I had to step in and save you from your own recklessness!'

Her indignation returned. 'What do you mean?'

'I expected at any moment to see you trampled to death beneath the horse's hooves.' Nathaniel glared down at her accusingly. 'What on earth did you think you were about, leaping into the fray in that way?'

'I assure you I knew exactly what I was doing.'

'Indeed?' Nathaniel scorned.

'I was put upon my first horse at the age of—' She broke off abruptly, lips closing firmly together as she realised she had said too much.

Or not enough, Nathaniel thought with considerable frustration. If it should turn out that Elizabeth Thompson was the daughter of some minor and impoverished gentleman, as he was seriously beginning to believe she might be, then his behaviour towards her earlier could place him in a very awkward position. A very awkward position, indeed…

'Yes, you were saying?' he encouraged persuasively.

Elizabeth straightened. 'Let me help you back to the house, my lord.'

'I am in pain, Elizabeth, not crippled!' Nathaniel gave a wince at the excess of aggression in his tone as she attempted to take his arm.

Her hand fell back to her side. 'Then perhaps, sir, you should look to your own actions before criticising my own.'

'How so?' Nathaniel frowned.

She gave a curt nod. 'If you had not become involved in a drunken brawl, then you would not have received the injuries from which you now suffer.'

'And if I received these injuries in the defence of a lady?' he offered drily, the waves of pain starting to recede now.

She raised sceptical brows. 'I find that very hard to believe. A lady of quality would never have placed herself in the position of needing such a defence,' she added as Nathaniel looked enquiringly at her.

That might well be true. Although, as Nathaniel's friend Lord Dominic Vaughn, Earl of Blackstone, had stated that he intended making the lady in question his wife as soon as was possible, it would perhaps be prudent on Nathaniel's part to keep that opinion to himself! 'I am sure that you would never place yourself in such a position,' he drawled instead.

Elizabeth frowned, obviously suspecting that he was mocking her. 'I am a lady's companion, my lord, not a lady,' she informed him haughtily as she resumed her walk back to Hepworth Manor.

A haughtiness that rendered Nathaniel no more convinced of that statement than Tennant had obviously been minutes earlier! 'But no less deserving of a gentleman's protection, surely?' He fell into step beside her.

Elizabeth looked at him sharply, the earl's features becoming clearer as they approached the candlelit house, harsh and uncompromising features that she found wholly disturbing to her already troubled peace of mind. 'The only person from whom I have needed protection this evening was you, my lord!' she sniffed.

'All evidence to the contrary, Elizabeth—it has been my experience so far in our acquaintance that you are more than capable of protecting yourself,' Nathaniel muttered with feeling.

She eyed him disdainfully. 'Perhaps that is as well.' The front door was duly opened by the butler, allowing the two of them to step inside out of the cooling night air. 'If you will excuse me, my lord?' Elizabeth kept her eyes demurely lowered in front of the butler. 'Mrs Wilson will be anxiously awaiting Hector's return.'

Nathaniel stood in the hallway, watching through narrowed lids as Elizabeth ascended the staircase accompanied by the scampering dog, making a note to speak to his aunt tomorrow as to exactly what she did or did not know about the young lady she had so recently employed.

'I will take brandy in the library now, if you please, Sewell,' he instructed the butler distractedly.

'Very good, my lord.'

Having settled himself beside the fire in the library, a much-needed glass of brandy in his hand,

Nathaniel turned his thoughts to that strange encounter with Sir Rufus Tennant.

He did not know the Tennant family well, had only been slightly acquainted with Sir Rufus's younger brother Giles, before his involvement in a scandal some years ago that had resulted in his taking his own life. He did not know Sir Rufus himself at all, the other man being eight or more years Nathaniel's senior. Reputed as being taciturn and somewhat reclusive, Sir Rufus's visits to London were infrequent, his forays into society non-existent, and without so much as a rumour or two regarding his romantic inclinations.

An occurrence that had, on one occasion, prompted Nathaniel's Aunt Gertrude into scandalously musing, after that gentleman had refused yet another of her invitations to dinner, as to whether or not Sir Rufus's…tastes might be in another direction entirely.

Tennant's request to call upon Elizabeth tomorrow would seem to imply his aunt's conclusions were entirely wrong.

'Sir Rufus Tennant is here to see you, madam,' Sewell announced loftily as he stood in the drawing-room doorway late the following morning.

Elizabeth looked up from her needlework as she sat unobtrusively at the back of the room, curious to see what Sir Rufus would look like in the light of day.

The gentleman who stepped into the room some seconds later was probably just under six feet tall, with dark hair in need of a trim in order to be completely fashionable, with the palest blue eyes Elizabeth had ever seen set in an austere but not displeasing face, his figure shown to advantage in the brown superfine, tan waistcoat and buff-coloured breeches, and brown black-topped Hessians that had obviously become somewhat dust-covered on the ride over here.

He paused in the doorway, those pale blue eyes narrowed as his gaze swept briefly over the two older ladies before coming to rest upon Elizabeth. He appeared to draw in a sharp breath, jaw tensing slightly, before he stepped further into the room to bow stiffly before Mrs Wilson. 'I trust you are well, madam?'

Elizabeth had mentioned last night's encounter to her employer over breakfast this morning, so Mrs Wilson, unsurprised to see him, smiled graciously up at her visitor. 'It has been far too long since we saw you last, Sir Rufus.'

That hooded pale blue gaze flickered briefly across to Elizabeth before returning to the older woman. 'I am, as usual, kept busy with estate business, ma'am. In fact, I only called this morning to ensure that Miss Thompson and your nephew returned safely from their walk yesterday evening.'

'Ah, yes.' Mrs Wilson's kindly gaze turned towards the now-blushing Elizabeth. 'Betsy has told me of what occurred. I trust that your horse suffered no ill effects from the encounter?'

'None at all, thank you, ma'am,' Sir Rufus assured.

'You will take tea with us, Sir Rufus?' Mrs Wilson nodded to Letitia to ring for Sewell.

'Thank you.' Sir Rufus nodded abruptly. 'I— do I have your permission to enquire after Miss Thompson's well-being?'

Elizabeth's blush deepened at the speculation that glittered briefly in Mrs Wilson's gaze as she nodded her permission before to all intents and purposes returning her attention to her own needlework. But Elizabeth knew that well-meaning but interfering lady well enough by this time to know that Mrs Wilson would be aware of every word exchanged between Sir Rufus and her young companion.

'Miss Thompson?' Sir Rufus stood before her now, that pale blue gaze piercing as he looked down at her.

'Sir Rufus.' Elizabeth nodded graciously, standing up to place her embroidery down on the chair behind her before curtsying briefly, not altogether sure that she was comfortable with his having singled her out in this way. 'I am pleased to hear of Starlight's good health.'

'Thank you,' he returned. 'I— Are you from these parts?'

'No, Sir Rufus, I am originally from H—' Elizabeth broke off abruptly, delicate colour once again warming her cheeks as she realised she would be revealing too much about herself if she were to announce she came originally from Hampshire. 'Herefordshire,' she announced firmly. 'But from the little I have seen, Devonshire is a very beautiful county.'

'Its cliff paths are perhaps not to be traversed at night, by either foot or horse,' he drawled ruefully.

'Perhaps not,' Elizabeth conceded with a smile. 'I trust the rest of your journey home was un-eventful?'

A nerve pulsed in that tightly clenched jaw. 'I am sure I could find nothing in the least disturb-ing after our own…momentous meeting.'

Elizabeth shifted uncomfortably as she realised that Rufus Tennant was attempting to flirt with her. Not in the least practised or smoothly—as if it had been far too long since he had done such a thing—but nevertheless he was attempting to flatter her, at least. 'It is very kind of you to say so, Sir Rufus.'

He attempted a smile. 'Perhaps—'

'How good to see you again, Tennant,' Nathaniel greeted briskly as he entered the room to stride over to where the older man stood beside Eliza-beth.

She had ample time, as the two men exchanged greetings, in which to note the contrasts between the two of them. Unfortunately to Sir Rufus's det-riment, she finally conceded grudgingly.

Nathaniel Thorne was probably ten years younger than Sir Rufus and possessed a vital-ity and smouldering good looks the older man so obviously lacked. Sir Rufus was dark where Lord Thorne was golden, and the younger man's hair was styled in the latest fashion. Lord Thorne's superfine hair was blond, and of a much more fashionable cut and with the same richness of colour as his eyes, its tailoring perfectly complimentary to his broad shoulders and tapered waist, the long length of his legs encased in tan pantaloons above brown Hessians polished to such a degree it was almost possible to see one's face in them, rather than dusty and mud-splattered as the older man's now were.

All of which only succeeded in arousing Elizabeth's sympathy for Sir Rufus's more homely looks…

Nathaniel could almost pick the thoughts out of Elizabeth's beautiful head as she looked at the two men from beneath the fan of her long, dark lashes. He sensed that she had compared the two of them, found Tennant wanting, but still preferred that gentleman's company to Nathaniel's own. Not surprising after the two of them had parted so at odds with each other the previous night!

He had given in to the temptation to kiss her

once again—a kiss that should never have happened, he knew, but which had nevertheless kept him tossing and turning sleeplessly in his bed for far longer than it should have done.

Admittedly it had been three weeks or more since Nathaniel had bedded a woman whilst visiting Gabriel at his palazzo in Venice, but even so merely kissing Elizabeth Thompson should not have affected him so deeply that he had been unable to dampen his arousal. Taking himself in hand to alleviate that arousal had not been in the least appealing, either, which was why Nathaniel did not feel in the best of humours this morning.

His temper had not been improved in the slightest upon entering his aunt's drawing room a few minutes ago to find Tennant at the back of the room in private conversation with Elizabeth.

The fact that he had felt that way at all had only succeeded in increasing his irritation concerning this completely inappropriate attraction towards Elizabeth Thompson. 'Perhaps we should rejoin my aunt, Tennant, and leave Miss Thompson to her needlework?' he suggested coolly as Sewell entered with the tea tray.

The other man looked at him with the pale, cold blue eyes of a fish. 'I—'

'Yes, do come and join Letitia and me,' his Aunt Gertrude invited lightly. 'I can then extend an invitation to Sir Rufus for the dinner party we are to have on Saturday evening,' she added warmly.

Tennant, although obviously displeased by the interruption, had no choice but to give a brief nod in Elizabeth's direction before strolling over to sit with the two older women.

Leaving Nathaniel alone with a quietly displeased Elizabeth…

Chapter Four

'Do you take some cruel delight in humiliating me?' she breathed accusingly.

'I did not wish you to make a fool of yourself by flirting with one of my aunt's guests,' Nathaniel came back coldly.

Elizabeth gasped at the insult, tears of humiliation glistening in her deep blue eyes as she looked up at him. 'Sir Rufus was the one to seek out my company, not the other way about.' Her voice was shaky with emotion.

Nathaniel glanced across at the older man as he attempted to converse politely with Mrs Wilson and Letitia Grant. Tennant was obviously ill at ease in female company; the occasional glowering glance he sent in Elizabeth's direction seeming to indicate that she was the only reason he was putting himself through such discomfort today.

Nathaniel's mouth twisted derisively as he turned back to Elizabeth. 'No doubt he would be quite a catch for a lady's companion.'

She gave a pained frown, not altogether sure what she had done to incur the earl's displeasure this time, only aware that she had. Sir Rufus Tennant might indeed be 'a catch' for a paid lady's companion—the same could not be said with regard to Lady Elizabeth Copeland.

'No doubt.' She kept her expression deliberately bland.

'Perhaps—'

'Are you not coming to join me in my endeavours to persuade Sir Rufus into joining our dinner party on Saturday evening, Osbourne?' Mrs Wilson looked slightly disapproving at her nephew's continued conversation with her employee.

'I will join you in a moment, Aunt,' he answered his elderly relative, once again lowering his voice as he spoke to Elizabeth. 'Of course, Tennant may be a little old for you…'

She raised dark brows. 'I doubt that a lady's companion has the luxury of worrying about such things as the age of one's husband, my lord.'

She glanced across at Sir Rufus. 'His looks and manner seem pleasant enough. And he appears to be a moderately wealthy man, too.'

'And is that important to you?' Nathaniel looked down the length of his nose at her.

Elizabeth's lashes were lowered. 'I am sure it would be important to most prospective brides, my lord.'

'As a bride's dowry is invariably of import to the groom,' he drawled pointedly.

Reminding Elizabeth that a dowry was something neither she nor her sisters possessed...

Their father had been the dearest of men, loving and kind, but always somewhat vague after his wife had left, resulting in him becoming slightly removed from his family and society to such a degree that he had not given his daughters' future after his demise the consideration that it deserved.

His death had been unexpected, so perhaps their father had believed Diana, Caroline and Elizabeth would all be safely married before that occurred. Although how that should have come about, when none of them were ever allowed to meet eligible gentlemen, Elizabeth was unsure.

Whatever his reasoning, the reading of Marcus

Copeland's will had revealed that he had made no provision for dowries for his three daughters, that lack of foresight instead leaving them to the guardianship and mercy of his distant cousin and heir, Lord Gabriel Faulkner.

Elizabeth smiled tightly. 'Then let us hope, for your sake, that the two Miss Millers and Miss Rutledge are all possessed of a large fortune.'

Nathaniel frowned darkly, not at all pleased with the way she had turned this conversation towards his aunt's less-than-subtle matrimonial intentions towards himself.

His two closest friends might have recently succumbed to the idea of marriage, Dominic intending to marry the masked beauty Caro Morton, and Gabriel, more sensibly, planning to offer for one of the three young ladies who had become his wards on his inheriting the title of Earl of Westbourne. But this didn't make Nathaniel feel any more kindly disposed towards the parson's mousetrap for himself. Indeed, he considered it his duty to uphold the very idea of bachelorhood for those others of his peers who had also so far managed to escape such a fate.

Elizabeth barely restrained her smile at the look

of disgust that had come over Nathaniel's face at the mere mention of matrimony in regard to himself, revealing to her, at least, that Mrs Wilson's hopes in that direction were likely to come to nought. 'You really should join your aunt and her guest, my lord.' She looked up at the earl challengingly, feeling that she had emerged the victor in that particular exchange.

Nathaniel looked down the length of his nose at her. 'I am used to doing as I please, not as others might wish me to do.'

She smiled briefly. 'One would never have guessed!'

Brown eyes narrowed at her obvious sarcasm. 'You—'

'Your tea is becoming cold, Osbourne,' Mrs Wilson cut in imperiously.

Alerting Elizabeth to the fact that she was seriously in danger of incurring that lady's wrath herself if she did not bring this conversation with her nephew to an immediate end. She did not so much as glance in the earl's direction again before crossing the room to stand before the older woman. 'Lord Thorne was merely advising me concerning the safest path for me to take in regard to Hector's walk.' She gave Sir Rufus Tennant a distracted smile as he rose politely to his feet.

'Of course.' Mrs Wilson gave her nephew an affectionate smile as he joined their group. 'Such a dear boy, always so concerned for the well-being of others…'

Elizabeth's snort of disbelief escaped before she had chance to stop it, a snort she quickly turned into a cough as she saw the way her employer frowned up at her. But, really, the mere idea of Nathaniel Thorne as a 'dear boy' who was 'concerned with the well-being of others' was perfectly ludicrous; the man was arrogance personified, and the only person towards whom he showed the least consideration, besides himself, was his aunt.

'I do hope you are not coming down with a cold, Betsy.' That lady delicately raised a lace handkerchief in front of her nose.

Elizabeth could see the irritating earl out of the corner of her eye, was completely aware of the mockery in the smile that now curved those sculptured, and oh-so-sensuous lips. 'I do not think so,' she assured the older woman mildly. 'I am probably just a little allergic to something in the room,' she added for the smirking earl's benefit. 'I am sure that it is nothing that a brisk walk outside in the fresh air will not cure.'

'I was about to take my leave.' Sir Rufus Tennant placed his empty tea cup on the table. 'Perhaps I might walk with you for a short distance?'

Elizabeth felt her heart sink at the suggestion. Her remarks to Lord Thorne a few minutes ago regarding Sir Rufus had been pure bravado on her part; she had absolutely no romantic interest in a man who was not only almost twenty years her senior, but so plain in appearance that she was almost ashamed to admit, as Lady Elizabeth Copeland, she would probably not even have noticed his existence.

'I am sure my knowledge of the area is far superior to Osbourne's,' that gentleman added haughtily.

Not only plain to look at, but pompous too, Elizabeth noted with an inward wince, making sure not to so much as glance in the earl's direction now, knowing that gentleman was sure to be frowning his disapproval, which was perhaps, contrarily, reason enough for Elizabeth to accept Sir Rufus's invitation. Except she really did not have the least romantic interest in the older man, as either Betsy Thompson or Lady Elizabeth Copeland…

She drew in a light breath. 'It is very kind of you to offer, Sir Rufus—'

'Very kind, indeed,' Mrs Wilson said warmly. 'Are the bluebells still out in the West Wood, Sir Rufus?'

'They are, ma'am.'

'Oh, then you must allow Sir Rufus to show you the West Wood in bloom, Betsy.' Her employer smiled her approval. 'Hector has always liked to frolic in the bluebell wood,' she added, as if that settled the argument.

Which, in fact, it did, Elizabeth accepted at the same time as she struggled with her inner frustration; Mrs Wilson's indulgence where her little dog was concerned was limitless, and if Hector liked to go to the bluebell wood then Elizabeth must surely take him there.

Chancing even the briefest of glances at Nathaniel Thorne beneath lowered lashes, in order to gauge his reaction to this conversation, had been a mistake. Horrible, horrible man—instead of disapproving he looked highly amused—no doubt because he was fully aware of Elizabeth's lack of enthusiasm for Sir Rufus's company!

Nathaniel's lips were pressed tightly together, as if to suppress the smile that was reflected in the laughing brown eyes that looked down at her so engagingly. 'I am sure you will greatly enjoy the bluebell wood, Betsy.'

If it were not for their listening and watching audience she would enjoy telling him exactly what she thought of him! 'I am sure that I shall.' She turned to Sir Rufus. 'If you would not mind waiting a few minutes more, I will go upstairs and collect my bonnet, sir.'

'Not at all.' He gave her a curt, unsmiling nod.

Elizabeth's steps were slow as she made her way up the stairs. In truth, she did not know quite what to make of Sir Rufus Tennant. Oh, he was polite enough in a brusque, no-nonsense sort of manner and did indeed seem desirous of her company, yet at the same time he made no effort to charm or cajole as a younger gentleman might have done in order to secure a lady's interest. She—

'I believe that is the first time I have been referred to as an allergy, Elizabeth.'

She turned so sharply on the stairs at hearing

that mocking voice directly behind her that she might have tumbled down them if Nathaniel had not reached out to clasp the tops of her arms to help her regain her balance.

Elizabeth moved out of that grasp as soon as she felt steady enough on her feet, rendered briefly breathless as she looked straight into the earl's rakishly handsome face as he stood on the stair two steps down from her. Standing so close to him, in fact, that she could see the golden shards of colour amongst the brown of his eyes and feel the warmth of his breath against her lips. As soft as a kiss…

Elizabeth stepped back and up another step to escape that sensual pull. 'I believe it is more an irritation than an actual allergy,' she bit out frostily.

'Are you ever at a loss for an answer?' The earl looked up at her admiringly.

'I sincerely hope not,' she said with satisfaction. 'And you should not have followed me, my lord,' she added, a perplexed frown on her brow; the role of lady's companion might not sit altogether comfortably on her shoulders, but for the moment that was indeed what she was.

'I did not "follow you", Elizabeth,' he denied. 'I only came to the drawing room at my aunt's behest so that I might say my hellos to Tennant. Having done so, I now have work to finish in the library.'

Elizabeth cheeks felt warm at the obvious rebuke. 'Work, my lord?'

'Try to sound a little less incredulous, Elizabeth,' Nathaniel drawled drily. 'Despite my recent stay in Venice, I am not completely a man of leisure,' he added irritably as her expression remained unchanged. 'As the Earl of Osbourne, I do have estates and such like to attend to.'

'I would have thought you had estate managers and a lawyer to do those things for you,' she commented.

'Well. Yes. Of course that is so,' Nathaniel acknowledged. 'But those people are directly answerable to me.'

'I see…'

His frown deepened. 'Why is it, do you think, that even the mildest of remarks from you sounds like a criticism?'

Elizabeth looked up at him with innocent blue eyes. 'I have absolutely no idea.'

'That is not your first untruth of our acquaintance,' Nathaniel muttered impatiently, 'but it is certainly one of the more obvious ones.'

Elizabeth instantly felt on her guard as she regarded him warily. 'I am sure I have no idea what you mean, my lord.' She had never been particularly good at deceit and prevarication; in fact, she was surprised that she had managed to maintain her role as a servant in Mrs Wilson's household for the amount of time she had without detection.

If, indeed, she had…

Mrs Wilson had been too caught up in other things since her nephew's return from Venice to trouble herself in questioning 'Betsy's' origins too deeply, but Lord Thorne had already made it obvious that he was starting to regard her as something of a puzzle that needed to be solved.

Indeed, his next comment confirmed it. 'Just as long as you are aware that, as my only living relative, my Aunt Gertrude's welfare is of the utmost importance to me,' he bit out pointedly.

Elizabeth looked alarmed. 'I trust you are not implying that I would in any way wish to do that kind lady harm?'

Nathaniel looked at her speculatively, noting

the pallor of her cheeks and the way her eyes had darkened. Guiltily? Or was it pain at Nathaniel having voiced his suspicions? 'Not deliberately so, perhaps,' he allowed slowly. 'But my aunt is apt to trust people rather than not—'

'Whereas you, no doubt, are apt to distrust them until proven otherwise?' she shot back.

His jaw tightened. 'Perhaps.'

There was no 'perhaps' about it in Elizabeth's eyes; Nathaniel Thorne had shown only too clearly these past twelve hours or so that the easy charm he chose to present to society—that Elizabeth had also believed to be the nature of the man—was, in fact, nothing but a front for his intelligence and shrewdness of mind. A shrewdness, now that he was back on his feet and out of bed, that was obviously causing him to question her motives for taking employment with his aunt.

She gave a cool inclination of her head. 'I will keep your concern for your aunt in mind. Now, if you will excuse me…? I have been gone so long Sir Rufus will think that I have changed my mind about taking our walk together.'

The earl gave a wry smile. 'A word of warning with regard to Sir Rufus…'

'Another one?' Elizabeth raised irritated brows.

That smile widened. 'It would seem to be my day for them.'

She sighed. 'And what do you now wish to tell me about him?'

Nathaniel considered what he knew of the older man's history. How Nathaniel, and most of society, had believed that the suicide of Tennant's younger brother several years ago, and the tragic nature of that death, might have temporarily unhinged the older man. Certainly Tennant's withdrawal from all society since then had been cause for speculation.

A withdrawal from female company, at least, which was now at an end, if the older man's reason for riding along the cliff path late the previous night was to be believed, along with the interest he had shown in Elizabeth Thompson by calling upon her today.

And if that interest should prove to be serious, to the point that Tennant actually made an offer for Elizabeth, surely it was then Tennant's prerogative to relate the tragic history of his own family to the young woman he intended to make his wife? What right had Nathaniel to interfere, after all, when any relationship between himself and his aunt's companion could go nowhere and was, in fact, highly inappropriate?

'It is of no import.' Nathaniel straightened dismissively. 'Enjoy your walk in the bluebell wood.'

Elizabeth remained on the stairs, looking down at the earl as he moved lithely down to the hallway below before disappearing in the direction of the library. Which was when she began to breathe again.

She had believed Lord Thorne's personal interest in her to be inappropriate, but the interest he was now taking in her past could only be considered dangerous.

'Whereabouts in Hampshire do you hail from, Miss Thompson?'

Elizabeth looked at the man who strolled along beside her in the bluebell wood that backed onto Hepworth Manor and then glanced behind them. It had been decided by Mrs Wilson, whilst Elizabeth was upstairs collecting her bonnet, that it was not altogether proper for Elizabeth to go walking alone with a single gentleman and that Letitia should go with them. Although much good that did when the other woman had become so distracted collecting up the fragrant blooms the moment they entered the wood that she now lagged far behind them.

Sir Rufus had chosen to lead his horse by the reins, a fact that Hector, released from his leash so that he might roam free, was taking much delight in. Sir Rufus was less than impressed, judging by the irritated glances he shot the little dog.

Elizabeth smiled. 'I believe I told you I am originally from Herefordshire, Sir Rufus.'

'Ah, yes, so you did.' He nodded, the bright sunlight not in the least kind to the narrowness of his features, but instead emphasising the lines beside his mouth and those pale blue eyes. 'Whereabouts in Herefordshire?'

'Leominster.' Elizabeth named the only town in Herefordshire she'd ever heard of. 'And have you lived all of your life in Devonshire?' she enquired politely.

He smiled briefly, that smile lightening the harshness of his features somewhat and, in doing so, lending him a mild attraction. 'I find very little to interest me in London society.'

As one who had never been into London society,

for obvious reasons Elizabeth found this statement intensely irritating. 'Not even the shops and entertainments?'

Sir Rufus gave a delicate shudder. 'Taunton is not too far a ride if I should need to shop. As for the entertainments, no, I do not miss them in the slightest,' he said brusquely.

No, this man did not in the least set out to charm, she acknowledged ruefully. But perhaps his frankness was to be admired? Considered a trait to be appreciated rather than a fault? Certainly her own father had shared Sir Rufus's opinion of the entertainments London had to offer...

'In that case, I am surprised Mrs Wilson was able to persuade you into accepting her dinner invitation for Saturday evening,' she remarked bluntly.

His expression softened somewhat as he looked down at Elizabeth. 'That particular invitation held another...attraction for me.'

She was not sure she was altogether comfortable with the almost flirtatious note she detected in his tone, especially as it seemed to sit so uncomfortably upon the stiffness of his otherwise tense demeanour. 'Mrs Wilson does have a particularly fine chef.'

'I was not referring to her chef—'

'No, Hector!' Elizabeth deliberately chose that moment in which to turn and chastise the little dog for harassing the long-suffering Starlight. 'I am afraid he is rather mischievous,' she excused as she went down on her haunches to re-attach the dog's lead.

Sir Rufus's features were once again austere. 'Mrs Wilson is somewhat…relaxed in her discipline of him.'

Elizabeth did not in the least care for the obvious criticism; Mrs Wilson might be over-indulgent with the little dog, but for the main part Hector did not take advantage of that indulgence. He was just naturally mischievous—and as such, totally lovable—by nature.

She straightened swiftly. 'I believe it is time that we were turning back.'

'Now I have offended you,' Sir Rufus guessed.

'Not in the least—'

'It is only that I consider animals should be treated the same as children, Miss Thompson: they are occasionally to be seen, and not to be heard from at all unless first spoken to,' he explained. If he was intending to charm his way back into Elizabeth's good graces, then he was failing abysmally!

She had never heard such nonsense, with regard to animals or children. She considered that both were to be loved and nurtured, to be enjoyed and not treated as part of the furniture until called upon. Indeed, her nanny had once told her that a man's attitude to children and animals said much about his nature. 'You are entitled to your opinion, of course, Sir Rufus,' she said coolly.

'I have offended you.' His grimace did absolutely nothing for his plainness of features. 'Perhaps on Saturday evening you might try to persuade me to a different point of view?'

And why on earth would she wish to do that, when neither Sir Rufus, nor his somewhat draconian points of view, were of any interest to her? 'I'm afraid that will not be possible, sir.'

He raised dark brows. 'Why not?'

Her smile was one of satisfaction. 'I am Mrs Wilson's employee, not a house guest. As such, I will not be a part of Saturday evening's dinner party.'

He looked most displeased at this information. 'Perhaps if I were to suggest to her—'

'I wish you would not,' Elizabeth cut in sharply. 'I assure you, I will be much occupied that evening, keeping Hector amused and out from under the feet of Mrs Wilson's guests.'

Sir Rufus shot the little dog a look of intense dislike. 'He should be placed outside in the stables for the evening with the other animals.'

A remark that immediately caused Elizabeth to wonder if she had ever taken such a ready dislike to someone before this? Probably not—she was gregarious by nature, enjoyed being with and talking to people. Well…usually—this man was unfortunately proving to be the exception.

'It really is time Letitia and I returned to Mrs Wilson,' she announced with some relief. 'I have very much enjoyed the walk in the bluebell wood,' she added, more for politeness's sake than actual truth.

Oh, she had very much enjoyed seeing and walking amongst the bluebells, it was only the company that had left much to be desired! How much more pleasant it would have been to have walked in the romance of the bluebell wood with a younger man. A handsome and charming man, set on seduction. A man with gold-coloured hair made even more golden by the sunshine, perhaps—

That way lay not only disappointment, but madness!

Lord Nathaniel Thorne was an even more unsuitable a companion for Elizabeth to share the romance of the bluebell wood with than the taciturn and austere Sir Rufus! Not only was he unattainable as a romantic interest for 'Betsy Thompson', but their earlier conversation, and the earl's connection to Lord Gabriel Faulkner, made him a man who was also a danger to her real identity of Lady Elizabeth Copeland and she wasn't ready to be unmasked just yet.

She gave Sir Rufus a bright and meaningless smile. 'I have no doubt there are things on your own estate in need of your attention.' That was a Caro ploy, Elizabeth realised with an inner wince of guilt; there was nothing that a man enjoyed more, her twenty-year-old sister had assured her conspiratorially on one occasion, than the opportunity to talk about himself and how very important he was.

His chest puffed out predictably as he straightened. 'Yes, of course, you are right. How considerate of you to realise that.' He nodded his approval.

Caroline had forgotten to mention that such flattery only made that man so much more appreciative of a woman's charms! Which, where Rufus Tennant was concerned, had not been Elizabeth's intention at all!

Instead of answering his comment, she turned to look for Letitia Grant. 'Oh, do let me take some of those from you,' she offered warmly as she moved forwards to take some of the heavy blooms from the other woman's arms, at the same time taking care to keep a tight hold on Hector's lead; it really would not do for her to have to resort to upbraiding Sir Rufus if he should dare to chastise the little dog in any way. 'I wish you a safe journey home, Sir Rufus,' she said, turning to dismiss him lightly.

He was already seated upon his horse, a frown between his eyes as he looked down at her. 'Those bluebells are the exact colour of your eyes…'

From any other man the remark would have sounded charming, but he somehow managed to make it sound more of a criticism than a compliment. 'Thank you,' Elizabeth murmured uncertainly.

He raised his hat to the two women. 'I will wish you both a good day.' After another intense glance in Elizabeth's direction, he pulled sharply upon Starlight's reins to turn the horse and canter away along the cliff path towards his home, his back and shoulders ramrod-straight as he made no effort to look back at the two women.

'How exciting, Elizabeth, that you should have attracted the attention of a man such as Sir Rufus!' Letitia twittered at Elizabeth's side.

She did not find his interest in her to be in the least exciting. In fact, she was sure she had never found anything in her short life less so!

Chapter Five

'So, now that you have had the chance to observe them, what is your considered opinion of the charms of Miss Rutledge and the two Miss Millers?'

Elizabeth gave a guilty start as Lord Thorne joined her as she stood at the back of Mrs Wilson's drawing room on Saturday evening, observing those three young ladies. Three rather silly young ladies, in her 'considered opinion', as they stood across the room giggling together like a gaggle of geese. Something that even she, who had no real experience of such things, knew no marriage-minded young lady should ever do; any gentleman remotely interested in a single one of them would be utterly daunted by the presence of the other two.

Elizabeth schooled her features into mild uninterest as she gave every appearance of ignoring the man standing beside her in the crowded and noisy room where the guests had gathered before they were called into dinner.

Elizabeth had unfortunately been drawn in to make up the numbers, the invitation to Sir Rufus having apparently made those numbers uneven, something that Mrs Wilson would not tolerate at her dinner table. Elizabeth's suggestion that Letitia would be much more suited to the task had been rendered null and void when Mrs Wilson revealed that Letitia already also made up one of the number, and that to remove her would only result in their being two more gentlemen than ladies, instead of one. Something else Mrs Wilson would not tolerate, apparently.

So it was, after two very busy days spent helping Mrs Wilson to organise her dinner party in order to ensure its success—two days when Elizabeth had also managed to avoid any further private conversations with her employer's nephew—she now found herself attending Mrs Wilson's dinner party, after all, having first removed all the lace from her blue silk gown in order to render it less fashionable. She was feeling distinctly uncomfortable amongst the local Devonshire gentry, all of whom were extremely well dressed and appeared well acquainted with each other already.

But even that was preferable to the company of the irritating earl! 'I am sure that any one of them would make you an admirable countess,' she answered noncommittally.

He eyed her mockingly. 'Did I detect a slight emphasis on the word *you* there?'

Elizabeth raised dark brows. 'I do not believe so, no.'

He gave an appreciative grin. 'Liar!'

She drew in a sharp breath. 'You are altogether too fond of levelling that accusation at me, my lord.'

Nathaniel sobered, his lids narrowing as he continued to look down at the young lady standing so coolly composed beside him. To all intents and purposes she should not have been noticeable at all in this room full of richly dressed and jewel-adorned women, and yet somehow it was the very simplicity of her appearance that had drawn more than one pair of admiring male eyes—including his own.

She wore only a thin ribbon the same blue as

her gown threaded through the darkness of her curls, and that gown was simplicity itself: high-waisted, with a scooped neckline that revealed the soft swell of her breasts, an inch or two of the soft ivory of her arms visible between the tiny puff sleeves and the above-elbow length of her white lace gloves.

She was, Nathaniel acknowledged with a frown, a perfect diamond set amongst much gaudier jewels. His mouth thinned. 'You must be disappointed that Sir Rufus is so late arriving?'

Having received a bouquet of white roses from that gentleman only yesterday—the first flowers she'd ever received from a gentleman—along with a note that simply read 'Tennant', she was not in the least disappointed by the man's late arrival this evening. In fact, she felt relieved at this delay in seeing him again, having absolutely no idea what the roses, or the brevity of the signature on the card that had accompanied them, was meant to convey. Red roses she could have understood as being a sign of admiration, or perhaps even yellow roses, but what did white roses signify? As for the terseness of the man's signature on the card…!

She had written Sir Rufus a short and polite note

thanking him for the flowers, of course, along with the news that she would be present at Mrs Wilson's dinner party, after all, in case he thought she had deliberately lied to him, all the time aware she did not know if she even liked him, or understood this apparently uncharacteristic interest in her.

Her uncertainty was not helped by the fact that she, and apparently every other woman in the room, had been rendered breathless by Nathaniel Thorne's godlike appearance this evening.

Elizabeth might have succeeded in ignoring the earl for the main part this past two days, but it was impossible to ignore such resplendent maleness that he displayed this evening, in his perfectly tailored black evening clothes and snowy-white linen. The many candles that illuminated the room turned his hair a deep, burnished gold, his eyes appeared a deep and glowing amber, and cast the handsomeness of his features into a sculpture of masculine beauty.

Certainly Sir Rufus Tennant—when he deigned to arrive—or indeed any of the other men present this evening, could not possibly hope to compete with such a vision of male elegance and smouldering sensuality!

'Very disappointed,' Elizabeth answered him stiltedly, her awareness of him so profound that the shortness of her fingernails dug painfully into the palms of her hands as she clenched them at her sides. 'And which of those three young ladies do you most find attractive?'

Nathaniel was not in the least surprised that Elizabeth had so neatly turned the conversation from herself and on to him; he had realised these past two days that she could be extremely evasive when she chose to be. Not that he had deliberately sought out her company during that time—he had decided it was becoming too much of a habit to kiss her whenever they happened to find themselves alone together. But still, it was impossible not to notice that she avoided his company as if he were possessed of the plague.

He gave every appearance now of considering the three young ladies who stood together across the room, although inwardly he found the style of their gowns over-fussy, and the constant giggling and surreptitious glances levelled in his direction extremely irritating. 'Perhaps Miss Rutledge is the most sensible of the three,' he finally allowed drily.

Elizabeth looked faintly surprised. 'And is sensibility a quality you require in a wife?'

Nathaniel knew he had been the one to introduce the subject this evening, but even so he found it strangely distasteful to discuss the merits, or otherwise, of any future wife he might choose with a young woman he had kissed with passion on more than one occasion.

Luckily he was saved discussing that subject further as his gaze narrowed on the man now striding purposefully across the room. 'I see Tennant has arrived at last and is even now making his way determinedly to your side,' he drawled derisively, the older man's progress not as straightforward as he would have wished, as neighbours who had not seen him at a social occasion of this type for years insisted on engaging him in conversation.

Elizabeth, having also noted Sir Rufus's arrival, had been madly occupied in thinking of ways in which she might avoid him. But with Lord Thorne's mockery so evident she had a complete reversal of feelings and instead bestowed the warmest of smiles upon the other man as he finally reached her side—not looking anywhere near as resplendent at the earl, of course, but tolerably attractive, none the less, in his black tailored evening clothes and snowy-white, if less fashionable, shirt and necktie.

'How lovely to see you again, Sir Rufus.' She gave an elegant curtsy as he turned to her after bowing abruptly to Lord Thorne. 'And I must thank you once again for the beautiful roses you sent me yesterday.' Elizabeth did not need to actually look at the earl to be aware of his start of surprise. Obviously the arrival of yesterday's roses had escaped his attention. 'I have them up in my room in the hopes they will last all the longer,' she added with deliberate sweetness.

'I grew them myself in my hothouse at Gifford House,' Sir Rufus informed her huskily, obviously pleased at her comments.

Nathaniel did not care if the man had given birth to the blooms himself—sending roses to a young woman he had only known a matter of days was surely unacceptable? Unless, of course, Tennant's intentions towards Elizabeth really were serious…

'Such perfect white buds,' Elizabeth continued.

White roses? Tennant had sent Elizabeth white roses? As a sign of the purity with which he regarded her, perhaps? Good God, whoever would have guessed that Tennant was a romantic?

Nathaniel could not even remember the last time he had sent a woman flowers. Or, indeed, if he ever had; women tended to take things like that completely out of context, to read emotions into such gestures that simply did not exist.

That Elizabeth had taken those blooms up to the privacy of her bedchamber would seem to indicate that she was not immune to such a gesture, either, even if that gesture had been made by an old stick-in-the-mud like Tennant.

'I believe your aunt is signalling that it is time for you to escort her in to dinner, Osbourne,' that stick-in-the-mud informed him loftily at the same time as he offered Elizabeth his own arm.

Leaving Nathaniel with no other choice but to respond to his aunt's tacit request that he do the same for her. But not quite yet… 'My aunt tells me there is to be dancing after dinner. I trust you will save the first set of dances for me, Miss Thompson?'

Elizabeth frowned up at Lord Thorne, knowing

from the challenging glitter in those amber-brown eyes that he was being deliberately irritating. Something he seemed to take delight in being whenever he happened to be in her company! 'I am sure that Miss Rutledge would appreciate that honour far more than I, sir.'

The earl gave a wolfish grin at the same time as those gorgeous eyes laughed down at her. 'The honour will be all mine, I do assure you, Miss Thompson.'

'But are you sure that your ribs will be able to stand the exercise, my lord?' she came back with that same saccharine sweetness with which she had thanked Sir Rufus for his flowers.

'I will ensure that they are.' That warm gaze continued to laugh at Elizabeth.

'Then I will claim the second set,' Sir Rufus put in impatiently.

'If Miss Thompson is not too fatigued from our own…dancing,' Nathaniel taunted.

'I am sure I will not be, Sir Rufus.' She glared her displeasure at the earl as she answered the other man, a look Nathaniel returned with mocking amusement.

'Until later, then, Miss Thompson.' Nathaniel

bent his head over her hand, then bowed tersely to Sir Rufus before he joined his increasingly impatient aunt and offered her his arm.

Elizabeth gazed after him in frustration, that irritation deepening as she saw that every other woman in the room was also watching the tall and rakishly handsome nephew of their hostess, some from behind the discretion of their fans, others openly admiring of the dashing figure he cut in the perfectly tailored evening clothes that emphasised the muscled strength of his shoulders.

Elizabeth gave a winsome sigh, knowing that as a mere companion to Mrs Wilson—worse, to Mrs Wilson's dog—she took altogether far too much interest in the arrogant Earl of Osbourne.

'Miss Thompson?'

And obviously not enough interest in the impatient man standing beside her with his arm still extended to escort her into dinner!

'Thank you.' She placed her hand upon Sir Rufus's arm, her face slightly flushed from the disapproval she read in the austereness of his features as they joined the line of guests moving slowly through to the dining room.

As might be expected from her lowly position

in this household, Elizabeth was seated far down the middle of the table, well away from the host and hostess. Mrs Wilson, aware of the roses that had arrived for Elizabeth yesterday, had placed Sir Rufus on Elizabeth's left side, with the slightly deaf and ancient Mr Amory, the local vicar, on her right.

The only consolation she could see to this arrangement was that as the host Nathaniel Thorne was seated at the head of the table, with the 'sensible' Miss Rutledge on his left, and the elder of the 'silly' Miss Millers to his right!

'I truly believed, after two hours spent in Tennant's company, that you were about to fall asleep in the sorbet!' Nathaniel grinned at Elizabeth as they later danced the first set together in the small candlelit ballroom at Hepworth Manor, the music provided by four musicians placed up in the gallery.

She looked at him with innocently wide eyes. 'You are mistaken, my lord; I very much enjoyed Sir Rufus's conversation. He was explaining to me the best way to grow roses.'

Those blasted roses again!

Amusement twinkled in those clear blue eyes as she continued, 'It would appear that it involves rather a lot of horse...manure.'

Nathaniel's shout of laughter was completely spontaneous, and drew several interested glances their way, glances that Nathaniel chose to ignore as he looked down at Elizabeth. 'He really is the most boorish of men,' Nathaniel said, shaking his head in disbelief.

Elizabeth shot Sir Rufus a slightly guilty glance as he glowered in their direction from the edge of the dance floor. 'We are being unkind...'

'In my opinion, one cannot be unkind enough about a man who spends two hours in the company of a beautiful young woman and can only think to discuss horse manure,' Nathaniel drawled.

The flush that warmed her cheeks was not entirely due to the exertion of the dance. The Earl of Osbourne, a man every woman in the room eyed so covetously, had just called her beautiful...

And what if he had? Admittedly she had so far received few compliments in her young life, but no doubt the earl had spoken just so to dozens... hundreds of other young women before her! 'I am sure that Miss Miller and Miss Rutledge did not suffer the same fate in your own company,' she retorted waspishly, having been aware, as she listened politely to the drone of Sir Rufus's voice—he had proved to be a man who did so love the sound of his own voice—of the giggles and simpering of those two young ladies at dinner.

'Let us hope not,' Nathaniel teased as they came together again in the dance. 'I do have something of a reputation to uphold, you know.'

Of course he did, Elizabeth reminded herself firmly. A disreputable and womanising reputation that he had no doubt enjoyed earning. The fact that she had become totally aware of the wretched man throughout the course of the dance, of the warmth of his hand through her glove whenever it clasped hers, the heated masculinity of his body when they came together, along with the slumbering sensuality in that dark brown gaze as he looked down at her, was of absolutely no import when she also considered how long and in whose company he had been nurturing that rakish reputation.

She lowered her dark lashes as she rose from her curtsy at the end of the set. 'No doubt you are intending to ask Letitia to dance the next set, my lord?'

It had not so much as occurred to Nathaniel to dance with his aunt's cousin, a woman aged in her mid-fifties, and whom he knew did not enjoy having attention drawn to her, which it surely would be if he were to invite her to dance. 'And why would I wish to do that?'

Elizabeth gave him a pained frown. 'Possibly because Mrs Wilson looked rather displeased when we stood up together for the first set of the evening.'

'Ah.' Nathaniel glanced across to where his aunt sat with several other older ladies, knowing by the fixed smile upon Aunt Gertrude's face that she was not listening to their conversation, her steely gaze fixed upon himself and Elizabeth as they stepped from the dance floor. 'I believe it might be more…politic to ask my aunt herself rather than Letitia.'

Elizabeth gave a gracious nod of her head. 'I am sure she will be most gratified.'

He bowed. 'As no doubt you will enjoy dancing the next set with Tennant. Perhaps he might even offer advice on how to grow tulips or daffodils next.'

'Oh, very droll, my lord.' She sniffed, her frown

turning to a gracious smile as Sir Rufus arrived to claim the next set.

'Osbourne,' he clipped abruptly.

Nathaniel raised haughty brows at the obvious dismissal, looking every inch the superior Earl of Osbourne as his stern gaze raked mercilessly over the older man. 'Have a care, Tennant,' he growled softly.

Sir Rufus gave a start. 'I beg your pardon?'

The earl eased the tension from his shoulders as he affected a charming smile. 'I was advising you to have a care for Miss Thompson's feet; I am afraid I may have inadvertently stepped upon one of them during the latter part of the set.' The two men continued to look at each other, eyes of pale and glittering blue and hard unblinking brown, neither man, it seemed, willing to yield in that silent battle of wills.

'I am feeling a little thirsty, Sir Rufus—perhaps we might find some refreshment before we dance?' Elizabeth's calm request broke into that tension. 'And I believe you were about to ask your aunt to dance the next set, my lord?' she added firmly.

What Nathaniel had been about to do, and what

he now wished to do, were two entirely different things—especially as the one involved planting a firm right hook on the pompous chin of one of his aunt's guests!

Instead he turned and took one of Elizabeth's gloved hands in his. 'I will seek you out again later in the evening,' he promised as he raised that gloved hand to place the warmth of his lips against it.

Elizabeth snatched her hand out of the earl's grasp as soon as she was able to do so without being overly obvious and watched him beneath lowered lashes as he left them to stroll across the room to talk to his aunt. Her palm burned beneath the lace of her glove from the touch of his fingers, the back of her hand aflame from the feel of those lips so close to her skin.

She knew that the intimacy had occurred only as a direct result of an irritating need on the earl's part to annoy Sir Rufus, but that did not make her own response any more acceptable as she sternly reminded herself that Nathaniel Thorne was a practised rake and a bounder, and his flirtatiousness in regard to herself—for whatever reason—was not to be tolerated.

She turned to smile at the glowering Sir Rufus. 'What a tedious young man the earl is, to be sure!'

That glower instantly faded as he returned her smile. 'I am relieved to hear you share my own opinion in that regard.' They strolled out to where refreshments were being served in the spacious hallway.

Elizabeth accepted the glass of punch he handed her, taking a sip to cool the guilty blush from her cheeks before answering him. 'Tell me again how you managed to produce that beautiful white bloom you have named Purity.'

'Ah.' He brightened considerably. 'Well, there...'

Elizabeth once again gave thanks for her sister Caroline's advice as Sir Rufus launched into a repeated explanation of how his obsession with growing roses had encouraged him to produce a hitherto-unknown bloom, and in doing so allowing Elizabeth to smile and nod on occasion without any real need to listen for a second time this evening.

The dance with Sir Rufus was not to be completely avoided, however, and they joined in the third dance of the set, Sir Rufus proving to be an adept dancer, if not a particularly graceful one. That the dance involved her twirling from partner to partner, with the elegantly graceful Lord Thorne as one of those, did not help the other man's cause.

Consequently Elizabeth was relieved when the set came to an end and she was claimed for the next by Mr Amory, followed by Viscount Rutledge, the latter an exceedingly charming widower of perhaps fifty or so years, his conversation, on the local area and his role as magistrate, proving to be of far more interest than Sir Rufus's roses. An interest for which Elizabeth was grateful when she saw Nathaniel Thorne take to the dance floor with Miss Rutledge on his arm and Sir Rufus with Mrs Wilson, fortunately in a dance in which the partners remained together rather than not—Elizabeth had suffered quite enough of the earl's and Sir Rufus's company for one evening!

Indeed, Elizabeth was so taken with the viscount's undemanding company that once the set came to an end she readily accepted his invitation, and his arm, to step out into the hallway for further refreshment.

'It would seem that you have captured the admiration of yet another middle-aged suitor.'

Elizabeth stood to one side of the hallway awaiting Viscount Rutledge's return with the glasses of punch, closing her eyes now as the annoying Earl of Osbourne spoke softly behind her.

Very close behind her if the way the warmth of his breath stirred the curls at her nape was any indication...

Chapter Six

Elizabeth drew in a deep breath, a smile fixed on her lips as she turned to face the earl standing so confidently in the hallway behind her. 'I am sure that Viscount Rutledge's attentions to me are nothing but a politeness on his part, my lord,' she dismissed coolly.

Nathaniel did not miss the unspoken implication that 'politeness' was a trait Elizabeth did not feel he, personally, possessed!

'Nor would I consider Sir Rufus to be middle-aged,' she continued.

But she would consider him to be an admirer…?

Quite rightly so, Nathaniel acknowledged with a frown. The other man was only eight and thirty, and passably wealthy. Observation of Tennant had also shown him to have been watching Elizabeth constantly throughout the evening, often with an intensity that bordered on rudeness. 'Do you not consider it a little greedy on your part, when there are several other single young ladies here this evening, to have so obviously bewitched all the single gentlemen present?' he rasped.

Her sapphire gaze swept over him dismissively. 'Not all, my lord.'

Nathaniel was not as convinced of that as she appeared to be; certainly he had found he had been watching her more this evening than was necessary—or wise—too.

Young women of Elizabeth Thompson's station in life, whilst perhaps suitable for marriage to a man of lower rank, were completely unsuitable for any role in an earl's life other than as his mistress; there was an air of independence about this young lady that said she would be totally averse to such a suggestion, from him or any other gentleman.

Which posed a serious question for Nathaniel as to what he was to do about his rapidly growing attraction towards her…

'Warm evening, is it not, Osbourne?' Viscount Rutledge returned to present Elizabeth with a glass of punch, a rotund man who invariably beamed good humour—even so, Nathaniel had heard, when the man was sending some poor devil off to be incarcerated in prison for several years!

'Very warm, sir.' Nathaniel replied.

'Perhaps you would care to take my punch and I will go back for another?' The older man offered him the second glass.

'Not at all,' Nathaniel refused evenly as he gave an inward shudder at the thought of drinking such a sweet concoction. 'I merely came over to secure Miss Thompson for the next set of dances.'

'Good for you.' The older man beamed. 'You will not regret it; I do not think I have met a partner so light on her feet for many a year.'

Elizabeth blushed, both at the obviously well-meaning compliment and the fact that Lord Thorne had not asked her to dance at all, but instead now placed her in the position of having to stand up with him for the next set or name him the liar he had earlier called her!

It was not that she did not find the earl an exciting man to dance with—he was possibly far too exciting—but she was unhappy about the fact that she had been so totally aware of him as they'd danced together earlier. She had also found herself watching him rather too closely as he'd danced with others. Elizabeth thought perhaps it was best for her peace of mind if she did not dance with him again this evening...

Her saviour came in an unexpected—but not necessarily unwelcome—form.

'Our dance, I believe, Miss Thompson?' Sir Rufus announced firmly as he joined their group.

Elizabeth had only said she would dance with him again later in the evening if there was time. 'Of course, Sir Rufus. If you will excuse us, gentlemen?' She handed her empty punch glass to the scowling earl before leaving on Sir Rufus's arm.

'Intelligent as well as pretty gel, that,' Giles Rutledge murmured as Nathaniel was left holding an empty punch glass rather than Elizabeth.

His mouth tightened as his narrowed gaze followed her progress back into the ballroom. 'So it would seem.'

Giles chuckled. 'Has she worked in your aunt's household for very long?'

For far too long in Nathaniel's frustrated opinion. In fact, it might have been better for all concerned if she had never come to work for his aunt at all.

* * *

'You really should tell Mrs Wilson if young Osbourne's attentions are becoming a nuisance.'

Elizabeth glanced sharply up at Sir Rufus as they danced. 'I have no idea what you mean, sir.' But, of course, she did. And no doubt Mrs Wilson would have something to say to her, either later tonight or first thing tomorrow morning, concerning her nephew's marked attentions towards her. The matter was not currently helped by the fact that Lord Thorne and Viscount Rutledge had returned to the ballroom and the former was once again watching her from beneath hooded lids.

Elizabeth had been invited to join the party this evening to make up the numbers, not, as Nathaniel Thorne had pointed out so mockingly earlier, to find herself engaging the attentions of every single gentleman present.

Although it was rather a pleasant feeling to be so popular, Elizabeth acknowledged ruefully, after years of being secluded in the country, where there was only her father, Squire Castle or his son Malcolm that her father had considered as suitable partners for his daughters to stand up with at the local Assemblies.

'That man is becoming a damned irritant,' Sir Rufus grumbled as he obviously also noted the younger man's presence. 'Every time I turn around, there he is at your elbow.'

Elizabeth doubted that too many people—most especially the women—would consider the Earl of Osbourne's attentions as an 'irritant'! Nor did she welcome the almost possessive tone she had heard in Sir Rufus's voice.

'I am sure he is just being kind.' Elizabeth kept her lashes lowered so that this pompously autocratic man should not see the anger glittering in her eyes; her role of humble companion, she had found, was becoming more and more difficult to maintain in a room full of her peers.

Diana had always acted as their father's hostess during the rare social occasions at Shoreley Park, but Caroline and Elizabeth had also been expected to make their guests welcome and see to their comfort. Here, amongst the local and landed gentry of Devonshire, she had found herself behaving in the same way, which surely was not a role that Betsy Thompson would ever have presumed to take upon herself!

Sir Rufus responded with a sceptical snort. 'Men

like Osbourne are not kind to beautiful young women out of the goodness of their hearts.'

She took exception to Sir Rufus's comment—despite having said exactly the same thing herself to the earl's face only days ago! It was one thing for Elizabeth to say it, quite another for this man to do so.

She looked up at him with deliberately innocent eyes. 'What other reason could there possibly be?'

'Why, the obvious one, of course!'

'Obvious, sir?' Surely this man would not dare to voice anything so outrageous in her presence?

'From all that I have heard, Osbourne prefers to take his mistresses from his inferiors.'

He would dare!

It was an indecent indiscretion Sir Rufus also seemed to become aware of as he began to bluster. 'Not that I am suggesting for one moment that you have in any way encouraged his attentions—'

'Perhaps that is as well!' Elizabeth came to a halt in the dancing. 'If you will excuse me, Sir Rufus? I—I feel I have danced enough for one evening.' She turned and walked from the dance floor, in the opposite direction from where Lord Thorne now stood conversing with Lady Miller.

'Miss Thompson!'

Unwisely, Sir Rufus had followed her. Even more unwisely, he had dared to grasp Elizabeth's arm and turn her to face him once again. She feared she really had suffered enough of this boorish man's company for one evening! 'Release me at once, Sir Rufus,' she spoke quietly, but the force behind her words was unmistakable.

A warning he quite rightly heeded as his hand dropped back to his side. 'I meant you no insult—'

Tears of humiliation had gathered on Elizabeth's lashes as she looked up at him. 'Whether it was your intention to do so or not, that is obviously what has occurred, sir.' Her chin rose proudly.

He attempted a placatory smile, but it was as though the gesture were not one he was familiar with. 'I do most sincerely apologise, Miss Thompson.'

'Your apology is accepted,' Elizabeth replied, very aware that those hot tears were close to falling down her cheeks.

'I had intended to ask Mrs Wilson if I might take you out driving in my carriage tomorrow afternoon,' he said.

Elizabeth bit her tongue to stop the sharp reply that sprang to her lips; unbelievably this man insulted her and then expected her to go out driving with him in his carriage tomorrow! 'I am afraid that will not be possible, Sir Rufus—'

'You can even bring that wretched animal with you if you wish,' he offered with obvious distaste.

A reluctant concession that only made Elizabeth all the more determined to refuse him. 'I am sure my time will be taken up tomorrow with helping to tidy away after this evening's festivities,' she said.

'Mrs Wilson has servants to do that—' He broke off with an uncomfortable wince.

'And I believe we have just decided I am one of them,' Elizabeth pointed out acerbically. 'Now you really must excuse me.' She did not trouble herself to wait for his reply, but instead quietly slipped out of the French doors that led out onto the terrace at the back of the house, moving to stand beside the metal balustrade and draw in deep breaths of air as she tried to stop those scalding tears from cascading down her cheeks.

And failed.

What an absolutely priggish man Sir Rufus Tennant was! How dared he—? Who did he think that he was—? To have insulted her so by implying—ooh!

Elizabeth was enraged. Incensed. Her evening totally ruined. Nor, she knew, would she ever again take for granted the feelings of her own maid Mary.

Not that she believed she had ever been unkind to that cheerful and obliging young lady, but having played the subservient role herself this past two weeks, Elizabeth better appreciated Mary's efforts on her behalf, and now realised that even the slight of taking those efforts for granted could be hurtful.

Had Mary ever had to suffer the unwanted attentions and insults of men such as Sir Rufus Tennant? If she had, then Elizabeth could only pity her—

'Elizabeth?'

Even if she had not instantly recognised those husky sensual tones as belonging to Nathaniel Thorne, she would have known it was he; the earl was the only person at Hepworth Manor who insisted on calling her by her given name.

And she was standing here like a ninny with

tears of humiliation scalding her cheeks and no doubt also causing her eyes to appear red and puffy!

Nathaniel, having witnessed Elizabeth's altercation with Tennant and her abrupt departure from the house, was not in the least reassured now by the fact that she would not so much as turn and look at him. 'Elizabeth—'

'Go away, my lord! Please!' she added less forcefully.

Nathaniel strolled across the terrace to stand beside her, the moonlight strong enough to allow him to see the whiteness of her knuckles as she tightly gripped the metal railing. A glance up at her averted face also revealed the evidence of tears on the paleness of the cheek visible to him. Nathaniel frowned as he reached out to grasp her arms and turn her to face him, to see more evidence of those tears on her other cheek. He looked down at her searchingly before taking her into his arms, the softness of her dark curls resting against his chest as his arms encircled the slenderness of her waist.

Perhaps not the most sensible thing for him to

have done, considering he had hardly been able to take his eyes off her all evening!

He had meant to offer her comfort and hopefully was doing that. But the close proximity of her soft and alluring curves, the beguiling feminine perfume of her hair, were all having their effect upon his own senses. Nathaniel could feel the stirring of his arousal—a fact that she would also soon become aware of if he continued to hold her so closely against him!

He put her slightly away from him. 'What did Tennant do or say to upset you so?' he demanded.

She shook her head. 'It is not important—'

'I disagree.'

'Please release me so that I may get my hand-kerchief from my pocket.' She looked up at him pleadingly.

A plea that Nathaniel acceded to as he saw the fresh tears escaping over her long lashes and down her cheeks, waiting until she had mopped them up before speaking again. 'Did Tennant proposition you?'

Elizabeth gave a choked laugh at that irony. 'No, of course he did not.'

'Then what did he do?' Nathaniel scowled down

at her darkly. 'And do not tell me he did nothing, because I will not believe you.'

She drew in a deep and steadying breath before answering him evenly. 'What you do or do not choose to believe is of no relevance to me.'

'Indeed?' he drawled drily. 'Then perhaps I should discuss this incident with my aunt.'

Elizabeth gasped. 'You will do no such thing—'

'And how do you intend to stop me from doing so?' He raised a mocking brow.

She glared up at him in frustration, knowing that the patient expression on his face was nothing but an illusion; she could feel the earl's inner displeasure as it came off him in waves.

Elizabeth was uncomfortably aware of how alone they were out here on the terrace, none of the other guests having yet felt the need to escape out into the cooling air, leaving the stillness of the night to enshroud just the two of them in its intimacy.

She shifted awkwardly. 'Perhaps we should go back inside.'

'Not until you have told me what Tennant did to upset you,' Nathaniel maintained stubbornly, the shield of his body not allowing her to go back inside without his agreement, which he had no intention of giving, not until he knew exactly what Tennant had said or done to reduce the normally stubbornly resilient Elizabeth to tears.

Seeing her distress had caused a tightening in his chest, at the same time as he felt an inner surge of violence towards the man who had caused it. He would know the reason why before he ripped Tennant to verbal, if not physical, shreds!

Elizabeth looked up at him beneath long and silky dark lashes. 'Are you really sure you wish to know, my lord?'

Her comment instantly alerted Nathaniel to the fact that he might have somehow featured in the way Tennant had hurt Elizabeth and he became even more determined to discover what had happened. 'Very sure,' he bit out tersely, a nerve pulsing in his tightly clenched jaw.

'Very well.' She gave a slight inclination of her head. 'Sir Rufus was concerned, owing to the fact that he seems to find you constantly 'at my elbow', as to your intentions towards me.'

'My intentions?'

The wariness in his tone was enough to make Elizabeth smile forlornly. 'He seemed to be under the impression that you choose your mistresses from the lower classes.'

'Good God!' The earl looked astounded. 'He actually said that to you?'

'Yes.' Elizabeth's smile widened as her sense of humour returned to her, no doubt due to the earl's genuine astonishment that Sir Rufus Tennant should have discussed such an indelicate subject with her at all. Elizabeth had been shocked at the time, but after Nathaniel Thorne's reaction she could not help but begin to find the incident amusing. She coughed delicately. 'He seemed to be under the impression that you might very shortly attempt to offer me that position, seeing that I fit your preferences.'

Considering Nathaniel's own thoughts had touched briefly on the same subject earlier this evening—and the way his erection throbbed achingly just from holding Elizabeth briefly in his arms a few minutes ago—he could have well done without Tennant's less-than-discreet remarks.

He eyed Elizabeth beneath hooded lids. 'And what were your thoughts on the subject?'

She gave a small trill of incredulous laughter.

'I assured him that it was not even a possibility, of course.'

Of course. So it was a pity that Nathaniel's own thoughts were still so undecided.

There was no doubting that he was attracted to this young beauty, or that it was an unsuitable attraction, considering her position in his aunt's household. But as he had watched her throughout the evening and felt himself drawn to the sensuous elegance of her body as she danced, had witnessed the easy charm with which she dealt with those around her, he had begun to wonder if it might not be possible to tempt Elizabeth away from her employment here and set her up in a discreet household of her own, where he might visit her whenever he felt so inclined.

Which, considering the arousal caused from just briefly holding the soft warmth of her feminine curves against his own would no doubt be often in the first few weeks of that arrangement!

But it was an arrangement he dared not even think of suggesting now after Tennant's hamfisted handling of the situation—which had perhaps been the other man's intent? he mused.

'My lord?' Elizabeth eyed him warily now.

Nathaniel sighed inwardly. 'It is usually polite to wait until one is asked before one says no.' Especially if the mere suggestion of it had reduced her to tears!

A frown appeared between her eyes. 'I merely thought to share the absurdity of Sir Rufus's suggestion with you, my lord.'

So not only had she found the suggestion so insulting it had reduced her to tears, but in retrospect she now found the very idea of such an arrangement absurd!

Neither of which was particularly flattering to a man's ego, Nathaniel acknowledged ruefully. Especially when the remark was made by the young and beautiful woman he found so physically arousing! 'You realise the reason for Tennant's interference, I hope?' he said.

Elizabeth was not so naïve that she did not realise exactly the reason for Sir Rufus's boorish behaviour. But if he had thought to endear himself to her by acting as her protector in the bluntly crude way he had tonight, then he was going to be sadly disappointed. A gentleman simply did not discuss such matters with a single young lady, no matter how lowly her station in life might appear to be.

She gave a shake of her head. 'I do not at all return Sir Rufus's interest.'

'You still have no inclination to accept an offer of marriage if he were to make one?'

'I do not.' Elizabeth barely managed to repress her shiver of revulsion at the very idea of marriage to a man such as Sir Rufus Tennant.

'I am glad to hear it,' Nathaniel said with obvious relief.

'Are you?' Elizabeth eyed him curiously. 'Why?'

He returned that frown for several long tension-filled seconds before answering evasively, 'Can you really see yourself incarcerated in the country for the rest of your life?'

As that had been Elizabeth's fate until a few short weeks ago, she had to suppress a smile! 'Devonshire is certainly a very beautiful part of England.' She shrugged.

'I doubt it would hold the same appeal if you were the wife of a pompous and self-opinionated man like Tennant.' Nathaniel's lips twisted into a moue of distaste.

'Perhaps not everyone finds Sir Rufus as… trying, as we do?' Elizabeth suggested fairly.

'I doubt that is true, considering he is still unmarried at eight and thirty,' Nathaniel said brusquely, having every intention of speaking severely to that gentlemen on the subject of Elizabeth Thompson before the evening came to an end.

'Perhaps he has remained unmarried through choice?' she mused.

'Perhaps.'

Elizabeth glanced at him thoughtfully. 'You speak as if you might know the reason for that choice.'

Nathaniel shook his head. 'I do not believe anyone knows Tennant well enough to know that.' Certainly not well enough to say with any certainty as to whether or not Sir Rufus had indeed been somewhat unhinged by the suicide of his younger brother all those years ago. 'I am merely trying to point out the oddity of a personable and reasonably wealthy man such as Sir Rufus still being unwed at the advanced age of eight and thirty.'

'In what way odd?' she pounced.

Nathaniel seriously regretted even broaching this subject. Not because he did not wish to turn Elizabeth's sympathy away from Sir Rufus—because he most certainly did—but Giles Tennant taking his own life had left a nasty taste in the mouths of all in society.

Affairs in society, and there were many, were usually conducted behind closed doors, well away from prying eyes and the sight, if not the knowledge, of one's spouse. That Giles Tennant had not only conducted such an affair with a married woman, but that the woman in question had actually deserted her husband and children to be openly at his side, had shaken society to its very foundations.

The two had been ostracised totally, of course; affairs were an accepted part of society, but a young man living openly with a married woman who had deserted her husband and children was not.

Even so, the two had remained in London, seemingly too much in love with each other to care that society now shunned them. And so Sir Rufus Tennant had been called upon to try to talk some sense into his younger brother. Which he had obviously failed to do; the couple had continued to live openly together for several more weeks before Giles had killed first his married lover, then himself.

Surely that was enough to unhinge even the most emotionally balanced of men, as Sir Rufus Tennant had always been considered to be?

'Lord Thorne…?'

'I apologise.' Nathaniel shook off the darkness of his memories at Elizabeth's softly spoken query; after all, it had been many years ago—he had only known Giles Tennant socially, and his married lover not at all. 'I was merely wondering if perhaps the reason for Sir Rufus's comments was because his own intentions towards you are no more honourable than he has claimed mine to be?' he suggested.

Her eyes widened. 'You believe he might offer to make me his mistress?'

'It is a possibility,' Nathaniel allowed grimly.

Elizabeth considered she had heard quite enough on that particular subject this evening! 'Then it appears I would be well advised to avoid being alone in the company of both of you.'

'Eliz—'

'I wish you goodnight, Lord Thorne,' she added firmly before turning swiftly on her heel and going back into the warmth and noise of the ballroom.

Well away from the disturbing company of Nathaniel Thorne.

Chapter Seven

'I wonder if you would mind leaving us for a while, Letitia?' Mrs Wilson smiled kindly at her cousin, as the three ladies sat together in the drawing room. 'I wish to talk privately to Betsy for a few minutes.'

The day following Mrs Wilson's dinner party had proved to be a busy one for Elizabeth, the morning spent, as she had predicted, in helping to tidy away, and the afternoon with receiving those ladies wishing to call and thank Mrs Wilson personally for such a wonderful dinner and entertainment the evening before.

Elizabeth had not seen Lord Thorne at all today, Sewell having informed Mrs Wilson at breakfast this morning that the earl had received several letters of correspondence that necessitated he spend most of the day in the library. Nor did he wish to be disturbed.

Weary from all the activity and visitors, Elizabeth had minutes ago excused herself from Mrs Wilson's presence with the intention of taking Hector for his afternoon walk. Her employer's request that she linger for a few minutes more so that she might 'talk to her privately' did not bode well…

'Do sit down again for a few moments, my dear,' Mrs Wilson chided gently as Elizabeth stood warily beside the doorway through which Letitia had just quietly left.

She sat down on the edge of a chair; Mrs Wilson was such a forceful woman it was impossible to ignore even her lightest request! 'Have I done something to displease you?' After the events of yesterday evening, Elizabeth suspected the worst. 'I assure you, I did nothing last evening to encourage the attentions of Sir Rufus or Viscount Rutledge.' Her cheeks coloured self-consciously as she omitted the name of the one man whose attentions were most likely to have caused Mrs Wilson's displeasure.

'It has been my experience that a beautiful

young woman does not have to do anything to encourage a gentleman's attentions,' Mrs Wilson stated drily.

'Perhaps not.' A frown puckered Elizabeth's creamy brow. 'Nevertheless, I assure you that I did not seek out the company of either of those gentlemen.'

'My dear girl…' Mrs Wilson gave a perplexed shake of her head '…you seem to be under the impression that I wish to chastise you for something you either did or said during the course of yesterday evening.'

'You do not…?' Elizabeth eyed the older woman uncertainly.

'Certainly not. Indeed, it has ever been the way of it that gentlemen will make fools of themselves over a pretty gel.' Her employer gave a contemptuous snort.

Then Elizabeth was completely at a loss as to why the other woman might wish to talk to her privately.

Mrs Wilson's gaze was piercing. 'You have been with me for several weeks now, and—tell me, are you happy in your employment with me?'

'Very much so.' Some of the tension left Elizabeth's shoulders—who could not be happy working in the household of such a kind lady as Mrs Gertrude Wilson, with the added boon of having darling Hector to care for?

'But it is not what you were born to, is it?'

Elizabeth realised that she had allowed herself to relax too soon as that shrewd gaze seemed to see right into the guilty heart of her. She turned her own eyes away to moisten dry lips, not quite sure how she should answer.

'Come now, Elizabeth,' Mrs Wilson encouraged. 'It is obvious to me that your voice and manners are those of a lady.'

The fact that the older woman had used her full name was in no way reassuring either! 'A lady fallen upon hard times, perhaps,' she explained evasively.

'Perhaps.' Mrs Wilson nodded slowly. 'I have become fond of you these past weeks, Elizabeth, and I would not like to think that… Are you in some sort of trouble? With your family, or possibly…' she shuddered '…the law?'

'Did Lord Thorne instigate these doubts in your mind about me, Mrs Wilson?' Elizabeth's impatience with that gentleman was barely contained.

'Osbourne?' The puzzlement on Mrs Wilson's face was enough to show that her nephew had not yet voiced his own suspicions to her.

'I assure you I am not in any sort of trouble, Mrs Wilson,' Elizabeth said honestly.

Oh, she had no doubts that when she and Diana met again, her sister would be most displeased with her, but Diana was never cross with either of her two headstrong sisters for very long, and no doubt in this case her relief at having Elizabeth returned to her would outweigh any serious upset. She could not care less what her new guardian, the scandalous Lord Faulkner, Earl of Westbourne, thought about her escapade, even if he ever came to learn of it, which was most unlikely as Diana would never betray her sisters like that.

'I am pleased to hear it,' Mrs Wilson said briskly. 'But you do not—there is nothing which you would like to discuss with me?'

Having grown up without a mother's guidance these past ten years Elizabeth felt the rise of an emotional lump in her throat at Mrs Wilson's obvious kindness. To the extent that she almost—almost—felt tempted to confide her present dilemma to the older woman. Indeed, only the knowledge that Mrs Wilson could not possibly continue to employ her, once she was made aware of Elizabeth's true identity and the offer of marriage from the Earl of Westbourne—a man Mrs Wilson was personally acquainted with and who was clearly a close friend of her nephew— prevented her from doing so.

'I assure you, there is truly nothing to discuss.' Elizabeth's situation, whilst it might possibly be a cause for awkwardness and embarrassment if her identity became known, in no way affected her employment here. 'Having no male relative on whom I can rely, I am in need of employment in order to support myself,' she added for clarification; Lord Gabriel Faulkner might be her father's third cousin or some such, but his relationship to Elizabeth was tenuous to say the least, notwithstanding his cold and clinical offer of marriage to her or one of her sisters!

'Very well.' Mrs Wilson accepted the end of the subject. 'There is just one other matter which I feel I must discuss with you...'

Elizabeth stiffened warily. 'Yes?'

Mrs Wilson smiled benignly. 'Sir Rufus approached me before he left yesterday evening and requested my permission to take you driving in his carriage. My dear, I appreciate he is not the most exciting of men.' Her employer chuckled at Elizabeth's dismayed expression. 'Indeed, it is the company of men like him that make me appreciate how lucky I was to spend almost twenty years of marriage with my darling Bastian!' She sighed in fond remembrance. 'However, boring as Sir Rufus Tennant undoubtedly is, I am duty-bound to remind you that he is nevertheless a titled and respectable gentleman.'

And beggars could not be choosers, Elizabeth acknowledged heavily. Except, even as Lady Elizabeth Copeland, she was nowhere near beggared enough to accept the attentions of a man as old and uninteresting as Rufus Tennant.

And it had absolutely nothing to do with her feelings for the young, virile and wickedly handsome Nathaniel Thorne!

Except, of course, it did…

Irritating as she found that gentleman, she could not deny that her heart beat faster whenever he was near, or that his kisses affected her in a way that was distinctly unladylike. Just thinking of those embraces now was enough to cause her breasts to swell and their rosy tips to tighten!

She shifted uncomfortably. 'I informed Sir Rufus yesterday evening that I had no wish to go driving with him in his carriage.'

'Boring but insistent.' Mrs Wilson frowned her impatience with the man. 'Do not worry, my dear, I will deal with Sir Rufus,' she declared. 'And if there ever comes a time when you do wish to speak with me about anything, then know that I have a sympathetic ear.' She smiled encouragingly.

An encouragement that was almost Elizabeth's undoing as she felt the sting of tears in her eyes. Diana was the most wonderful of sisters, a stalwart to both Elizabeth and Caroline since their mother's defection, much more so than their Aunt Humphries, who had lived with them for many years; Mrs Wilson's offer of sympathy made Elizabeth realise how much she had missed having an older woman to share her youthful uncertainties with.

She stood up. 'You are very kind, Mrs Wilson,' she said, her voice husky with emotion.

'A secret probably better not confided to

Osbourne—otherwise I shall never succeed in marrying him off!' The older woman laughed affectionately.

'I am afraid it is far too late to keep that particular secret, Aunt; I have long been acquainted with your kindness,' Nathaniel drawled as he straightened from the doorway where he had been standing for the past several minutes as an unwilling eavesdropper on the ladies' conversation.

A fact that obviously displeased Elizabeth Thompson as she rounded on him accusingly. 'A lady must surely be allowed some secrets, my lord.'

Nathaniel strolled further into the room, aware that she was not now referring to his aunt's kindness. Just as he was aware of how lovely Elizabeth looked today in a gown of buttercup yellow, her dark curls artlessly arranged about the delicate beauty of her face and emphasising the deep blue of her eyes. Eyes that had become deep and stormy as she glared her ire at him. 'As long as that lady realises it is those very secrets that deepen and hold a man's interest…' He watched through narrowed lids as delicate—and guilty?—colour warmed her cheeks.

'You have finished your correspondence for the day, Osbourne?' his aunt asked.

He shook his head. 'I am merely tired of being confined indoors, Aunt, to the extent that I have come to enquire if I might not accompany Miss Thompson and Hector on their afternoon walk?'

Elizabeth had not been at all pleased by Lord Thorne's interruption of and his eavesdropping on her conversation with Mrs Wilson; she was even less so now at the thought of being alone with him again.

They had parted badly the evening before—when did they not?—and Elizabeth certainly had no intention of continuing that *risqué* conversation. 'Are you sure you are well enough after the… exertions of yesterday evening, my lord?'

'And what 'exertions' might those be, Miss Thompson?' he asked pointedly.

Reminding Elizabeth far too strongly of being held in this man's arms against the warmth and hardness of his body as they danced together… 'Why, the dancing and conversation, my lord.' She sincerely hoped that Mrs Wilson did not guess the reason for the blush that coloured her cheeks.

Nathaniel's mouth quirked. 'I may have been

indisposed these past few days, but I assure you I am not yet so decrepit that a little dancing and company render me prostrate the following day.'

The warmth deepened in her cheeks at her intimate knowledge of just how decrepit this man was not! 'I am sure I did not mean—'

'Stop teasing Elizabeth, Osbourne.' Mrs Wilson came to her rescue.

His brows were raised as he turned to look enquiringly at his aunt. 'I thought you preferred she be called Betsy?'

'It no longer seems...fitting,' Mrs Wilson explained. 'And I am sure that a walk in the fresh air will be good for the both of you,' she added. 'I believe that a short lie down upon my bed will serve me better!' She was smiling as she stood up to leave.

Elizabeth's eyes widened warningly on the earl as she saw the heated speculation in his gaze as he glanced across at her after his aunt's announcement. As if he were envisaging the benefits of the two of them lying down on a bed together...

It was an image that both alarmed and excited her. It would no doubt be very exciting to lie on a bed beside the wickedly handsome Nathaniel

Thorne. Just as her inexperience in such matters made her unsure and positively alarmed at what might follow!

Diana, as their Aunt Humphries had previously done with her, had dutifully talked to her two younger sisters concerning what to expect in the marriage bed when that time came. But Elizabeth had only needed to be held in Nathaniel Thorne's arms, to be kissed by him, caressed by him, to know that there could be much more between a man and a woman than simply lying upon one's back and allowing her husband to take his pleasure.

What of that tingling in her breasts when he held or kissed her? The hardening of those rosy tips when he touched her there? That hot damp-ness that bloomed expectantly between her thighs whenever he was near? There simply had to be more between a man and a woman than Diana had described!

A curiosity to know what that 'more' was had been well and truly awakened in Elizabeth by the obviously experienced Earl of Osbourne...

'You really meant what you said yesterday eve-ning about not wishing to go for a drive in Ten-nant's carriage with him...'

Elizabeth glanced at the earl beneath her straw bonnet as the two of them once again walked along the cliff path—Hector firmly secured to his lead!—in the sunny light of day this time, the views of the Devonshire coastline magnificently displayed before them. Scenery that was wasted on Elizabeth at the moment as she could think only of Lord Thorne's presence beside her and those earlier, disturbing thoughts of intimacy…

The earl's comment revealed that he had overheard much more of her conversation with Mrs Wilson than Elizabeth had previously realised. 'I rarely say what I do not mean, my lord,' she said as she paused to allow Hector to investigate a particularly aromatic display of wildflowers.

'Then you are unusual among your sex, Elizabeth,' he said drily, very elegant in a dark blue superfine with a silver-brocade waistcoat and pale grey pantaloons, black Hessians gleaming brightly, his hat sitting rakishly atop his blond locks.

'Perhaps that is only so amongst the members of my sex that you have so far…encountered, my lord,' she came back tartly as they continued upon their way.

Putting him firmly and decisively in his place, Nathaniel acknowledged appreciatively. Just as he appreciated that Elizabeth's observation was probably a correct one. He tended to stay well away from young and marriageable ladies of the *ton*—being ever wary of the parson's mousetrap!—and also the more beautiful of the married ladies, who were often interested in playing society's games in the bedchamber whilst their husbands conducted their own affairs. It was a game Nathaniel had never felt inclined to play, having an aversion to entanglements with married ladies, whatever their social standing. Which left him to dally with only the young and widowed ladies of society, or the occasional actress who caught his eye.

Despite Tennant's outrageous remarks to Elizabeth yesterday evening, Nathaniel did not take advantage of young ladies employed by himself, his friends, or his aunt!

Which begged the question, what was he now doing once again alone in Elizabeth's company, torturing himself with what he could not have?

Nathaniel had decided after last night that perhaps he should stay away from her if his smallest attention to her was to be the subject of gossip by people such as Tennant. Indeed, he had busied himself answering correspondence in the library all day in an effort to do just that. Only to find, after meeting Letitia in the hallway earlier, that he was drawn to the room where she had left his aunt and Elizabeth talking quietly together.

He had stood in the doorway and watched her unobserved for several minutes. Admiring the beauty of her profile. Appreciating the elegance of her bearing. Coveting the swell of her breasts visible above the low neckline of her yellow gown.

Not what he should be thinking of whilst out walking alone with her on a cliff-top with only the good-natured Hector to act as chaperon! 'I expected I might receive a correspondence from my disreputable friend Westbourne this morning,' Nathaniel said the first thing that came into his head—a head he realised was once again filled with thoughts of taking Elizabeth in his arms and kissing her senseless!

She stiffened, no doubt in disapproval. 'You did not?'

'No.' He grinned at her obvious displeasure. 'No doubt he is being kept busy about his own affairs.'

'Oh?'

He nodded. 'You will no doubt be surprised to learn that almost seven months ago he was given guardianship of three young ladies.'

Elizabeth was obviously not in the least surprised to hear that—how could she possibly be when she was one of them! 'One can only feel sorry for those unfortunate young ladies,' she said cuttingly.

The earl chuckled huskily. 'Knowing Westbourne, I have no doubt they will all three very shortly fall in love with him.'

'Indeed?' Elizabeth eyed him frostily, knowing that this one certainly would not! And she believed that her two sisters had more sense than to do so, either.

'Most women do, you know,' Nathaniel admitted ruefully.

'Then they must be particularly stupid women,' Elizabeth bit out tartly, uncomfortable discussing her new guardian like this. Unless... 'And why would you think that I might be in the least interested about anything concerning Lord Faulkner?'

The earl shrugged. 'I was merely making conversation.'

'About a man whom you already know I disapprove of?'

He grimaced. 'Perhaps in the hopes that you would realise there are men of much worse reputation than I!'

Elizabeth eyed him speculatively. 'I had not realised there were degrees of being disreputable.'

'Oh, certainly there are.' He grinned down at her. 'I, for example, am considered only moderately so.'

'Whereas Lord Faulkner is considered completely beyond the pale.' Elizabeth nodded sagely. 'I see.'

The earl frowned his irritation. 'Now see here, Elizabeth—' He broke off as she smiled up at him teasingly. 'You are funning me,' he realised slowly.

Indeed she was. And from his reaction, it was not something that occurred very often, particularly from a woman...

As the daughter of an earl, Elizabeth knew that the title of the Earl of Osbourne wielded much power and influence, in society as well as in the House. As such it would only be his very closest friends and family, such as Lord Gabriel Faulkner and Mrs Wilson, who would dare to talk to him in this irreverent way. Which was perhaps part of the reason for his seeking out Elizabeth's less-than-respectful company in the way that he did?

Well, she certainly had no intention of behaving like a simpering ninny in order to dispel that interest, batting her eyelashes at him and giggling at his slightest remark, as the Misses Miller and Rutledge had done the previous evening! Even if she had a genuine wish to dispel any interest he might have in her—which, the more time she spent in his company, she was not at all sure she did have...

This man might often irritate and annoy her, but he also excited her, made her feel truly desirable for the first time in her young life. After years of living almost the life of a nun, hidden away in the country under the vigilant and watchful eye of her father, it was heady flattery indeed to know that a man as handsome and sought after as Nathaniel Thorne found her company pleasing. That he found *her* pleasing.

There was also the added boon of her teasing having succeeded in diverting the conversation from the potentially dangerous subject of the Earl of Westbourne. 'Only mildly funning you, my lord,' she allowed drily. 'And what, in this rising scale of being disreputable, would you consider Sir Rufus Tennant's level to be?' she prompted mischievously.

'He does not register at all,' Nathaniel dismissed scornfully.

'No?'

'Tennant's younger brother was the disreputable one in that family,' he revealed.

Her eyes widened. 'Was?'

Nathaniel frowned his annoyance, both with this return of the conversation to the elder Tennant and with the fact that he had allowed himself to be so irritated by it he had resorted to repeating gossip. 'Giles Tennant succeeded in killing himself several years ago.'

'But how sad for Sir Rufus!' Elizabeth gasped, obviously deeply moved by this revelation.

He had obviously succeeded in arousing her sympathy for the older man, Nathaniel realised impatiently. 'Do not feel too sorry for him, Elizabeth; Giles had shot and killed his married lover before he took his own life,' he said harshly.

Elizabeth came to an abrupt halt, swaying where

she stood, the colour draining from her cheeks, her chest becoming so tight that she could barely breathe. Surely—surely it was not possible…? Could it be the case that Sir Rufus Tennant's brother had been the lover of her own mother?

But the coincidence of events was undeniable; the young men of the *ton* were known for being rakish and outrageous, but how many of them could there possibly be who had actually shot and killed their married lover before then killing themselves?

'Elizabeth?'

'I—how shocking.' Her throat felt so parched that she could barely speak, her head abuzz with the possibilities. 'How long ago did this happen?'

'What difference does it make when it occurred?' he asked curiously.

'I—well, I would know then whether or not I ought to offer Sir Rufus my condolences when next I see him,' Elizabeth invented breathlessly.

'You should not,' the earl announced definitely with a dark scowl.

'But—'

'Elizabeth, it happened years ago. Damn it, I only revealed the scandal to you at all in order to demonstrate that there is likely an emotional instability in that family,' he explained.

And now that he had, Elizabeth needed to know more. To know everything that there was to know about the murder of Giles Tennant's lover followed by his own suicide. She felt a desperate need to know whether Sir Rufus was the older brother of the man for whom her mother had deserted both her husband and three young daughters ten years ago…

Chapter Eight

'Are you all right?' Nathaniel looked down at her frowningly as he saw how pale her face had become, her eyes wide and darkly shadowed, both those things reminding him all too forcibly that, for all she gave the impression of self-reliance, she was in fact a very young lady employed by his aunt. And in his annoyance with Rufus Tennant's persistent interest in her, Nathaniel had related something that Elizabeth obviously found extremely shocking.

Annoyance…?

Was it just annoyance Nathaniel felt at Tennant's persistence, or could it be some other emotion? Something much more ugly? Such as resentment at the other man's interest in her?

Surely not? Resentment would seem to imply jealousy of a sort, and jealousy was an irrational emotion; Nathaniel was not an irrational man. Decisive, even arrogant, but he did not believe he was ever irrational.

He was attracted to Elizabeth certainly, but surely no more so than he had found himself attracted to dozens of other women over the years. Attractions that had invariably been successful in their outcome…

Something that certainly could not be said of his current attraction towards the elusive, even slightly mysterious, Elizabeth Thompson. Was that perhaps the real reason for his current irritation? It was certainly a more agreeable explanation than his previous one had been!

Elizabeth still felt dazed, knowing that her more-than-obvious reaction to Lord Thorne's disclosure of the scandal involving Sir Rufus's brother must seem strange—and the very last thing she wished to do was arouse the earl's suspicions as to her personal interest in that subject.

No, if she wished to know any more of it, to confirm if her suspicions were true or not, then she must talk to Sir Rufus himself.

'I—I believe we have walked far enough for one afternoon, my lord.' She gave a tight smile as she tugged lightly on Hector's lead so that she might turn back towards Hepworth Manor.

Nathaniel fell into step beside her. 'I apologise,' he said. 'I have obviously upset you by speaking of the scandal involving Tennant's brother.'

'But you did not speak of it,' Elizabeth denied. 'Not in any detail, at least,' she added with a frown. 'You did not reveal the name of his married lover, for example…'

'Nor will I.' His mouth was tight. 'I should not have said the little that I did. It is not a suitable subject upon which to converse with you. What I said distressed you enough, Elizabeth.'

Elizabeth would be ever grateful that he had mentioned it at all. Especially if it should turn out that Giles Tennant had indeed been her mother's young lover…

It at least gave her the opportunity to speak with Sir Rufus, a man who would likely know more of the past scandal that had resulted in her mother's death—something that neither Elizabeth nor her sisters had so far been able to learn.

It had not occurred to any of the sisters to question their father too deeply when their mother first left them; they had all been too young and greatly traumatised by that desertion, and their father had been prostrate with grief. And later, once the three sisters were old enough to voice their curiosity about the past, their father had refused absolutely to discuss his wife, or the scandal surrounding her death, with any of them.

Of course, Sir Rufus could prove to be just as intractable on the subject of his brother's demise, and, even if he was not, Elizabeth's hopes might all be dashed if he were to reveal that his brother's death had absolutely no connection to that of Harriet Copeland.

But until Elizabeth had the opportunity to speak with Sir Rufus again she had no way of knowing that. Which was why, once she had returned to Hepworth Manor, Elizabeth now had every intention of accepting Sir Rufus's invitation to go out riding in his carriage with him.

'I am merely tired, my lord, and not in the least upset by your conversation,' she said to explain the abruptness of her decision to return to Hepworth Manor.

Nathaniel felt a sense of dissatisfaction with Elizabeth's answer, aware there was something… different about her in these past few minutes.

And she was correct; it was not distress that he now sensed in her emotions, but something else. Something he did not understand, which he found highly displeasing.

He eyed her closely from beneath the brim of his hat. 'Perhaps you should have followed my aunt's example and rested in your room instead of coming outside for a walk.'

'Perhaps,' she echoed evasively.

Nathaniel's frustration increased. 'It is my intention to call upon Viscount Rutledge tomorrow.'

'An excellent idea.' Elizabeth nodded coolly. 'I am sure Miss Rutledge will think so too,' she added mockingly.

His mouth firmed at her obvious taunting. 'Perhaps you would care to come with me?'

'And cast a shadow over Miss Rutledge's pleasure in seeing you again?' She shook her head.

'I was thinking more along the lines that Rutledge might be pleased at a visit from you,' Nathaniel said satirically.

'Of course...' She appeared to give the matter some thought as Hector lingered to investigate a rabbit hole. 'No, I believe it would be better if you were to go alone, my lord. Besides,' she continued firmly as Nathaniel would have spoken again, 'I am really not at liberty to just disappear with you on a visit to one of Mrs Wilson's neighbours.'

'You are if I say that you—' Nathaniel broke off with an annoyed growl. 'Never mind.' He scowled. 'I believe I will leave you and Hector to finish the walk back at your leisure.' He glanced down at the little dog as he continued to dig his way further into the rabbit hole. 'I have some more correspondence to deal with before dinner.'

'Have a care, my lord, or all this work may make you as dull as you believe Sir Rufus to be!' Elizabeth jeered.

Nathaniel felt utterly frustrated as he returned that teasing gaze, knowing that he only intended shutting himself away in the relative privacy of the library at Hepworth Manor in order to prevent himself from doing something totally irresponsible—such as making love to Elizabeth again.

He raised a mocking eyebrow. 'I do not believe there could possibly be another man alive as dull as he!'

Until a short time ago Elizabeth would have totally agreed with him. But if her suspicion as to his connection to her mother's young lover should prove to be correct, Elizabeth knew she would then consider him the most interesting man of her acquaintance!

Not at all in the way that she found Nathaniel Thorne interesting, of course; the earl had awakened feelings inside her, hidden desires that she had so far been totally unable to rationalise. Or resist…

She gave a graceful shrug of her shoulders. 'No doubt one person's idea of dullness might be another's idea of stability and steadfastness. Both of them desirable qualities, I am sure you will agree?'

'I trust nothing I have said to you today has influenced you into feeling so much sympathy with Tennant that you are now reconsidering your refusal to go out riding in his carriage with him?' The earl scowled down at her darkly.

Elizabeth deliberately kept her lashes demurely downcast. 'Mrs Wilson was at pains earlier to point out that gentleman's good qualities to me…'

'You are reconsidering!' Nathaniel could not keep the disbelief from his voice.

Limpid blue eyes looked up to meet his. 'Perhaps.'

'You are being ridiculous—'

'I am?'

Nathaniel could not miss the slight inflection in her voice. Or the reason for it. He was the one behaving ridiculously. Especially when he still had no idea what to do about his own attraction to her. For many reasons—not least the disapproval of his Aunt Gertrude—setting Elizabeth up as his mistress would appear to be a non-starter.

'Maybe if I were to recount the sad tale of my own parents having both drowned, during a sea voyage across the Atlantic when I was but seventeen years old, you might feel the same sympathy towards me!' he muttered disgustedly.

'And is that what happened?' she asked gently.

He inclined his head. 'It is.'

She looked pained. 'That is indeed a tragedy...'

'But not tragic enough to garner the same sympathy as Tennant, apparently,' Nathaniel snorted.

'You do have your Aunt Gertrude to support you, whereas Sir Rufus appears to have no one,' she pointed out.

He frowned. 'You are too soft-hearted by far.'

'I am what I am, my lord.'

'And being you, will no doubt do exactly as you wish!'

Elizabeth gave an impish smile. 'That is exactly what I have been doing these past few weeks, yes.'

Nathaniel wished he had the same freedom of choice. But his responsibilities, to both his title and his estates, decreed that he did not. 'In that case, if you will excuse me…' He bowed to her before turning on his heel.

Elizabeth, watching him stride forcefully away from her, could not help but admire the width of his shoulders, his tapered waist and the long muscled legs encased smartly in black Hessians. The May sunshine seemed to turn his hair to a rich and burnished gold. A thick and silky gold that Elizabeth's fingers itched to touch…

She gave a heavy sigh, knowing that her apparent change of interest in Sir Rufus Tennant had put yet another rift in her relationship with the earl. One that was for the best, perhaps—there was absolutely no future in the growing attraction she felt towards Nathaniel Thorne, either in her role as lady's companion, or as Lady Elizabeth Copeland. The best that she could hope for was that they would not part as bad friends when the time came. She—

'I had thought the man would never leave!'

Elizabeth had been too lost in those disturbing thoughts of Lord Thorne to notice the approach of the other man, but she turned sharply now to look up at Sir Rufus Tennant as he sat astride Starlight, the shadowing brim of his hat hiding the expression in his pale blue eyes, although his comment would appear to imply that he had been observing them for some minutes before approaching her. 'How nice to see you again, Sir Rufus,' Elizabeth spoke with a warmth that was forced rather than felt; it took only seconds in this man's company to know that she found him no more pleasing despite the fact that he might hold the answer to some of the secrets of her mother's past.

He slid smoothly down from the saddle to stand at her side as he removed his hat before bowing slightly. 'I was riding over to Hepworth Manor in the hopes that I might speak with you.' He replaced his hat upon his dark head.

And instead he had found Elizabeth out walking and in conversation with the Earl of Osbourne. A conversation Sir Rufus had deliberately chosen not to interrupt…? 'I am sure Lord Thorne would have welcomed the opportunity to speak with you too.'

Sir Rufus gave a scathing snort. 'I have no patience with rakes such as he!'

Elizabeth immediately felt herself bristle on the earl's behalf; if he truly were the rake Sir Rufus described him as being, then surely he would have taken advantage of the opportunity of their being alone together just now in which to make further advances to her? The fact that he had not surely implied he could not be as disreputable as Sir Rufus—and she—had previously implied.

Nevertheless, Elizabeth was also aware that she would require Sir Rufus's good will if she wished to ask the necessary questions of him, so she needed to tread carefully. 'He is still very young, Sir Rufus,' she said noncommittally.

He looked pleased by Elizabeth's apparent dismissal of the good looks and charm of a man ten years his junior. 'Would you care to continue walking along the cliff path with me?'

Considering she had minutes ago been walking in the other direction… 'That would be lovely,' Elizabeth accepted brightly. 'But what of Starlight?' She reached up to stroke the grey on his silky soft nose.

'I will tether him to one of the trees for the time we are gone; he will come to no harm here.' Sir Rufus suited his actions to his words before strolling along the pathway beside her. 'I believe I owe you an apology, Miss Thompson,' he spoke awkwardly, as if he were unaccustomed to admitting he was ever in the wrong. 'I…spoke out of turn yesterday evening and sincerely apologise if I offended you.'

'Think no more about it, Sir Rufus.' Elizabeth's smile was brittle.

'I cannot help but think of it.' He stopped to turn and gather one of her gloved hands into his. 'I obviously disturbed you with my comments about Osbourne and the last thing I wish to do is upset you, Elizabeth,' he added gruffly.

Elizabeth swallowed hard, not at all sure she was comfortable with having her hand held in Sir Rufus's, let alone the almost feverish glitter she saw in those pale blue eyes as he looked down at her so avidly. 'I admit I felt upset at the time, but I am not anymore,' she said as she gently but firmly removed her hand from his.

'I simply wanted to warn you of the possibility of Osbourne taking advantage of you—'

'I believe it would be for the best if we did not speak on that subject again. I assure you, Lord Thorne is my employer's nephew to me, and nothing more.' She turned to continue walking along the pathway.

Sir Rufus fell into step beside her, not speaking for several minutes. 'It is a beautiful day, is it not?'

The weather was certainly a safer subject for them to discuss than Nathaniel Thorne! 'Beautiful,' Elizabeth echoed distractedly; it was one thing to have decided she must speak with Sir Rufus at the earliest opportunity, quite another to suffer his almost possessive interest in her, let alone know how to broach such a personal subject as a brother he had never so much as mentioned to her.

'Do you find you like Devonshire?' Sir Rufus prompted politely.

'It is very pretty.'

Sir Rufus nodded his satisfaction with her answer. 'There is nowhere else quite like it.'

Elizabeth looked at him beneath lowered lashes. 'And what of your family? Do they also prefer the simplicity of Devonshire to the rush and bustle of London?'

His expression settled into its usual austerity. 'I have no family.'

Her eyed widened innocently. 'Oh, but I was sure that Mrs Wilson mentioned your having a younger brother?' Elizabeth's heart was pounding so loudly in her chest at the lie that she was afraid Sir Rufus might actually hear it.

His jaw clenched. 'I had a younger brother. He died some years ago.'

'I did not mean to be insensitive.' Elizabeth stopped on the pathway to place her gloved hand lightly on Sir Rufus's arm, hoping that her sympathetic expression did not betray the inner frustration she felt with his having omitted to say exactly how many years it was since his brother had died.

A nerve pulsed in Sir Rufus's cheek. 'You could not have known,' he accepted smoothly.

'You have no other family?'

'None to speak of, no.'

She nodded. 'Your brother must have been very young when he died.'

His expression hardened. 'I would prefer not to talk of it if you do not mind.'

Elizabeth minded very much, at the same time as she accepted that Sir Rufus did not know her well enough as yet to confide the intimate details of his family with her. Indeed, he did not appear to be the type of man who ever felt the need to confide in anyone, about anything.

'Of course,' she accepted lightly; after all, she did not at all wish to alert Sir Rufus as to the depth of her interest in his brother's death—or her possible connection to the woman Giles Tennant might have killed. 'I should not have intruded upon what is obviously a sensitive subject to you.'

A dark scowl appeared between those pale blue eyes. 'It is not a sensitive subject at all; merely one I see no point in discussing any further.'

His tone was such that it was impossible for Elizabeth to continue probing right now. But it was a subject she had every intention of returning to at the earliest opportunity. 'Mrs Wilson has given her permission for me to go riding with you in your carriage tomorrow if that is convenient with you?' She looked up at him expectantly.

Allowing her every opportunity to see the look of triumph that suddenly lit those pale eyes. 'Tomorrow afternoon will suit me perfectly.'

'Wonderful!' Elizabeth smiled at him. 'Now I really should be getting back to Hepworth Manor—'

'So soon?' Sir Rufus now scowled darkly.

'Mrs Wilson relies on my advice when choosing her gown for dinner,' she added affectionately, if not quite truthfully.

But even this brief time in Sir Rufus's company had been taxing on Elizabeth's nerves and revealed he was not a man that she felt in the least comfortable with, let alone enjoyed his company. Besides which, she had nothing else she wished to talk to him about and had already shown enough curiosity about his brother for one day.

'If you really feel that you must.' Sir Rufus still looked less than pleased.

'I do.' Elizabeth once again placed her hand briefly on his arm. 'After all, I would not wish to abuse Mrs Wilson's kindness when she had already given permission for us to go driving together tomorrow.'

'Of course not.' Sir Rufus seemed perfectly happy to accept her going now that he was safe in the knowledge of seeing her again tomorrow, although that look of satisfaction faded somewhat when he looked down at the scampering Hector. 'I trust there will be no need to bring that dog with you?'

Elizabeth was once again reminded that she had been advised that a man who did not like dogs and children was not to be trusted. Admittedly, at this moment in time Elizabeth was only sure that Sir Rufus did not like dogs, but even so... 'I am sure not.' She smiled tightly. 'After all, there would be no exercise for him sitting in a carriage.'

Sir Rufus looked relieved as he attempted to explain his aversion. 'I was once bitten by a dog when I was a child, you understand.'

'Ah.' Elizabeth nodded. 'I assure you, Hector is the most good-natured of animals. Perhaps the dog that bit you was ill or in pain?' Or perhaps Sir Rufus had been as cold and unpleasant in his earlier years as he was as a man...

He looked down at her coldly. 'That is no excuse for such unacceptable behaviour.'

Elizabeth feared even asking what had happened to that poor dog after he had bitten him! 'Animals can sometimes sense when one is...not comfortable with them.'

Those blue eyes became glacial. 'Afraid, you mean?'

'Not at all,' Elizabeth hastened to say as she realised the tangle she was falling into. 'I, for instance, did not grow up with cats and tend to be slightly wary in their company.'

Some of the tension left Sir Rufus's shoulders. 'Cats are like horses, independent creatures all. I simply cannot abide the way dogs grovel and whine for attention.'

Elizabeth decided that was quite enough on that particular subject too—if they continued in this way there would be no safe subjects left for them to discuss! 'Until tomorrow afternoon, Sir Rufus.' She dropped him a brief curtsy.

He nodded in response, a slight softening in his icy demeanour. 'I am already looking forward to it.'

Which was more than Elizabeth was!

She did not like Sir Rufus in the least, Elizabeth realised with a sinking heart as she turned to walk slowly back to Hepworth Manor. She found him pompous, opinionated and even slightly cruel when he talked of darling Hector.

Perhaps she should not have agreed to go driving with him at all. Perhaps, now that she was over her first shock at the things Lord Thorne had told her about Giles Tennant, and thinking more clearly, it would have been wiser to ask Mrs Wilson if she had any knowledge of Sir Rufus's younger brother; Mrs Wilson was not a woman who cared for gossip, certainly, but that did not mean she would not know exactly when and how Giles Tennant had died. And also the name of the married lover he had killed before taking his own life.

Yes, perhaps it would have been more sensible on Elizabeth's part to have spoken to Mrs Wilson on the subject rather than suffer several hours alone in Sir Rufus's company tomorrow...

Chapter Nine

'By the time you return from your carriage ride with Tennant tomorrow afternoon my aunt will have organised the vicar reading the banns at church on Sunday and spoken to the seamstress concerning the style and time it will take to make your wedding gown!'

Elizabeth closed her eyes briefly as she came to a halt in the vast and otherwise deserted entrance hall of Hepworth Manor. Having excused herself and left the other two ladies drinking tea in Mrs Wilson's private parlour, following yet another sumptuous dinner—and an embarrassingly speculative conversation concerning Elizabeth's carriage ride with Sir Rufus tomorrow!—she had been anticipating the privacy of her bedchamber. Instead of which, it appeared she must once again deal with the mocking Earl of Osbourne before she could make good her escape.

She turned slowly to face him now, sincerely hoping she retained her coolness of expression as she took in the fact that the earl had removed his jacket and necktie since leaving the dining room, and now stood in the doorway of the library wearing only a pale blue brocade waistcoat over a white silk shirt that was unbuttoned at the throat, revealing the beginnings of that light dusting of dark golden hair which Elizabeth knew from the days he had been incapacitated in his bed covered his muscled chest before dipping down below the waist of his pantaloons…

She clasped her hands together to hide their trembling and the return of the temptation she felt to touch the silky softness of his already slightly ruffled golden hair as she drew in a ragged and shallow breath before answering him frostily. 'I am sure that your friends find you highly amusing, my lord, but I am afraid, this evening at least, your particular brand of humour is completely wasted on me!'

Nathaniel leant a shoulder against the door frame as he observed her through narrowed lids.

Aware, from the stirring of his arousal just from looking at her in the pale peach gown that left the tops of her shoulders and a large expanse of her breasts bare, that he had probably imbibed too much brandy since dinner to have engaged her in conversation at all.

An unusual occurrence for him, no matter what she might think to the contrary. Indeed, Nathaniel did not believe he had overindulged to this degree since his years in the army, when it had seemed the bitter taste of battle could only be expunged by downing a bottle of the excellent brandy which Gabriel had invariably kept in his luggage for just such occasions.

The reason for his overindulgence this evening was due to a battle of quite another kind and could be placed squarely at the slippered feet of the young lady now standing so aloof and unattainable across the entrance hall. Elizabeth looked absolutely enchanting, the peach colour of her gown giving her skin a creamy hue and her lips a pearly rose tint, both of which he found highly desirable, the candlelight also lending an ebony sheen to the darkness of her curls. A fact he had been totally aware of throughout the whole of the time they had been sitting at the dinner table.

His mouth twisted derisively now. 'Why especially this evening?'

Elizabeth looked even more irritated. 'Because I fear you have all misunderstood my reasons for agreeing to accompany Sir Rufus tomorrow.'

'Indeed?' He raised blond brows in interested query.

Her mouth firmed. 'Yes.'

'Then perhaps you would care to come into the library and explain those reasons to me?' He stood to one side in invitation for her to enter.

Elizabeth did not care to explain herself to anyone, least of all the unsettling Nathaniel Thorne! Indeed, the lack of formality to the earl's appearance rendered the whole idea of her being completely alone in the library with him a disturbing one.

Even if—in complete contradiction to the way she felt at the thought of being alone with Sir Rufus Tennant—it was a temptation she found hard to resist.

'I think not,' she answered primly. 'You are obviously slightly…indisposed—'

'I am slightly inebriated, Elizabeth, not "indisposed",' Nathaniel corrected drily before straightening. 'With emphasis on the *slightly*.'

'Even so…'

'Are you going to behave like the lioness or the mouse, Elizabeth?'

Her eyes flashed deeply blue. 'I do not believe I am either of those things, my lord. I simply consider it inadvisable to be alone in a gentleman's company at any time, but especially when he has been drinking brandy.'

'The demon drink, hmm?'

'Not at all.' She frowned as he continued to mock her. 'Indeed, my father considered it a panacea to anything that might ail him,' she added affectionately.

'And what, do you imagine, might be ailing me this evening?'

Her frown deepened. 'I have no idea.'

'No?' the earl challenged before his eyes narrowed shrewdly. 'You used the past tense just now when referring to your father.'

Colour warmed her cheeks at the realisation she had revealed too much yet again to the highly observant earl. 'Perhaps that is because my father is dead, my lord.'

'I see,' he murmured slowly. 'And what things might have "ailed" your father before he died that he felt the need to imbibe brandy in order to ease them?'

Elizabeth shifted uncomfortably. 'No doubt the usual ones of a father with several young daughters.'

'So there are more of you at home?' Nathaniel drawled thoughtfully as he stored that knowledge away for future reference. 'Older or younger?' he prompted sharply.

She gave him a wary look. 'The number and age of my siblings is irrelevant, my lord—'

'Perhaps you should allow me to be the judge of that?' He eyed Elizabeth challengingly.

'No, I do not believe that I should.' She met that challenge unblinkingly. 'Now if you will excuse me…? I was on my way to bed when you…engaged me in conversation.'

Nathaniel gave her a wicked smile. 'I have no objection whatsoever to continuing this conversation in your bedchamber. In fact, I believe I might prefer it.' He straightened with the obvious intention of joining her.

'That was not what I meant at all!' Elizabeth gasped as that becoming blush once again coloured her cheeks.

He came to a halt. 'The library or your bedchamber; it is your choice, Elizabeth.'

She drew her breath in. 'I do not see that as being any choice at all, my lord!'

'The library.' Nathaniel glanced into the room behind him, the glow of the fire adding to its air of intimacy. 'Or your bedchamber.' His gaze swept over Elizabeth, from her slippered feet to her dark curls, before slowly shifting to the top of the staircase.

She appeared agitated. 'You are being unreasonable, my lord—'

'I am giving you a choice, Elizabeth.' His voice was steely. 'It is completely up to you which one you make.'

The choices he'd given her were, in her mind, no choices at all; whichever she chose she would then be alone with him.

A lioness or a mouse…?

Lord Thorne had meant to challenge her with

that taunt and unfortunately he had succeeded; Elizabeth was certainly no longer a mouse—if, indeed, she had ever been one—but as yet she did not feel she was quite the lioness. 'The library,' she announced before sweeping past him to enter that candlelit room. The reason for the discarding of the earl's jacket and necktie was immediately obvious to her; the fire in the hearth rendered the library very warm indeed on this mild spring evening.

The half-full decanter of brandy sitting on the table beside the fireside chair, along with a glass containing a measure of that liquid, and an open book placed across the arm of that chair, were clear indications of what the earl had been doing when he'd heard her outside in the entrance hall.

Elizabeth was wearing peach-satin slippers to match her gown and had often been complimented as to how light she was upon her feet—all of which seemed to suggest that the earl had left the library door open for the very purpose of hearing her walk past.

She was frowning slightly as she stood on the rug before the fire and turned to face him. 'What did you wish to discuss with me, Lord Thorne?'

Nathaniel wondered if she had any idea how regal she looked as she stood bathed in the glow of the firelight: her eyes were a cool blue, her nose short and perfectly straight above the full and enticing bow of her lips and challengingly raised chin, her bearing one of extreme haughtiness.

Whoever this young lady's antecedents were, Nathaniel would stake his reputation on there being a duchess or a countess amongst them. Perhaps, in view of his tendency to imbibe brandy, the father Elizabeth had spoken of a few minutes ago had been born on the wrong side of the blanket, possessing all the genes of a gentleman if not the legitimacy, genes he had then passed on to his own children?

Each day seemed to add but another layer of mystery to Elizabeth's background. She was an enigma he found himself being increasingly drawn to, despite wishing it were otherwise.

Elizabeth looked across at Nathaniel warily as he softly closed the door behind him and moved across the room to stand only inches in front of her.

'Elizabeth.'

She felt the husky timbre of his voice all the way

down the length of her spine. A tingling, shivering, quivering of awareness that warmed her from the inside out, bringing a flush to her cheeks and a brightness to her eyes, whilst her lips felt swollen and sensitive as she ran the moistness of her tongue across them. As for the rest of her body…!

She ached in places she had only ever talked about in whispers with her sisters: her breasts and between her thighs. The hard nubbins at the tips of her breasts chafed against the soft material of her gown, and between her thighs once again felt hot and slightly damp.

She looked up at the earl beneath the curtain of her long lashes. 'My lord…?' Could that soft and breathy voice really belong to her?

Nathaniel could not resist touching her any longer as he lifted his hand to gently touch the dark curls at her temple, the tips of his fingers tingling as they touched the silkiness of her skin. 'We were discussing the reason for my having enjoyed several glasses of brandy this evening…'

Those dark lashes fluttered nervously, briefly revealing the dark blue of her eyes. 'We were?'

'Yes,' he confirmed with a small smile. 'Elizabeth, do you have any idea of the effect you have upon me?'

The creaminess of her throat moved as she swallowed. 'I—perhaps,' she allowed bravely.

Nathaniel's answering laugh wasn't entirely happy. 'And do you have any idea how unsuitable such an attraction is?'

Elizabeth started to feel cross. 'I believe you are being insulting, my lord.'

'What the devil are you still calling me that for? We are well past the stage of you calling me anything but Nathaniel,' he announced, glaring down at her.

She blinked nervously. 'It is most improper—'

'This is even more so…' And with that, he gathered her up into his arms before lowering his head and fiercely claiming her mouth with his. He had been wanting, aching to kiss Elizabeth again for hours—no, days, it seemed—and now he took full advantage of the fact that he once again held her beguiling softness in his arms.

There was no gentleness in him as his lips devoured hers with the force of a storm that swept away any resistance in its path. It was all she could do to cling to the broad width of his shoulders as she knew herself lost to everything but the passionate demand of that kiss.

Elizabeth almost forgot to breathe beneath that avalanche of heat, aware of nothing and no one but Nathaniel's mouth and the warm caress of his hands as he moulded her curves against his much harder ones before cupping her bottom and drawing her into him intimately.

He broke the kiss, breathing hard as he moved his lips to the slender column of her throat, her neck arching in invitation as she felt the heat of that questing mouth against her flesh, her whole body aflame with feeling.

Her fingers finally got what they had been craving when they became entangled in the heavy gold of Nathaniel's hair. She trembled as his hand moved to cup beneath her breast and the warmth of his lips pressed against the bared swell of flesh visible above the scooped neckline of her gown.

'How beautiful you are, Elizabeth,' he groaned hoarsely, his breath a hot caress against her fevered flesh as he unfastened several buttons at the back of her gown so that he might tug the bodice and shift down and bare her breasts to his enraptured gaze. He drew one of the swollen nubbins into the heat of his mouth and rasped his tongue over and around that sensitive tip as she sighed and moaned her delight with his touch.

Looking down at Nathaniel as he embraced her—his eyes were closed, lashes long and golden against his perfectly sculptured cheekbones, his lips moist and demanding about the tip of her breast—was the most erotic experience of Elizabeth's life.

She couldn't even think about denying either of them this sensual pleasure as he swept her up in his arms and carried her across the room to lower her onto the chaise that stood in front of the window. He straightened to throw off his waistcoat and then pull his shirt over his head, revealing the strapping still about his chest and the muscled strength of his shoulders bathed in candlelight before he knelt beside the chaise, his eyes hot with desire as he looked his fill of her bared breasts. His heated gaze moved up to capture hers as his hands cupped beneath those sensitive orbs before he lowered his head to place a lingering kiss on first one swollen and aching nipple, then the other.

Elizabeth trembled anew and she drew in a

shuddering breath as she felt the rasping of his tongue against her sensitive flesh. 'Nathaniel...'

'Yes—Nathaniel!' he encouraged throatily. 'Say it again, Elizabeth!'

'Nathaniel...' she repeated breathily as his lips explored the dark hollows at her throat, the long column of her neck, the softness of her earlobe before once again capturing her lips in a kiss that seared and seduced in its intensity as that clever tongue of his swept between her lips to capture and claim her.

Elizabeth's hands moved up to touch his chest before exploring the hard contours of his back and shoulders, totally lost to the seduction of that kiss even as she marvelled at all the other sensations she was being bombarded with—the warmth of Nathaniel's skin as his muscles shifted and moved beneath her lightly caressing fingers, the silky hair on his chest that was slightly abrasive against her highly sensitised breasts.

Nathaniel dragged his mouth from hers to look down at her with fevered dark eyes as his hands framed the pale beauty of her face. 'You are temptation incarnate, Elizabeth,' he muttered. 'Deep, dark, wanton temptation!'

Those blue eyes widened. 'But I did nothing—'

'You tempt simply by existing,' he declared gruffly, his arousal an unbearably hot, hard, pulsing need.

'But—'

'Feel how much I want you!' He captured one of her hands in his and brought it down to touch that rigid throbbing need, his breath releasing in a tortured groan as he felt those slender fingers against his responsive flesh, instantly knowing that he wanted more. Needed more! 'Touch me,' he begged even as he unfastened the buttons at the front of his pantaloons, allowing himself to spring free. He took her hand in his and wrapped her fingers about him before he showed her exactly how to squeeze and stroke him.

Elizabeth had never experienced anything so wondrous. Nathaniel's arousal was hard and pulsating in her fisted hand. Steel encased in velvet. He quivered all over as she ran her thumb lightly over the sensitive tip.

Her gaze widened as she saw the expression on his face as he sat back upon his booted heels and let her stroke him; it was almost one of agony rather than enjoyment, a dark flush to his cheeks. 'Am I hurting you?' she gasped, ceasing her caresses.

'God, no!' he groaned. 'Do not stop, Elizabeth…!' he entreated even as his fingers wrapped about hers as he encouraged her to begin a rhythmic caress of that silken length.

She swung her legs to the floor as he released her to continue that caressing rhythm alone, aware of his passionate gaze on her bared breasts as she sat up to look down at what she held clasped in her stroking fingers. He was beautiful, truly beautiful, and so very thick and long.

Elizabeth's eyes widened as she saw the bead of creamy moisture that escaped the tip, quickly followed by another, that liquid moistening her fingers. She licked her lips, wanting, wanting—

She acted on instinct as she slid to the floor in front of Nathaniel, on her knees before him as she lowered her head to flick her tongue over him, tasting the salty liquid, and then tasting him again, and again, finding him as addictive as she did his aching moans of pleasured response.

'Dear Lord!' Nathaniel exclaimed weakly as pleasure beyond measure coursed through him, both at the erotic vision of Elizabeth on her knees before him and the feel of her hot, lapping tongue flickering over his arousal before she took him fully into the heat of her mouth. He was all the more aroused because he knew that her actions were purely instinctive rather than practised.

His fingers became entangled in the darkness of Elizabeth's curls as he gave himself over to the pleasure she bestowed upon him so completely, his back arching, his teeth tightly clenched together as he surrendered to the need to thrust himself slowly and rhythmically into the moist, sensuous cavern of her caressing mouth, her slender fingers barely able to meet around the base of him.

Would Nathaniel have allowed Elizabeth to continue her delightful ministrations if the sound of his aunt's and Letitia's voices outside in the hallway had not permeated his ecstasy-driven brain? Would he have succeeded in destroying her innocence totally by allowing her to take him to the explosive conclusion he so desperately needed?

Perhaps—he could never remember being this out of control and totally at the mercy of a woman's mouth and hands before, but he hoped he would have been able to pull back before it was too late to stop himself from releasing completely.

As he pulled back now, his hands cradling each side of Elizabeth's face as she looked up at him, her gaze slightly unfocused, obviously completely unaware as yet of the other women's presence outside in the hallway. 'We are not alone in the house,' Nathaniel reminded her in a hoarse whisper.

She blinked dazedly before looking about the room, as if half expecting to find another person had entered without her knowledge. Once she was assured they had not, her darkened gaze returned to his. 'I do not—'

'Shh,' he warned. 'Listen.'

Elizabeth became very still as she did as he asked, her face paling as she heard Mrs Wilson and Letitia talking as they went up the stairs together.

As she realised that only a thin piece of wood was standing between herself and complete exposure as the wanton Nathaniel had just minutes ago accused her of being!

Chapter Ten

'There is no need to look quite so stricken, Elizabeth,' Nathaniel murmured as he stood beside the fireplace, the force of their lovemaking, and the pain from his now aching ribs rendering him completely sober. He had righted his pantaloons in the past few minutes and pulled on his shirt to leave it hanging loosely over the top of them to hide his still-burgeoning arousal. No doubt it would remain that way for some time to come!

'How can I not be stricken?' Elizabeth had refastened her gown, but her curls were still in disarray and her face was now flushed with mortification. She could not even meet his gaze as she stood across the room from him. 'What if Mrs Wilson had decided to come into the library to say goodnight to you?'

'She did not,' Nathaniel said soothingly.

'But—'

'There are enough things to worry about to-night, without troubling yourself over something that did not happen,' he said wryly, reaching for his brandy glass and downing the contents in one swallow, welcoming the burning sensation down his throat before that warmth hit his stomach.

Elizabeth breathed in indignantly. 'Of course I must trouble myself—what things…?' she prompted warily as the rest of his comment obviously pierced that indignation.

Nathaniel eyed her with a touch of exasperation. 'Such as how we are to continue here together in future.'

'Continue?'

'Really, Elizabeth…' he sighed '…you are not usually so lacking in intelligence.'

'I am not in the least lacking in intelligence now, my lord—'

'Call me Nathaniel!' he ordered as he moved forwards suddenly. Only to come to an abrupt halt as she instantly took a step away from him. His eyes narrowed. 'Have I shocked you so much you are now frightened to even be near me?'

It was not Nathaniel whom Elizabeth was frightened of, but her own responses to him!

As for being shocked? How could she not be shocked at her own forwardness? How could she not wish to run away to her bedchamber and hide beneath the covers on her bed at the thought of the intimacies they had just shared? That she had allowed herself to indulge in?

For self-indulgence it had certainly been to give in to the desire she had known to not only touch Nathaniel with her hands, but with her lips and tongue… Elizabeth could still taste him now, that addictive, salty-sweet taste. Could still feel the velvet softness of his skin as it encased the long and throbbing length of his arousal, a living, moving entity almost beyond his control.

All of it so much…different, to what Elizabeth had imagined it might be. And all of her behaviour was so shocking to herself that she could not even look Nathaniel in the eye, but instead concentrated her gaze somewhere over his left shoulder. 'I will tell Mrs Wilson first thing tomorrow that I must leave her employment—'

'Why must you?' he demanded.

Now Elizabeth did look at him, her heart faltering in her chest at the coldness of his expression as he looked down the length of his aristocratic nose at her. Looking so unlike the man who had made love to her only minutes ago and who had become lost in the pleasure of her hands and mouth upon his body…

She looked quickly away again, her face aflame with memories of those intimacies. 'One of us must leave—'

'If that is true—'

'You surely cannot doubt it!'

'—then surely that one should be me?' Nathaniel finished coolly.

Elizabeth gave a rueful shake of her head. 'Mrs Wilson would far rather her nephew remain here than the young woman she hired as companion to her dog.'

'I would not be too sure of that if I were you,' Nathaniel drawled. 'I have no doubt that my aunt loves me, but she adores Hector!' he added drily in answer to her questioning glance.

He had meant to make her smile—instead, those deep blue eyes filled up with tears. This was a mess to be sure, Nathaniel accepted heavily, at the same time as he accepted he was the one to blame for it. Bad enough that he had touched Elizabeth so intimately, but to have encouraged her to return those intimacies, by undoing his pantaloons and guiding her hands onto his naked body, was surely unforgivable!

The shocked bewilderment on her pale young face surely attested to that…

Nathaniel released a heavy sigh. 'I will explain to my aunt in the morning that business necessitates I leave Hepworth Manor immediately.'

'She will then wonder why did you not mention it this evening,' Elizabeth pointed out.

His mouth thinned. 'To which I shall reply that I am unaccustomed to having to explain myself. To anyone,' he added grimly.

Elizabeth gave a wan smile. 'Your aunt is not just anyone. Neither is she accustomed to being refused.'

Nathaniel could not miss the emphasis on the word *she*. Neither could he deny the claim; his Aunt Gertrude was indeed a formidable and forthright woman who would demand more explanation than he might wish to give. He also realised his aunt still had concerns over his injuries, despite them starting to heal nicely.

What a tangle. What an awful mess this was, to be sure. Maybe if he had not been so angry with Elizabeth for having changed her mind concerning accompanying Tennant on a drive tomorrow, then he would not have drunk the brandy, would not have encouraged her to come into the library at all, would not have kissed and caressed her, before encouraging her to do the same to him—

Damn it, yes, he would! Nathaniel knew he would have done all of those things whether or not he had imbibed brandy; the fact that he was now completely sober showed he had not drunk anywhere near enough brandy to blame his behaviour on that. He had wanted to make love to Elizabeth, had wanted her to make love to him in return.

God, the way she had kissed and caressed him…

Nathaniel had never experienced anything like it in his life before. Oh, he had been with women during his years in the army, and since, all of whom were experienced in every way there was to give pleasure to a man, but never before had he felt such uninhibited pleasure at the hands and mouth of an innocent young lady.

Never had he been so lost in pleasure, so out of

control in a lady's presence that he was in danger of releasing himself into the heated moistness of her mouth!

And he had been in danger of doing exactly that, he acknowledged self-disgustedly. Had been on the very brink of losing all control when he'd been brought to his senses so abruptly by his relatives' voices.

Just looking at Elizabeth's mouth now, imagining those soft and delectable lips about his shaft, was enough to make him pulse and ache anew, warning him that he must leave here as soon as was possible, if for no other reason than to find a woman, an experienced woman, to ease that ache before he made a fool of himself again!

He turned away from even looking at the enticement of Elizabeth's pouting pink lips. 'I will speak with my aunt in the morning and make my excuses.'

'I really wish you would not, my—Nathaniel,' she corrected swiftly as he shot her another scowling glance. 'I had not intended my employment with Mrs Wilson to be of long duration in any case.'

Dark eyes narrowed. 'Why not?'

Elizabeth frowned at him. 'I do not have to explain my reasons to you—Nathaniel!' she gasped as he crossed the room in two long strides to take a firm grasp of her arm.

'Do not "Nathaniel" me in that recriminating tone.' He looked at her intently. 'If you leave here tomorrow, where will you go? To whom will you go?' he added suspiciously.

She met his accusing gaze calmly. 'Once I leave here it will be none of your business where I choose to go.'

His mouth compressed. 'Or to whom?'

'Exactly.' Elizabeth nodded.

He raised arrogant blond brows. 'I think you underestimate my powers of persuasion.'

'I think you underestimate my own ability to withstand that persuasion, my lord,' she came back just as firmly, her expression defiant as she deliberately freed herself from his grasp.

He released a frustrated breath. 'I refuse to allow you to just leave here without saying where and to whom you will be going.'

'You do not have the right to refuse me anything,' she insisted vehemently.

This young woman was going to be the death

of him, Nathaniel decided grimly. The slow and agonising death of him!

How could it be any other way, when she pleasured him to the heights of release one minute, before then sweeping him to the depths of frustrated impatience the next? When just the thought of her disappearing as completely and as suddenly as she had entered his life was enough to throw him, a man who rarely if ever lost his temper, into a state of such dissatisfaction it could not be called anything else but that?

For all that he might now play the part of the fashionable man about town, his years in the army had made him a man accustomed to action; Elizabeth's decision to disappear back from whence she had come, with no intention of telling him or anyone else where that might be, rendered him totally impotent. A situation that was totally unacceptable, to both the soldier and the earl.

He looked down at her between narrowed lids. 'Perhaps in that you are right, Elizabeth.'

'Of course I am right—'

'I am, however,' he continued firmly, 'completely at liberty to tell my aunt that my actions this evening are the reason for your decision to leave her employment.'

Elizabeth gasped in horror. 'You would not!'

'I believe you know me better than to believe that,' he drawled.

Elizabeth knew this man more thoroughly, more intimately, than any other man alive! As he had said, that was the whole point of her decision to leave Hepworth Manor—it was because of the intimacy that had just occurred between them that she could not stay.

'Why would you do such a thing?' She glared up at him.

He shrugged. 'I will know myself to be wholly responsible if you leave here so rashly and find yourself in difficulties. And I find guilt is not an emotion that sits easily upon my shoulders.'

And they were such broad shoulders too, Elizabeth acknowledged privately. Broad and muscled shoulders that she had moments ago caressed and—Lord, she must stop this! Must put those intimacies firmly from her mind or she would send herself mad thinking about them.

She straightened proudly. 'You would only succeed in shaming us both if you were to tell Mrs Wilson of the real reason for my departure.'

Nathaniel became very still, his expression unreadable. Shame them? Elizabeth considered their lovemaking to be shameful? Ill-advised, perhaps, even shocking in its intensity, but shameful? No, unlike her, he did not consider their time together as being in the least shameful. But perhaps she was looking for more from him?

His mouth twisted. 'Do you expect to hear my name, rather than Tennant's, read out in connection with yours at church on Sunday?'

Elizabeth gasped. 'I beg your pardon?'

Nathaniel raised an eyebrow at her. 'A single word of tonight's events in the right ear—Viscount Rutledge's, perhaps?—and I would be expected to make an offer for you.'

Elizabeth drew herself up haughtily. 'I have no intention of my name being read out in church on Sunday in connection with either you or Sir Rufus.'

This young woman never ceased to surprise him, Nathaniel realised ruefully. Most women in her circumstances, when faced with the choice of casting herself back out into the capriciousness of the world, or the possibility of compromising an earl into marriage, would surely have chosen the latter. Not so Elizabeth…

'Now if you will excuse me…' She turned to leave.

'Elizabeth!'

She turned slowly, unwillingly to face him, her chin nevertheless proudly high. 'There is nothing more to be said, Nathaniel.'

There was much that still could, and should, be said, he acknowledged honestly. But he knew this was not the right time, with emotions still running so high.

He nodded curtly. 'We will talk again in the morning.'

'I will be leaving in the morning,' she announced emphatically.

'And what of your carriage ride with Tennant in the afternoon?' Nathaniel asked quietly. 'Sir Rufus will no doubt be very disappointed if you send him a note informing him that not only are you not accompanying him, but that you are leaving the area completely.'

In truth, Elizabeth had forgotten all about Sir

Rufus Tennant and her agreement to go for a carriage ride with him tomorrow afternoon.

Of course she had forgotten him; Elizabeth defied any woman not to have forgotten such a plain and uninteresting man as Sir Rufus Tennant after knowing the pleasure of Nathaniel Thorne's lovemaking!

'I am sure Sir Rufus will perfectly understand.'

'Somehow I doubt that very much,' Nathaniel drawled. 'I have never seen a man quite so set upon capturing a woman's affections.'

'You are deliberately exaggerating his interest in me in order to cause me embarrassment.' Elizabeth's face was flushed with displeasure.

No…Nathaniel did not feel he was in the least exaggerating Tennant's single-minded interest in her. In fact, he did not believe he had ever seen another man quite as determined in his pursuit as Tennant was with regard to Elizabeth these past few days. Well, her decision to leave Devonshire would at least remove her from that cloyingly unpleasant situation…

'If you choose to think so,' Nathaniel said curtly.

'I do,' she stated firmly before once again turning to leave the room.

Nathaniel watched her go, his expression thoughtful as he turned back to gaze down at the fire. His behaviour tonight had not only been ill-advised, but recklessly out of character, to the point that it would have been completely his own fault if Elizabeth had been the type of young woman to take advantage of the situation and demand that he marry her forthwith. Much to the delight of the gossiping and malicious old biddies of the *ton*, no doubt; the Earl of Osbourne trapped into marriage by a young lady without money or title!

He should be feeling both relieved and thankful at his narrow escape, but instead of that relief Nathaniel found he could only remember that Elizabeth had denounced their lovemaking as being shameful…

'—simply cannot understand what can have happened to him!' A distraught and anxious Mrs Wilson paced the cavernous hallway of Hepworth Manor the following morning, her face pale and lined, revealing every one of her three-and-forty years of age.

She was totally justified in her distress, Elizabeth acknowledged with a heavy heart; Hector had been allowed outside into the garden by one of the footmen whilst the ladies and Lord Thorne had finished breaking their fast, only for that young man to find absolutely no sight nor sound of the little dog when he went back outside to collect him only a few minutes later.

A comprehensive search of the grounds by several of the footmen and housemaids had not improved that situation, until the butler had felt he had no choice but to come into the breakfast room and inform his mistress of Hector's disappearance.

Nathaniel had risen to his feet immediately, ordering his horse to be saddled as he first comforted his aunt before swiftly quitting the house.

The earl had been gone for almost an hour now, with Mrs Wilson becoming more and more distressed with every minute that passed…

Not, Elizabeth accepted, the ideal time for her to inform her employer of her decision to leave this morning. Not the day for such an announcement, in fact, when no doubt Mrs Wilson would become prostrate with relief once the little dog was found.

If he was found…

What no one had so far mentioned—would dare to mention in Mrs Wilson's hearing—were the steep and rocky cliffs that bordered the grounds of Hepworth Manor. Cliffs that would be deadly if a little dog like Hector were to accidentally fall over one of them.

And so for the moment Elizabeth was keeping her own counsel with regard to her decision to leave, knowing there was no possibility of her deserting Mrs Wilson in her hour of need when that lady had been so kind to her.

Instead she paced the hallway at that lady's side as she murmured soothing words of comfort and reassurance. 'Lord Thorne will find him, I am sure.'

'But what if—yes! Yes, of course, dear Nathaniel will find him.' Mrs Wilson drew herself up determinedly. 'He will return shortly, no doubt with an abashed Hector in his arms.'

It was Elizabeth's dearest wish that this should prove to be the case. She had grown as fond of Hector these past two weeks as she was of Mrs Wilson; indeed, she could not think of one without the other.

'Do stop snivelling, Letitia!' Mrs Wilson told her cousin irritably as that lady sat on a chair beside the front door sobbing into a lacy handkerchief. 'It serves no purpose whatsoever and is only succeeding in making your eyes and nose exceedingly red.'

'But I feel so responsible.' The older woman continued to sob inconsolably. 'I should have gone outside with Hector. Should have—'

'Do not be ridiculous, Letitia.' Mrs Wilson sighed. 'Hector is six years old, has stayed here many times and has never before wandered off on his own in this way when let out first thing in the morning.'

Which was all perfectly true; the footman always let the little dog outside first thing in the morning and Elizabeth took Hector for a longer walk once the two of them had eaten their breakfast. For Hector not to have even returned for that breakfast was unusual in itself; the little dog loved food almost as much as he loved his doting mistress.

Elizabeth, after spending a virtually sleepless night in her bedchamber, had not had any appetite for her own breakfast this morning, too disturbed by her behaviour with Nathaniel in the library the evening before to be able to think of eating.

Not that there had been any evidence of that disturbing incident on Nathaniel's handsome face and appearance this morning as he ate his way through a large cooked breakfast and drank several cups of tea whilst conversing lightly with his aunt about mutual acquaintances.

He had even spoken to Elizabeth twice, once to comment that she was looking rather pale this morning, and the other to request that she pass him the sugar bowl. The first she had completely ignored, and the second she had done without replying.

Mrs Wilson drew in a shaky breath. 'What can be keeping Nathaniel?'

Presumably his inability to find Hector, Elizabeth acknowledged worriedly. Quite what Mrs Wilson would do if the earl returned without the little dog—

All the ladies turned anxiously towards the door as a loud knock sounded on the other side of it, accompanied by what sounded distinctly like Hector's familiar bark.

Chapter Eleven

'I simply cannot thank you enough for returning my darling Hector to me unharmed, Sir Rufus.' Mrs Wilson beamed up at that gentleman over the top of the little dog's head as she still cradled him possessively in her arms some ten minutes or so after he had been returned to her.

Nathaniel, having just returned from his own fruitless search for Hector, only to find him already returned to his doting owner, now stood beside the unlit fireplace, observing the scene taking place across the drawing room, his mood broodingly pensive as all three of the ladies talked to and looked approvingly at the older man. An approval that Tennant was obviously lapping up as greedily as a cat with a saucer full of cream.

Which could only be called sour grapes on his part, Nathaniel acknowledged self-derisively. It was purely because Elizabeth, whilst stroking and petting Hector, was smiling up at Tennant…

He was not sure which annoyed him the most—that she was not stroking and petting him in that happy way, or that she was smiling so brightly at Tennant when she had not been able to meet Nathaniel's own gaze at breakfast this morning.

Sour grapes, indeed!

'It is my pleasure, I assure you, Mrs Wilson.' Sir Rufus accepted the accolade of praise. 'I simply happened to be riding by when I heard his little whines of distress.'

Nathaniel's aunt repressed a horrified shudder. 'My poor darling could have been trapped in that rabbit hole for hours if you had not found him when you did.'

Doubtful, when Nathaniel had been on his way to explore the woods after first riding the length of the cliff path in search of the mischievous dog, at which time he would no doubt have heard Hector's whines for himself. But he had not done so, and now had to accept that Rufus Tennant was the hero of the hour. 'Indeed, we are in your debt, Tennant.' He gave the other man a stiff bow.

'Not at all, Osbourne,' the other man dismissed

smoothly. 'Knowing how Mrs Wilson dotes upon her pet, I am only too pleased this unhappy circumstance had such a satisfactory ending.'

'Can I persuade you into taking tea with us, Sir Rufus?' Mrs Wilson beamed at him.

'Unfortunately estate business dictates that I be at home this morning,' he refused regretfully. 'But I will be returning this afternoon in order to collect Miss Thompson for our carriage ride.' Sir Rufus smiled down at that young lady in such a proprietary way that Nathaniel had to grind his teeth together in order to stop himself from making a sharp comment. In fact, he had decided during the night, as he once again tossed and turned, unable to sleep after that unsatisfactory conclusion to his encounter with Elizabeth in the library, that the only positive thing about her decision to leave Hepworth Manor today was that, although it was taking her away from him, it would also succeed in removing her from Tennant's more-than-obvious attentions.

'I am very much looking forward to it, Sir Rufus,' Elizabeth answered the other man brightly.

Nathaniel's scowl darkened. 'But I had thought—'

'Yes?' Elizabeth turned to him sharply, the

warning in her clear blue gaze enough to inform Nathaniel not to bring up the subject of her departure.

Did that mean that she had changed her mind and intended to stay, after all, possibly because Mrs Wilson's worry over Hector this morning made it a less-than-ideal time for Elizabeth to inform her employer of her decision to leave? Or could her change of mind be because Tennant's rescue of the little dog now meant that she thought more kindly of the other man than she had previously?

It was a possibility that did not please Nathaniel in the slightest. 'I believe it might come on to rain later this afternoon,' he murmured instead of his intended comment.

'I am sure that Sir Rufus has a suitable carriage if that should prove to be the case,' Elizabeth dismissed as she turned away from the brooding earl.

Really, did the man have no sense of his aunt's emotional state? There was no way she was going to resign today and risk further upsetting Mrs Wilson when she'd already been so distraught!

She found it ironic that Sir Rufus should have been the little dog's rescuer. Indeed, considering the man's less-than-favourable opinion of Hector, his rescue of the little dog was to be doubly admired.

Although Hector seemed less than grateful for that rescue as he bared his teeth in a growl at Sir Rufus as that gentleman moved closer to bend over Mrs Wilson's hand as he took his leave!

'I do apologise for Hector's lack of manners, Sir Rufus.' Mrs Wilson became flustered as Sir Rufus reeled back in alarm. 'How ungrateful of you, Hector!' She frowned at her pet disapprovingly as she stood up to place the still-growling dog into Elizabeth's arms. 'Perhaps you could take Hector to the parlour and give him a bath after his adventure?'

'Of course.' Elizabeth turned to give Hector's rescuer a brief curtsy. 'I will see you this afternoon, Sir Rufus.'

'I will be here promptly at three o'clock,' he assured her warmly.

'I will walk outside with our guest, Aunt.' Nathaniel moved away from the fireplace to accompany the other man out into the cavernous hallway. 'You did my aunt a great service today, Tennant,' he allowed grudgingly.

'Only too happy to oblige.' The man's expression was amiable as they stepped outside together.

Nathaniel nodded tersely as one of the grooms aided Sir Rufus in mounting his horse. 'I trust, in the circumstances, you will not keep Miss Thompson too long from her employer this afternoon?'

Sir Rufus looked down at him beneath the brim of his hat. 'I have noticed you seem to take a… great deal of interest in Miss Thompson's welfare.'

Nathaniel's expression remained coolly removed in the face of this challenging accusation. 'As a member of my aunt's household, Elizabeth naturally falls under my guardianship.'

'With the indulgent Mrs Wilson no doubt acting as her protector within that household?' the older man sneered.

Nathaniel drew in a sharp breath at the obvious insult. Perhaps a merited one, considering his own less-than-gentlemanly behaviour with Elizabeth yesterday evening, but nevertheless… 'Exactly what are you implying, Tennant?'

'Why, nothing at all, Osbourne.' Sir Rufus gave a dismissive smile that did not reach the coldness of those pale blue eyes. 'Except you are fortunate in having such a doting aunt as Mrs Wilson.'

And this man's implication, although still un-stated, was obvious. 'I think it best if I wish you good day, Sir Rufus.' Nathaniel's gaze was just as icy.

'Until this afternoon.' The older man nodded before pulling on his horse's reins to turn and ride away.

Nathaniel lingered outside to watch until the other man had ridden out of his sight, his thoughts as dark as the scowl upon his brow, his distrust of Tennant—in spite of his having rescued Hector—having intensified during these past few minutes' conversation. That the other man still suspected Nathaniel of having less-than-honourable inten-tions towards Elizabeth had been made as clear to him as if Sir Rufus had actually thrown down a gauntlet of challenge.

Intentions Nathaniel would be hard pressed to deny after making love to Elizabeth, and encour-aging her to make love to him in return, the previ-ous evening.

'What is wrong?'

Elizabeth drew in a deep and calming breath

before she looked up from soothing the healing balm onto Hector's front leg following his bath before the fire. Hopefully, her expression was one of cool uninterest as Nathaniel stood in the doorway of the small parlour. 'Hector has suffered a slight graze on his leg following his adventure down the rabbit hole.' She gently wrapped the little dog more securely in a warming towel.

'Indeed?' The earl moved into the room on long and graceful legs encased in beige pantaloons and brown-topped Hessians. 'I wonder how that occurred?'

'No doubt in his efforts to escape his confinement.' Elizabeth held the dog in front of her protectively.

Nathaniel gave her a rueful smile. 'He did not seem particularly grateful for Sir Rufus's efforts earlier.'

'No, he did not.' She grimaced. 'Which was unfortunate, considering that Sir Rufus is less than comfortable in the company of dogs.'

The earl arched golden brows. 'Indeed?'

'A bad experience as a child, I believe.' At least, Elizabeth had assumed Sir Rufus had been a child at that time. At the moment she was too aware of the intimacies she had shared with Nathaniel the previous evening to be able to remember exactly what Sir Rufus had said about the incident. Of kissing Nathaniel. Touching him in a way that made her blush just to think of it!

Despite the worry of Hector's disappearance this morning, Elizabeth knew she had thought of little else since leaving this man's presence the previous evening. She'd had no idea, for example, of how beautiful a man's arousal could be, both to look at and to touch. Long and thick and firm, yet so velvety soft to the touch. Nor had Elizabeth realised how delicious he would taste. An addictive creaminess, which, despite the hours that had passed, she was sure she could still savour on her tongue—

'It does not look like a graze.'

Elizabeth's attention returned to the man she had been remembering making love to, her breath catching in her throat as he stood close beside her in order to examine the cut on Hector's front leg. So close that she could feel the heat of his body and see the long sweep of his golden lashes against his beautiful cheekbones.

'What do you mean?' She examined Hector's leg

for herself, noticing for the first time that some of the skin looked bruised about the small cut. 'No doubt he became entangled in some brambles or some such thing before becoming trapped.' She smiled indulgently at the sleepy little dog as he lay comfortably in her arms. 'Otherwise he seems none the worse for his escapade.'

'And what about you, Elizabeth?' Nathaniel's gaze was narrowed on the flushed beauty of her face, noting the slight shadows beneath those deep blue eyes that would not meet his—due to a similar lack of sleep the night before, perhaps? 'Are you none the worse for last night's escapade too, Elizabeth?' he prompted gruffly.

The darkness of her lashes quickly rose, then as quickly fell again after she shot him a searching glance. 'I believe the less said about yesterday evening the better!' Her tone was waspish.

His mouth thinned with displeasure. 'And the reason for the obvious change in your plans to leave here today?'

She moved to place the now-sleeping Hector in his basket beside the fire. 'I could hardly risk upsetting Mrs Wilson further by informing her of my impending departure.' She straightened, her gaze very direct. 'Unless, of course, you are set upon it, in which case—'

'I am not in the least set on it, Elizabeth.' Nathaniel voiced his own impatience with the situation. 'It was your decision to leave here, not mine.'

'Because the situation has been made intolerable.' She did not add the reason was their lovemaking the previous evening, but nevertheless he still heard that statement in the flatness of her tone.

His jaw clenched. 'You believe encouraging Tennant's advances will make that situation more bearable for you?'

'Of course I do not.' Elizabeth eyed him impatiently. 'And I do not consider a carriage ride as encouraging him. Having to remain here for perhaps a day or two longer, and Sir Rufus's gallantry this morning in rescuing Hector, meant that I could not possibly refuse to accompany him this afternoon.' She gave a defiant sniff. 'Besides which, I am as grateful as Mrs Wilson to Sir Rufus for having safely returned Hector to us.'

An occurrence that gentleman had been relishing greatly only minutes ago, Nathaniel acknowledged as his frustration with Tennant's air of self-satisfaction increased. At the same time he realised he was currently behaving like some young idiot of the *ton*, resentful of the fact that another man had dared to approach the woman he was interested in.

Nathaniel could not deny he was deeply attracted to Elizabeth—as had been clearly demonstrated by his responses to her the previous evening. But his own lack of control during their lovemaking did not give him the right to protest about another man having the same interest in her. Even if, at this moment in time, he did feel like strangling him.

He looked down at Elizabeth now. 'I believe it fitting that you take one of my aunt's maids with you this afternoon to act as chaperon.'

Her chin rose challengingly. 'For my own protection or Sir Rufus's?'

Nathaniel's jaw tightened. 'For your own, of course.'

Elizabeth gave a slight inclination of her head. 'If you feel it is necessary…'

'I do.'

Elizabeth had found this entire conversation to

be painful. They were lovers—the aching sensitivity of her breasts this morning attested to that!—and yet not. Strangers, and yet they were not that either. In truth, she no longer had any idea what they were! Nor did she wish to know; her plans to leave Hepworth Manor were only temporarily delayed, not put off completely.

'Was there anything else you wished to discuss with me, my lord? If not,' she continued firmly as his eyes glittered his dislike of the formality, 'I believe I should rejoin Mrs Wilson in the drawing room.'

'By all means.' He nodded tersely.

That dismissal did not prevent Elizabeth from being completely aware of his darkened gaze upon the stiffness of her back and shoulders as she left the parlour, only relaxing that defensive posture once she was outside in the hallway, her breath leaving her in a shakily relieved sigh as she leant back weakly against the coolness of the wall.

She had called the situation between herself and Nathaniel intolerable, but it was so much worse than that. She apparently found it impossible to even cope with the natural function of breathing when in his company…

* * *

'After our discussions on the subject at dinner the other evening, I thought that after our drive you might perhaps care to view the roses in my hothouse at Gifford House?'

The threatening rain mentioned by Nathaniel earlier this morning had not yet made an appearance, allowing Sir Rufus to call for Elizabeth in an open carriage which he drove himself. Elizabeth was seated beside him and Mrs Wilson's maid and Sir Rufus's groom were seated less comfortably at the back of the carriage.

It had been something of a relief for Elizabeth to take this opportunity to escape the claustrophobic atmosphere that now existed for her at Hepworth Manor; her cheeks were flushed and eyes bright from her enjoyment of this fresh and beautiful May afternoon. 'I would like that very much, Sir Rufus,' she said, so relieved to be out and about—far away from the disturbing presence of Nathaniel Thorne!—that she did not even care if that visit to the hothouse involved another discourse on the merits of horse manure as fertiliser for those roses!

Sir Rufus looked pleased with her answer. 'You will not be disappointed, I assure you.'

Elizabeth was not predisposed to be in the least disappointed. Indeed, she had managed to dismiss her previous misgivings about Sir Rufus completely after his rescue of Hector this morning and had accepted now that he was perhaps just a man ill at ease in society. Which was not a fault in his character, she thought, merely an awkwardness brought about by a lack of social intercourse.

He certainly seemed friendly and amiable enough this afternoon as he pointed out the local landmarks during their drive, the spectacular scenery another balm to Elizabeth's ragged nerves. So much so that by the time they drove along the driveway to Gifford House, she was feeling relaxed enough in his company to contemplate introducing the subject of Sir Rufus's younger brother. The real reason, after all, that she had accepted his invitation.

'It is such a big house for you to live in alone, Sir Rufus.' She looked up admiringly at the pleasantly situated three-storey red-bricked house as he helped her alight onto the gravel driveway.

'I have lately begun to have hopes that might

not always be the case.' He tucked his hand proprietarily into the crook of her arm as they ascended the steps to the front door.

Ah. In her eagerness to broach the subject of Giles Tennant, Elizabeth had overlooked what Sir Rufus's interpretation of such a remark might be! She gazed up at him with innocently wide blue eyes. 'You are perhaps intending to have family come to stay for the summer?'

He gave her a chiding glance. 'I believe I have already told you I have no family.'

'Of course you did.' Elizabeth gave a false laugh, grateful for the presence of Mrs Wilson's maid following at a discreet distance behind them. 'What a beautiful hallway!' she announced not quite truthfully as they entered the house to stand in an entrance hall much less cavernous than the one at Hepworth Manor and yet which somehow felt so much colder.

In truth, it was not to Elizabeth's taste at all, comprising of dark tiles upon the floor and the heads of game such as stag and deer mounted upon the walls—no doubt animals shot by Sir Rufus himself on his rides through the local woods and countryside. Whilst Elizabeth accepted that hunting was a way of country life, she had always been grateful that her father had never chosen to bring home trophies such as these from his own outings with the hunt.

'Perhaps we might go straight to the hothouse?' she suggested brightly, anxious to escape the glassy-eyed stares of those heads mounted upon the walls.

Sir Rufus raised dark brows as he handed his hat and cane to the waiting butler. 'You would not prefer to take tea first?'

Tea might dispel some of the chill Elizabeth was now feeling, but not if the drawing room should also have these same unpleasant trophies displayed upon its walls. 'I believe I am too eager to see the beauty of your roses to bother with tea just now.' She made no effort to remove her own bonnet or pelisse, the chill of the house seeming to seep into her very bones after the warmth of the sunshine outside.

Sir Rufus beamed his approval. 'Then that is what we shall do!' That smile faded as he turned dismissively to the young maid who still accompanied them. 'You may go along to the kitchen with Campbell.'

Annie looked uncertain at the suggestion, leading Elizabeth to question whether Nathaniel had issued the girl with instructions not to leave Elizabeth's side during her outing with Sir Rufus. She did not doubt that the earl was arrogant enough to have done so!

'Well, go along, girl,' Sir Rufus snapped his impatience with Annie's hesitation. 'We will ring for you when it is time for Miss Thompson to leave.'

The maid shot Elizabeth a last lingering glance before turning to follow the butler through the door leading to the stairs down to the kitchen at the back of the house.

Leaving Elizabeth completely alone in Sir Rufus Tennant's company.

Chapter Twelve

Nathaniel had not intended to ride anywhere near Gifford House when he set out that afternoon. And yet that was exactly where he now found himself, seated astride Midnight as he reined in at the end of the driveway leading up to that austere red-bricked residence, scowling as he saw the open carriage standing in front of the house and attended by a groom as evidence that Tennant and Elizabeth were together inside somewhere. With Elizabeth no doubt basking in Tennant's obvious admiration for her—

He was being unfair now, Nathaniel acknowledged broodingly. Rufus Tennant had as much right to pay Elizabeth attention as the next man. Their interlude the previous evening certainly did not give Nathaniel exclusivity where that young lady was concerned, especially when he could see no future in it. Besides which, Tennant—damn him!—had proved himself to be the hero of the hour.

Yes, very likely Elizabeth no longer found Sir Rufus quite so boring as she once had and was even now bestowing those bright and beautiful smiles upon the other man as he proudly showed off his home to her.

A home which Nathaniel was beginning to suspect the other man intended offering to share with Elizabeth.

'How busy you have been, Sir Rufus!' Elizabeth was truly impressed with the numerous blooms displayed in the extensive hothouse attached to Gifford House. As much as she was relieved at the warmth inside the glass building following the chill she had felt inside Gifford House itself.

'I have enjoyed growing roses since I was a boy,' that gentleman announced proudly as they strolled the pathways between the dozens of colourful and scented blooms.

'An interesting hobby, to be sure.' Elizabeth nodded politely.

'I believe it has become more of an obsession

than a hobby,' Sir Rufus admitted. 'Indeed, it has been a lifelong wish of mine to produce an original bloom.'

'And have you succeeded?' Having just spotted a display of the bloom Purity sent to her only two days ago, Elizabeth was anxious to divert Sir Rufus's attention.

'Indeed I have,' that gentleman confirmed as he led the way to the far end of the hothouse where a rose grew in separate splendour from the rest of the blooms.

It was indeed a beautiful flower, Elizabeth acknowledged: a huge cream-coloured bloom lightly tinged with peach at the ends of the petals and giving off a strong and heady perfume as Elizabeth bent over it admiringly. 'And what have you named your rose, Sir Rufus?'

'Nothing as yet. I once thought to name it Harriet's Innocence,' he added with a frown. 'But now that I have at last been successful I am not so sure…' He looked down at her with an intensity that Elizabeth found slightly uncomfortable.

So much so that for a few moments she almost missed the significance of the original name Sir Rufus had chosen for his rose.

Harriet…

The same name as Elizabeth's own mother. Could that be a coincidence?

Nathaniel had absolutely no idea what he was about knocking on the front door of Gifford House, his riding crop tapping impatiently upon one muscled thigh as he waited for the butler to open the door in answer to that knock.

By rights he should have just continued on with his ride back to Hepworth Manor. Except Nathaniel had found he could not. He had not liked the idea of Elizabeth going riding in Tennant's carriage with him this afternoon in the first place; the fact that gentleman had now brought her back to his home, with only one of Mrs Wilson's young maids as chaperon, Nathaniel considered to be completely improper.

At least, that is what he had told himself when he urged Midnight into a gallop down the drive, before throwing the reins to the attendant groom and sliding from the saddle to run up the steps to the front door. Nathaniel considered that any further soul searching into his reasons could wait until after he had returned a suitably chastened Elizabeth to the safe guardianship of Mrs Wilson at Hepworth Manor.

Elizabeth straightened slowly, bewildered as to what significance Sir Rufus's original choice of name for his rose might have. Or if it had any significance at all...

She was unsure as yet as to whether or not Giles Tennant had been the young gentleman with whom her mother had run off to London. Although she would now say not; surely Sir Rufus would never have thought to name a rose after the woman responsible for his brother's disgrace and suicide?

No, that would make no sense at all, Elizabeth realised heavily, meaning that she must have been mistaken all along, that there was, after all, no mystery attached to the death of Giles Tennant that related to the Copelands in any way.

None of which in the least changed the covetous way in which Sir Rufus was now looking at her!

Elizabeth realised belatedly that she should not have agreed to come to his hothouse alone with him, that she had placed herself in a position of vulnerability by doing so. Sir Rufus might be inclined to believe she welcomed his attentions.

She stepped away from him. 'I believe it is time I returned to Hepworth Manor, Sir Rufus,' she announced briskly. 'Mrs Wilson will be—Sir Rufus…!' Elizabeth gasped in protest as she found herself suddenly pulled into that gentleman's arms and crushed against his chest as he rained kisses upon her face. 'Sir Rufus, stop this at once!'

'You are so beautiful, Elizabeth!' He continued to hold her firmly in his arms as he kissed her throat and ears, knocking her bonnet askew as he did so. 'So innocent. So—'

'Sir Rufus, please!' Elizabeth attempted to fight against the muscled strength of his shoulders, only to find herself held prisoner by the steely arms that surrounded her and now held her so close that it was impossible for her to move at all. 'You—' All further protest was silenced as Sir Rufus claimed her lips with his own.

It was a kiss totally unlike the ones Elizabeth had shared with Nathaniel and afforded her none of the same pleasure. Sir Rufus's lips, overly moist, were also hard and demanding upon hers as he bent her back in his arms, kissing her with an insistence that bordered on painful. She—

'Perhaps I have called at an inconvenient time…?' There was no missing the hard edge to that otherwise pleasant tone.

However Sir Rufus seemed unaware of the earl's presence as he continued to kiss Elizabeth with a thoroughness she found unpleasant at best and nauseating at worst. In fact, if Sir Rufus did not cease this attack in the next few moments Elizabeth was afraid she would be forced to succumb to a faint for the first time in her life!

'Tennant!'

The sharpness of Nathaniel's voice finally seemed to permeate whatever haze of passion Sir Rufus had been lost in, his eyes a stormy blue as he raised his head to look down briefly at Elizabeth and gather her possessively to his side before turning to look at the man standing further down the hothouse. 'How dare you enter here uninvited?' he demanded furiously.

'Your butler would no doubt have announced me if you had not been…otherwise occupied at the time.' Glacial brown eyes swept disdainfully over the older man. 'As it was, I thought it wise to dismiss him and announce myself.' That icily cold gaze now shifted onto Elizabeth, she having at last managed to free herself from the confinement of Sir Rufus's arms and to step away from him.

She could only imagine how this situation must have looked when Nathaniel entered the hothouse. Certainly she did not need a mirror to know that her bonnet was completely askew, her curls along with it, her eyes bright with unshed tears, cheeks flushed and her lips feeling as if they might actually be swollen as well as bruised.

If that wasn't enough, the disgust she could see in Nathaniel's expression clearly showed he believed her to have encouraged Sir Rufus's advances!

Elizabeth's nausea returned. 'My lord—'

'I will give you every opportunity to explain yourself later, Elizabeth,' Nathaniel bit out between clenched teeth before turning the full force of his obvious anger upon Sir Rufus. 'In the meantime, I will be borrowing your carriage, Tennant, in order to drive Elizabeth back to Hepworth Manor. Your groom will return with it later—'

'Now see here—'

'I advise—unless you wish me to challenge you here and now?—that you not attempt to argue the point, Tennant.' Nathaniel was so furious that he was in danger of striding the short distance that separated them and putting to good use the hours he had spent practising in the ring and for which he had something of a reputation amongst the gentlemen of the *ton*.

A fact Tennant was also well acquainted with if the pallor of his cheeks was any indication. 'The fighting of duels is forbidden by the Crown,' he spluttered.

Nathaniel gave a humourless smile. 'Then it is as well there is no member of the Crown here at this moment to witness it, is it not?'

'Nathaniel—'

'I have suggested that you wait until later to explain yourself, Elizabeth.' The mildness of his tone was totally belied by the livid glitter of his gaze as it once again swept over her with utter disdain.

'But—'

'You will be silent!' Nathaniel was so angry—with Elizabeth, for her naïvety in placing herself in this tenuous position, as much as with Tennant

having taking advantage of that inexperience—
that he was seriously in danger of losing his composure altogether.

Something he never did.

As an only child of loving parents, Nathaniel
knew he had been self-willed during his youth,
with a wildness to match. Following the shock of
his parents' death, and his long acquaintance with
his arrogantly self-assured Uncle Bastian, as well
as Gabriel Faulkner and Dominic Vaughn, he had
learnt to control that wilful temper and to behave
on most occasions with the same indifference as
his two best friends. Seeing Elizabeth in Tennant's arms being thoroughly kissed by the other
man, had pierced that icy control so deeply that
he badly longed to beat Tennant to a pulp before
shaking Elizabeth until her teeth rattled in her
head. Or making love to her so passionately she
was in no doubt as to whom she belonged with!

Which would not do at all. 'Come, Elizabeth,'
he instructed harshly, waiting until she had hesi-
tantly crossed the short distance to his side, his
hand firmly about the top of her arm, before turning his attention back to the other man. 'It would
be better for all concerned if you did not call at

Hepworth Manor again until after I have taken my own leave.'

Sir Rufus's eyes narrowed to icy slits. 'I do not take seriously threats from dissolute rakes such as yourself!'

Elizabeth drew in a sharp breath, knowing by Nathaniel's sudden stillness that the other man had just overstepped a line and had delivered an insult Nathaniel could not ignore.

Not that she would not relish the idea of Sir Rufus being taken down a peg or two after the way he had manhandled her only minutes ago, but she did not want to risk Nathaniel suffering any harm, either socially or physically. Socially, he ran the risk of being banished by the *ton* on instruction from the Crown for the fighting of a duel. And physically… A single glance at the tensed muscles beneath Nathaniel's perfectly tailored black superfine, and the lithe fitness of the rest of his body, was enough to tell her that he was more than capable of besting the older man in any show of physical strength, even with his still-healing injuries.

Nevertheless, Elizabeth knew that her coming here alone with Sir Rufus was directly responsible

for the tense situation that now existed between these two men. 'Could we just leave now,
Nathaniel? Please?' She turned to look up at him
beseechingly. 'I am feeling decidedly unwell,' she
added encouragingly.

For several more tense seconds she feared her
pleas would be unheard as the men continued to
glare coldly at each other, then she felt some of the
tension ease from Nathaniel's body as his fingers
loosened slightly about her arm and he drew in
a long controlling breath before addressing the
other man contemptuously. 'Just as I do not take
seriously an insult from a man who attempts the
seduction of a young and unprotected lady!'

Those pale blue eyes continued to meet the
challenge of Nathaniel's for several long seconds,
leading Elizabeth to fear that the earl's disdainful
remark might have only added fuel to the fire.

Until Sir Rufus's pale blue gaze shifted onto
her, becoming softer, almost pleading. 'I apologise, Elizabeth, if any of my actions just now…
frightened you. I should not have allowed myself
to be so overcome by your beauty that I forgot
your innocence.' He bowed deeply in apology.

It was an apology that did nothing to dispel the

revulsion she now felt at the memory of those moist and demanding lips upon her own, of being held helpless in Sir Rufus's hard embrace as he plundered her mouth with a thoroughness that made her feel ill just to think of it.

But those memories had no place in a situation that was still so edged with the potential danger of an illegal duel being fought over her. 'Your apology is accepted, Sir Rufus,' she said stiffly before turning away from him to once again look pleadingly up at Nathaniel. 'May we please go now, my lord?'

Nathaniel was still fighting the inner need he felt to pummel the other man to within an inch of his life and enjoy every moment of doing so for daring to so much as touch Elizabeth, let alone kiss her!

Instead he looked across at the other man coldly as he repeated his earlier statement. 'Your carriage and groom will be returned to you later today.'

Nathaniel kept a firm hold of Elizabeth's arm as he strode back into the house, through the dark hallway and back outside into the fresh and invigorating spring air, drawing several deep breaths into his lungs before approaching the carriage standing ready on the driveway.

'Tie my horse to the back and get on, man,' he instructed the groom tersely as he helped Elizabeth to climb safely into the carriage before stepping up to sit beside her and take up the reins. 'Not a word until we are safely back in the privacy of Hepworth Manor,' he warned between gritted teeth as Elizabeth turned on the seat with the obvious intention of speaking to him. Nathaniel was fully aware of the listening groom seated behind them if Elizabeth was not.

She looked somewhat bewildered before frowning. 'But what of Mrs Wilson's maid?'

'Is it not a little late for you to have remembered that young lady's existence?' Nathaniel asked even as he drew the horses up sharply and turned to the groom. 'Go and fetch the maid,' he ordered.

'She is in the kitchen,' Elizabeth added, waiting until the young groom had run off to the back of the house before turning back to Nathaniel. 'The situation you witnessed just now was not what it seemed, my lord.'

'No?' He looked coldly down the length of his arrogant nose at her. 'It appears to me you are a young lady who habitually embroils herself in unseemly "situations", Elizabeth. Or perhaps it is as I once suggested and you've been doing your best to procure a proposal from either Tennant or myself?'

Nathaniel had meant to wound, and he had succeeded. Elizabeth drew in a sharp breath at this painful reminder of her wanton behaviour in his arms the evening before, realising it rendered her defenceless in the scene Nathaniel had just interrupted.

For her to claim that her unrestrained response to Nathaniel's lovemaking had been due to feelings which she dared not even acknowledge to herself would only leave her open to further ridicule and his certain rejection.

He was unlike any other man of Elizabeth's acquaintance. Certainly she could never have found a man such as Sir Rufus Tennant in the least attractive after knowing the kisses and intimate caresses of Nathaniel Thorne!

'You are being unfair, Nathaniel,' she told him emotionally.

'If I am, then you will have plenty of opportunity to challenge that unfairness once we are safely returned to Hepworth Manor,' he assured her grimly as the groom thankfully returned with the maid at that moment and the two of them jumped onto the back of the carriage, allowing Nathaniel to urge the horses onwards.

There was silence in the carriage for several minutes until Elizabeth spoke with a softness intended only for his ears. 'Will you—do you intend telling Mrs Wilson of this—regrettable situation?'

'I believe I will have to tell her something. If I do not, she will wonder why one of her closest neighbours, the man who only this morning rescued her "darling Hector", has suddenly taken it into his head not to call on her again,' he replied just as quietly.

Elizabeth caught her bottom lip briefly between her teeth before speaking again. 'You believe Sir Rufus will heed your advice and not call at Hepworth Manor again whilst you are staying there?'

Was that relief or disappointment he heard in her voice? Or perhaps just morbid curiosity? Was she was romantic enough, naïve enough, to relish the idea of two men fighting a duel over her honour?

'Mourning the separation from your middle-aged admirer already, Elizabeth?'

Her cheeks became even paler. 'You must know that I am not.'

'Must I?'

She sucked in a painful breath. 'Yes.'

Nathaniel sighed. 'I have no wish to talk of this any further just now, Elizabeth,' he said, knowing his murderous feelings towards the older man were still barely held in check—a somewhat disturbing admission from a man who had for years prided himself on the ease of his self-control and leading him to the conclusion that perhaps it was indeed time that he returned to his life in London...

He had still received no reply from his own correspondence to Gabriel, so had no idea whether or not either Westbourne or Blackstone were even in town. But even if they were not, Nathaniel would surely be able to find some other amusing company to occupy him, female company that would surely put Miss Elizabeth Thompson firmly from his mind as well as ease his aching need for physical release.

Yes, returning to London, to the bed of an experienced courtesan, now held an allure Nathaniel knew it would be foolish of him to ignore.

Chapter Thirteen

As chance would have it, there was no opportunity for Elizabeth and Nathaniel to talk privately when they returned to Hepworth Manor, Nathaniel having remained outside to see to the return of Sir Rufus's carriage and groom, and Mrs Wilson immediately demanding that Elizabeth attend her in her private parlour.

'Sit down and tell me all, my dear!' Mrs Wilson beamed up at her conspiratorially as she patted the chaise beside her.

Elizabeth ignored the invitation, just as she intended resisting the other woman's obvious intention of demanding the details of her outing with Sir Rufus—no doubt Nathaniel would regale his aunt with those scandalous details soon enough. 'I am feeling rather dusty from the carriage ride, so would you mind very much if I went upstairs to my bedchamber to freshen up first?' She smiled in an effort to lessen the other lady's obvious disappointment.

'No, of course not. But—ah, you are returned too, Osbourne.' She turned to smile at her nephew as he strode into the parlour, a frown appearing on her brow as she saw the grimness of his expression. 'Well, I must say that neither of you look at all refreshed from being out and about on such a beautiful day.' She looked positively put out by the fact.

Elizabeth hardly dared look at Nathaniel, a single glance having shown her that he looked no less approachable now than he had during the carriage ride back to Hepworth Manor, his jaw firmly set, the expression in his eyes hidden by hooded lids.

But those two things were enough to tell her of his continued displeasure. 'If you will both excuse me…' Her head was lowered as she crossed the room on slippered feet; if it was now Nathaniel's intention to tell his aunt the details of her disgrace, then Elizabeth would rather not be present when he did so.

Nathaniel reached out and took hold of Elizabeth's arm as she reached his side. 'There is no reason for you to leave on my account,' he told her.

Elizabeth looked up at him beneath the dark fringe of her lashes. 'I had already stated my wish to go up to my bedchamber before you came in, my lord.'

Nathaniel's mouth tightened. 'In the face of great opposition, I am sure,' he drawled, knowing his aunt well enough to realise she would have wished to know every detail of Elizabeth's afternoon spent in Sir Rufus's company. Certain details of which Elizabeth would no doubt be reluctant to confide.

Elizabeth grimaced before murmuring softly. 'I have decided to leave the disclosure of my disgrace in your own capable hands, my lord.'

He frowned darkly. 'I—'

'What are the two of you whispering about over there?' his aunt demanded truculently, obviously displeased at being excluded from their conversation.

Nathaniel gave Elizabeth a last searching glance before releasing her arm to step across the parlour to join his aunt. 'I am sure we have delayed Miss

Thompson long enough, Aunt.' He lifted the lid on the teapot and, discovering it was still warm, attended to pouring himself a cup, at the same time allowing Elizabeth to make good her escape.

His aunt looked perplexed as she noted the young girl's hurried departure. 'You do not suppose that Sir Rufus behaved in any way improperly towards Elizabeth, do you?'

Now was the time for Nathaniel to tell his aunt of the scene he had walked in on earlier, to reveal Elizabeth's behaviour with Tennant.

Except by doing so Nathaniel knew he would be damning Elizabeth, and for all that she had behaved recklessly by going to Gifford House with Tennant accompanied only by his aunt's maid, Nathaniel found he did not, after all, wish to see her belittled in his aunt's eyes. Elizabeth obviously held a sincere affection for the older woman, an affection Mrs Wilson's concern now indicated she returned.

'I doubt that very much, Aunt.' He made a show of sipping the lukewarm tea.

His aunt still gazed distractedly towards the doorway through which Elizabeth had so recently departed. 'What do you make of her, Osbourne?'

Nathaniel almost choked on his mouthful of tea, swallowing the brew down with an effort before answering. 'Why should you imagine I might make anything of her, Aunt?' he returned with a wary guardedness.

His Aunt Gertrude gave him a reproving look. 'I may occasionally give the impression of giddiness, Nathaniel, but do not take me for a fool,' she advised.

'I should never dream of doing so.'

His aunt nodded. 'Then you cannot help but be aware that there is a mystery attached to that girl. And, unless I am mistaken, you are as intrigued by it as I.' She eyed him speculatively.

Yes, he was, Nathaniel acknowledged heavily. Still. Despite, only hours after making love to her himself, having found Elizabeth locked in the arms of another man, being passionately kissed...

Elizabeth could never before remember feeling so bereft as she did now as she paced the confines of her bedchamber, easily able to imagine the conversation taking place downstairs in the parlour between Nathaniel and his aunt as he revealed her disgrace to that lady.

It would serve little purpose for Elizabeth to claim her innocence in the matter; she had been found in a compromising position—by Nathaniel Thorne, of all people!—with a man of only a few days' acquaintance. Moreover, she knew that in her eagerness to be alone with Sir Rufus, so that she might question him further in regard to his brother, she and she alone was responsible for having placed herself in that vulnerable position. That she had received an answer without the need to voice so much as a single one of her queries was of little comfort when Elizabeth knew that Nathaniel now looked at her with contemptuous and suspicious eyes.

How could she have been so stupid, so reckless, when Sir Rufus had already shown such a partiality for her company, as to place herself so completely at his mercy in that way? In doing so, she had obviously earned Nathaniel's disdain. That was what hurt Elizabeth the most. Not her own lack of caution. Not Sir Rufus having taken advantage of her naïvety. No, it was Nathaniel witnessing both those things which now upset her so.

What must he think of her now? What must he feel for her now?

As if Elizabeth really needed to ask herself either of those questions—it was obvious that he considered her to be either naïvely gauche or calculatingly manipulative in order to secure an offer of marriage. And what could Elizabeth possibly say in her own defence if Nathaniel accused her of such? Certainly not that she had acted unthinkingly, out of a single-minded need to discover whether or not Giles Tennant had been her mother's lover. She—

Elizabeth stopped her pacing and turned sharply as a knock sounded on the door to her bedchamber. 'Yes?' she prompted warily; more curiosity from Mrs Wilson she could perhaps cope with without breaking down completely, more accusations from Nathaniel she could not.

It was a pity that when the door opened it was indeed Nathaniel standing outside in the hallway. 'I believe we have an unfinished conversation, Elizabeth?'

She closed her eyes briefly before opening them again, only to find herself the focus of the full force of the contempt glittering in Nathaniel's dark gaze. 'I doubt your aunt would consider this an appropriate place for any sort of conversation between her nephew and a single young lady.'

Nathaniel easily heard the nervousness lurking beneath Elizabeth's outward show of confidence. 'There is no reason for my aunt to ever know of it.' He stepped inside the bedchamber and closed the door behind him. 'Are you feeling unwell?' He frowned at the unmistakable pallor in her cheeks, visible now that she had removed her bonnet.

She gave a humourless smile. 'I have been made love to against my will by one man, and accused of encouraging those advances by another gentleman in order to procure an offer of marriage, so, yes, I am feeling a little…agitated!'

Nathaniel's brows rose. 'You did not appear to be resisting Tennant's advances when I entered the hothouse.'

Those blue eyes sparkled with indignation. 'Perhaps that is because Sir Rufus made it impossible for me to free either my arms or my lips in order to do so!'

Nathaniel looked suddenly livid. 'He forced his attentions upon you?'

Elizabeth hesitated in replying in the affirmative, aware as she was of Nathaniel having all but challenged the older man to a duel earlier; a challenge he would feel duty-bound to repeat if she, an employee of his aunt's, were to confirm that Sir Rufus had kissed her against her will. Besides which, perhaps her going to Gifford House with Sir Rufus and entering the hothouse with him unchaperoned could be considered encouragement enough for what had followed?

She sighed. 'I believe my own lack of...experience in such matters likely encouraged Sir Rufus in his misunderstanding of the situation.' Elizabeth was aware of how ridiculous that claim must sound after her wanton behaviour in Nathaniel's own arms the evening before, but it was all she had to offer.

What a tangle this was, to be sure—to be disgusted by the mere touch of one man, whilst at the same time unable to resist the attentions of another.

Perhaps her father had been in the right of it, after all, in refusing to allow his three young daughters to enter London society; Elizabeth, at least, had shown just how ill equipped she was to deal with the advances of older and so much more experienced gentlemen than herself.

She lowered her lashes. 'I believe I may have forgotten to thank you earlier for your...timely intervention.'

Nathaniel gave a hard and humourless smile. 'Any more "timely" and I may have come upon the two of you in a situation not easily forgotten by any man, let alone one who has been as intimate with you as I!'

Elizabeth gasped as the deliberate insult. 'You would dare to talk of that now?'

'Oh, I would dare any number of things,' he said as he moved further into the bedchamber, those dark and glittering eyes narrowed. 'As it is, you may be comforted by the fact that I have not as yet revealed this afternoon's...indiscretion, to my aunt.'

Her chin rose proudly. 'Why not?'

Nathaniel's smile was completely lacking in humour. 'You almost sound disappointed, Elizabeth.'

She shook her head. 'Only surprised, my lord. It appears to me, in view of your obvious suspicion of me, that this would have been the ideal opportunity for you to persuade your aunt into immediately terminating my employment, rather than allowing me to leave of my own free will tomorrow.'

Instead of which Nathaniel had informed his aunt that he would be the one leaving Hepworth Manor the following day… His Aunt Gertrude had not taken the announcement well. Indeed, she had argued against it for several minutes after Nathaniel had told her of his decision to begin his journey back to London come the morning. Arguments Nathaniel had overridden by explaining that, after almost a week and a half of being confined to his bed, he had affairs of business to attend to in town that he could no longer ignore.

When, in actual fact, Nathaniel knew the real reason for his departure stood before him… Face pale, dark curls tousled, her gown less than pristine, Elizabeth still held an attraction for him from which he needed to distance himself if he were to find any peace of mind at all.

'Indeed it would,' he conceded coolly. 'But, as you said earlier, it would hardly have been fair to discuss that situation with a third party until I was conversant with all the facts.'

'And now that you are…?'

Now that he was, Nathaniel wanted nothing more than to return to Gifford House and tear Tennant limb from limb!

Such a violence of emotions was complete anathema to him. Unacceptable. Inexplicable. So much so that Nathaniel believed that the safest course of action was to put as many miles between himself and Elizabeth as was possible, and at the earliest opportunity.

He straightened determinedly. 'I have informed my aunt that I shall be leaving Hepworth Manor in the morning—'

'But why would you do such a thing when I have already stated that I will be leaving here tomorrow?' Elizabeth gasped, too disconcerted by this announcement to even attempt to hide her dismay at the thought of him going.

Heavy lashed lids now hid the expression in those dark eyes. 'I acknowledge that our own behaviour together has been less than wise, but I advise you not to be under any misapprehension that it gives you the right to question my future actions!'

Elizabeth felt as if she had received a slap to

her cheek. Indeed, the coldness of Nathaniel's tone was delivered with the same precision as a physical blow. 'I apologise.' She kept her lashes downcast so that he should not see the pain she was sure must be in her eyes at this verbal set-down. 'I was merely surprised at the suddenness of your decision to leave here, that is all.'

Elizabeth was not a courtesan, or a young and lonely widow of the *ton* from whom Nathaniel usually picked his mistresses, but a young, single woman of genteel, if impoverished, quality, who had no choice but to work as a lady's companion in order to support herself. As such Nathaniel could not in all conscience bed her, let alone offer her the role of his mistress for the several months it would take for him to become bored by her charms, as in doing so he would be robbing her of the only two things she had to offer a prospective husband—namely her reputation and her innocence. Indeed, in the present circumstances, Sir Rufus Tennant was more than a suitable match for a young woman such as Elizabeth.

Unable—unwilling!—to offer her anything more himself, Nathaniel knew he had no other choice but to bow gracefully out of Elizabeth's life and so leave the way open for some other man—even Sir Rufus—to pay his addresses to her.

The fact that he still felt like pummelling the other man to within an inch of his life for so much as looking at Elizabeth, let alone touching her, told him that his departure had better be sooner rather than later!

'Enjoyable as yesterday evening was, the truth is that I have other…commitments in town, which are desperately in need of my attentions.'

Simply from the way he said 'other…commitments' Elizabeth knew that he was referring to a woman. No doubt an older, more experienced woman, who, unlike Elizabeth, was more than a match for his extensive physical experience. An older, more experienced woman 'desperately in need of his attentions'…

Nathaniel could not have stated any more clearly that he had merely been toying with her. That she had been but a diversion until he felt able to take up his previous life. Until he felt his health was returned enough to enable him to give his mistress those 'attentions'!

Had she ever felt such misery before this? Elizabeth wondered numbly. Had she ever before so badly wanted, needed, to scream and shout at the depth of the hurt she was feeling?

She had certainly never felt the need to scratch and claw a faceless, nameless woman, whose only crime was to welcome a more-than-willing Nathaniel Thorne into both her arms and her bed.

Elizabeth moistened the numbness of her lips before speaking. 'In that case it remains only for me to wish you a safe journey tomorrow, my lord.'

Nathaniel's intention had been to put the necessary distance between himself and Elizabeth, both physically and socially—something that he had obviously succeeded in doing if the cool remoteness of her expression now was any indication. Such a neutral expression, in fact, that he contrarily wanted nothing more than to kiss her in order to find the warm and vibrant woman he had held in his arms the evening before.

An action guaranteed to further complicate an already unacceptable situation...'I accept your good wishes,' he said distantly. 'Will you now consider staying on here yourself?' he could not resist enquiring.

Would she? Elizabeth wondered. Could she?

Could she remain here in Devonshire, with all its attendant memories, after Nathaniel had returned to his life—and his mistress—in London?

She still had no idea whether or not Lord Gabriel Faulkner had quit Shoreley Park, or if he was perhaps still lurking there, with every intention of remaining until he had persuaded one of the Copeland sisters into marrying him. Nor could Elizabeth go back to London now that she knew Nathaniel was to be there; after the set-down he had just given her, she dared not run the risk of his accusing her of having followed him there!

She released her breath in a sigh. 'I believe I shall.'

'Do not look so forlorn, Elizabeth,' the earl mocked her. 'Perhaps Tennant will come up to scratch after all and offer you marriage!'

Elizabeth's eyes flashed deeply blue as she looked across at him. 'And if he were to do so, I would have no hesitation in refusing him!'

Nathaniel raised blond brows at her vehemence. 'Would that not be rather…foolhardy, given your present circumstances?'

She frowned warily. 'Foolhardy in what way, my lord?'

He gave an impatient snort. 'Obviously if you were to marry Tennant you would become Lady Tennant.'

Elizabeth was already Lady Elizabeth! And much good it did her at this point in time...

'There is that to consider, of course.' She eyed Nathaniel scornfully. 'You are quite correct in advising me not to act too hastily, my lord.'

Nathaniel eyed her impatiently, his frustration barely held in check. Could Elizabeth seriously be considering accepting if Rufus Tennant should offer her marriage? And had he himself not just advised her to consider such an offer carefully before refusing?

Yes, Nathaniel had done that—but only in the belief that Elizabeth would indeed refuse such an offer of marriage. Damn it, just the thought of her in Tennant's bed every night was enough to effect a return of his earlier feelings of violence. As to his feelings concerning Tennant's hands upon her deliciously curvaceous body—!

But if not Tennant, then it would someday be another man whom eventually wedded and bedded her...

'I believe this conversation is now over, my

lord,' Elizabeth prompted as he now seemed in no hurry to quit her bedchamber. Something she dearly needed Nathaniel to do—before she could no longer hold back the hot tears burning the backs of her eyes and threatening to fall!

This had to be the very worst day of her life. The disappointment of realising that Sir Rufus's brother offered no answers in regard to her mother's death, followed by the indignity of suffering Sir Rufus's kisses; to then be discovered by none other than Nathaniel Thorne, a man who had kissed and caressed her with such passion the evening before; now to be advised by that same gentleman that she should seriously consider any offer of marriage Sir Rufus might make to her—whatever tender emotions she might have felt towards Nathaniel Thorne must now surely be at an end?

'Lord Thorne!' she repeated sharply as he still made no answer.

His mouth had thinned, his jaw set disapprovingly. 'I wish you every happiness in your future… endeavours.'

Elizabeth gave a curt inclination of her head. 'And I wish the same for you.'

There was nothing more to be said, Nathaniel realised impatiently. Nothing more to be done. Just this stilted leave taking, between two unlikely people who had been thrown together, and whom circumstances had allowed to become closer than normal propriety permitted.

Nevertheless… 'Elizabeth—'

'We have said our goodbyes to each other, Nathaniel; let that be an end to it,' she said with quiet finality.

Goodbye.

Yes, this was their goodbye, Nathaniel realised with a frown. Any further conversations between the two of them would take place in the presence of his aunt or Letitia and be all the more formal because of it. He would miss their verbal sparring. Would miss the parry and thrust of those private conversations. Deeply regretted that he would never hold Elizabeth in his arms again, that he would never kiss her again. Never caress her—

'I really must ask you to leave my bedchamber now, my lord,' Elizabeth insisted waspishly.

Nathaniel straightened abruptly, his bow brief

and his expression coldly remote. 'No doubt I will see you at dinner.'

'No doubt.' Her curtsy was just as formal.

Elizabeth stood and watched as Nathaniel walked from her bedchamber, knowing that any further meetings between the two of them before his departure tomorrow would be as Lord Nathaniel Thorne, Earl of Osbourne, and Miss Elizabeth Thompson, the young and impoverished companion of his aunt.

Chapter Fourteen

'I want to know how this could have happened!' Nathaniel's voice was cold with suppressed fury as he stared down at Midnight lying prostrate in the straw in his stall, the stallion obviously in great pain and discomfort. 'And why!' he added forcefully, hands clenched into fists at his sides.

Finch, a man in his fifties and the head groom of his aunt's stables at Hepworth Manor, looked no less grim as he straightened from examining the black stallion. 'He must have eaten something, my lord.'

'Such as what?' Nathaniel looked pointedly at the horses in the neighbouring stalls as they munched happily—and healthily—on their early-morning feed.

The groom shook his head. 'He was perfectly well when I checked at eleven o'clock yesterday evening, and he went down too fast for it to have been anything else.'

Nathaniel had not been in the best of moods this morning even before he came out to the stables to check on Midnight and instruct he be prepared for his departure today.

Dinner yesterday evening had been a stilted affair, with his aunt and Letitia making most of the conversation and Nathaniel and Elizabeth not even looking at each other, let alone attempting to speak, which had not made for a comfortable night's sleep. Nathaniel had hoped to talk to Elizabeth over breakfast this morning, so that at least they did not part acrimoniously, only to be thwarted in that plan when she'd sent down her apologies and the explanation that she had a cold. His Aunt Gertrude had immediately gone upstairs to check on her young companion, of course, returning several minutes later to confirm that Elizabeth did not look at all well and that she had advised her to spend the rest of the day in her bed.

To now come out to the stables and find his horse stricken with some unexplained illness was positively the last straw as far as Nathaniel's already tautly strung patience was concerned. That he would not be leaving today, as planned, was more than obvious; he intended getting to the bottom of Midnight's sudden malaise. It was a lesson he had learnt too well whilst in the army; a soldier saw to the comfort of his mount before thinking of his own.

'Do what you can for him.' Nathaniel said to Finch as he straightened from the stallion's side. 'If there is no change by midday...' He scowled at the thought that they might have to put the horse out of his misery.

'Let us hope it does not come to that, my lord,' the head groom replied. 'I have given him a purge and that may well bring about some positive results.'

In the meantime Nathaniel had no choice but to go back into the house and instruct his valet to delay his expected departure; he might yet have need of the clothes already packed into numerous trunks and loaded into the carriage.

'We do not seem to be particularly lucky with the health of our animals at present, Osbourne,' his aunt sympathised when he informed her of the reason for the postponement of his journey, the brightly alert Hector sitting comfortably upon her silk-covered knees and showing absolutely no sign of his own misadventure of yesterday.

Nathaniel frowned. 'No, we don't, Aunt.'

'Excuse me, madam, but these have just arrived for Miss Thompson…' Sewell stood in the doorway of the parlour, a huge bouquet of cream roses, each petal tipped with a peachy hue, obscuring most of his rigidly held torso. 'I was unsure, in view of Miss Thompson feeling indisposed this morning, as to whether or not I should take them up to her bedchamber.'

Nathaniel scowled at the array of beautiful blooms, knowing Tennant was responsible for sending them. 'Leave them on the table there, Sewell,' he instructed the butler, waiting until the older man had left the room before striding over to remove the card nestled amongst the blooms and unashamedly reading the message written there: *Please accept these roses as an apology for my behaviour yesterday and as evidence of my deep regard for you. I have decided to name the rose 'Elizabeth's Innocence'. Tennant.*

'Why are you reading a private missive to Elizabeth, Nathaniel?' His aunt sounded shocked at his impropriety.

Nathaniel's fingers tightened about the card as he turned to face his Aunt Gertrude, uncaring that he crushed it in his palm. 'Will you excuse me, Aunt?' He picked up the bouquet of roses with the obvious intention of leaving the room.

'I—but—' Mrs Wilson looked completely non-plussed by this strange behaviour. 'You cannot go up to Elizabeth's bedchamber, Nathaniel!' She rose to her feet, her expression scandalised. 'Let Sewell or one of the maids take up the roses, if you must. You simply cannot—'

'Oh, I simply must, Aunt,' he said.

'But—what will the servants think?' His aunt raised an agitated hand to her ample chest.

He gave a humourless smile. 'I will not tell them, Aunt, if you do not.' He made good his escape before his aunt could think of any further objections she might make, having no intention of heeding them in any case.

Already agitated at Midnight's malaise, and ir-ritated at his delayed departure, he now found the arrival of Tennant's roses as being the final insult, when she would not so much as leave her bedchamber to make her goodbyes to him. It was the excuse he needed so he could go to her...

Last night Elizabeth had cried for so long and so miserably that she had absolutely no difficulty in convincing Mrs Wilson that she was brewing a cold. Her throat was sore and her eyes were surely red enough from weeping to be convincing.

Nathaniel, not a virus, was the reason for those humiliated tears, of course.

He had barely been able to look at Elizabeth at dinner the previous evening, let alone speak to her, all of his few remarks directed to his aunt or Letitia Grant. By the end of the evening she had been consumed with misery to know Nathaniel now believed her to be nothing more than a scheming young woman in search of a wealthy husband.

Going down the stairs this morning, and pretending a calmness she did not feel, as Nathaniel took his leave of them all was totally beyond her present fragile state of emotions.

Why she should be so utterly downhearted at his bad opinion of her she refused to consider; she only knew that her misery was very real as well as very painful. She—

Elizabeth's gaze turned sharply towards the door as it was thrown open unceremoniously. Nathaniel was standing in the doorway, a huge bouquet of roses in his arms. The grimness of his expression, and the distinctive colour of those blooms, was enough to alert her to the fact that the roses were certainly not a peace offering from him.

She moistened dry lips before speaking. 'I had thought you might have left by now, my lord.'

His eyes narrowed stormily. 'You mean, perhaps, that you had hoped I had.'

'No, I—'

'Perhaps I should have been gone by now if my horse had not been struck down by a mysterious illness.' He kicked the door closed behind him and came to stand beside the bed, looking down at her. 'These, as you have probably already guessed, have just arrived for you.' He dropped the bouquet of roses on top of the rumpled bedcovers. 'This came with them.' His top lip curled back in a sneer as he threw a crumpled card down as well.

Elizabeth pulled herself further up the bed and leaned back against the pillows, taking her bedcovers with her to protect her modesty as she did so, before smoothing out the crushed card and reading the message written there. 'Sir Rufus is obviously a man lacking in all understanding! He behaved unacceptably towards me yesterday.' She put the card onto the table beside the bed with a moue of disgust before moving the roses to one side, showing no pleasure in their presence.

The burn of Nathaniel's ire had sent him up here like a bullet being fired from a pistol, but he calmed somewhat at Elizabeth's own lack of interest in receiving the roses from Tennant, or being in the least flattered that they were being named for her.

His anger faded completely as Nathaniel drank in the loveliness of her loose dark curls displayed across the pillows behind her and framing the pale fragility of her face, some of the silky strands falling across the gentle rise and fall of her breasts visible beneath her white silk nightrail.

The lessening of his temper finally allowed him to realise the consequences of his recent actions; he had defied his Aunt Gertrude, and propriety, by coming upstairs to the bedchamber of her young and unmarried companion, especially as he should not even have known where it was situated, as well as coming in without permission!

Facts borne out by the trepidation with which those dark blue eyes now looked up at him beneath the fringe of their long dark lashes.

He stepped back from the bed in the hopes he might appear less threatening. 'Elizabeth, I apologise for my lack of—I should not have—dash it, what is wrong with you?' He instantly forgot his previous intention of being conciliatory as he finally took a proper look at her without strong emotions clouding his eyesight.

There was nothing wrong with her, except she'd had no will or inclination to leave her bed this morning simply in order to watch Nathaniel ride away from her. 'I believe I have a slight cold, my lord,' she said mendaciously, knowing her voice and looks would serve to confirm that diagnosis, as it had to his aunt earlier.

His mouth thinned. 'A certain part of your anatomy will remain far from cold if you dare call me "my lord" once more when we are alone together!'

Elizabeth felt the heated colour in her cheeks. 'I did so because I believed that was appropriate for the level of our...acquaintance now, my—

Nathaniel,' she hastily amended as his face darkened ominously.

He raised arrogant blond brows. 'And I believe
I will inform you whether something is or is not
appropriate for you to do. What do you intend
doing about Tennant's roses?' His gaze sharpened
as he abruptly changed the subject.

Elizabeth looked down at the beautiful flowers
as they lay on the bedcovers beside her, inwardly
lamenting that such an obnoxious and insensitive
man should have been responsible for their very
existence. 'I shall not do anything about them,
my—Nathaniel.' She sighed heavily. 'They are
undoubtedly beautiful flowers, but to even acknowledge them would offer an encouragement
to Sir Rufus which I do not feel.'

Nathaniel felt even more of the tension ease
from his shoulders. 'If that is genuinely the way
that you feel in regard to Tennant, then I believe
you are being wise in your lack of action.'

'What do you mean "if"?' Elizabeth asked. 'Do
you still doubt my lack of interest in that gentleman?'

Damn it all, did she have to take offence at every
word that left his mouth? 'Of course I do not. I

merely—oh, never mind,' he said wearily. 'Should I ask my aunt to arrange for a physician to call upon you?'

'For a simple cold?' She shook her head. 'I am sure I shall be perfectly well enough to go down-stairs by dinner time.' She frowned suddenly. 'Did I hear you say earlier that your horse is unwell?'

Earlier, when Nathaniel had first burst into her bedchamber behaving like a maniac surely bound for Bedlam. God knew what his Aunt Gertrude was thinking of his actions at this very moment!

'You did,' he confirmed, knowing he was going to receive a severe grilling from his aged relative when he returned downstairs. 'Some discomfort of the stomach, which the groom has attributed to Midnight having eaten something during the night that he should not have.'

She looked concerned. 'Are any of the other horses in the stables suffering the same discomfort?'

Nathaniel inwardly applauded her presence of mind in asking exactly the same question as he had earlier. 'No,' he replied. 'The head groom has some hopes of Midnight rallying, but it means that I shall not, after all, be leaving here today.'

'Oh.'

Was that disappointment or relief he read in her expression? The first would be the logical choice, of course, but the situation between them had never been particularly logical. 'In which case, I shall be pleased to see you well enough to join us downstairs for dinner this evening,' he said slowly.

That delicate colour returned to her cheeks. 'So that you might have the opportunity to once again ignore me as you did yesterday evening?'

Nathaniel heard the rebuke in her tone. 'I had thought that was the way you wished it to be between us in future.'

Her eyes sparkled with temper as she looked up at him. 'To be overlooked as if I do not exist? To be made to feel vilified, unworthy and undeserving even of conversation?'

'Now see here, that simply was not the way of it at all!' Nathaniel protested firmly. 'I did not think you in the least unworthy and undeserving—'

'I believe I am best placed to state how being ignored by you made me feel, Nathaniel.' She sat up, the dark curtain of her long curls falling forwards across her breasts and reaching almost to her waist. 'And, as such, I'm telling you that you behaved abominably towards me last night.'

He was now too aware of the wildness of her beauty, and the lack of formal clothing between them, to feel able to give his full attention to her accusation. Nevertheless, he did his best to answer her honestly. 'I did not deliberately mean to hurt you, Elizabeth,' he said gruffly.

'Then it is a pity that is exactly what you suc-ceeded in doing.'

Sweet heaven, she looked so deliciously appeal-ing, lying there pouting at him, that he just wanted to gobble her up! Remove that nightrail and reveal the slender delicacy of her naked curves before tasting and sipping from every inch of her—indeed, he could almost taste her—the perfumed perfection of her skin, the tight little buds that tipped the swell of her breasts, the creamy damp-ness between her thighs...

Oh, to the devil with it!

What on earth was he doing here? In fact, what had been the thinking behind his invasion of her bedchamber when he knew her to be still abed? Had he been thinking at all, or just acting instinctively, because his temper was already out of sorts even before Tennant's roses arrived?

His impulsive behaviour this past few minutes was so beyond his normal studied control that he felt totally unable to answer any of his own questions, especially with her still lying there, displayed so temptingly before him.

Elizabeth sensed a subtle shift in the tension that now existed between them. A tension, an awareness, that had not been present a few seconds ago, the very air in the room now seeming to be filled with a waiting expectation.

She slowly moistened her lips. 'Perhaps it is time that you left my bedchamber, Nathaniel.'

He quirked an eyebrow at her. 'My aunt made it more than clear to me that I should not come here at all.'

'Mrs Wilson knows you are here?' she squeaked.

Nathaniel grimaced. 'Unfortunately she does.'

Elizabeth's heart sank in her chest. 'What must she think of me?' she gasped her dismay.

'Of you?' he said. 'I believe it is my reputation that has suffered in my Aunt Gertrude's eyes.'

Elizabeth somehow doubted that. Not only did Mrs Wilson adore her nephew—he really could do no wrong in her indulgent opinion—but it was invariably the woman whose reputation suffered in situations such as these. 'You must leave immediately.' Elizabeth threw back the bedclothes, stood up and grabbed her robe before slipping her arms inside and tying the sash firmly about her waist. 'This instant! What are you doing?' she exclaimed as she suddenly found herself being pulled into his arms, the softness of her breasts crushed against the firmness of his waistcoat-covered chest.

He gave her a wicked little grin. 'I should have thought my intent was more than obvious, Elizabeth.' His lips nuzzled the sensitive column of her throat.

Of course his intent was obvious unless one was an imbecile, which she certainly was not. Nor could she deny that she enjoyed being in Nathaniel's arms again, feeling his lips exploring the arched delicacy of her throat. But such behaviour was not wise when Mrs Wilson might decide at any moment that her nephew had been in Elizabeth's bedchamber quite long enough and came up the stairs in search of him.

'I cannot seem to keep my hands from you,'

Nathaniel muttered as one of his hands cupped beneath her breast, the soft pad of his thumb moving across the already engorged tip.

'You must!' Even as she voiced her husky protest Elizabeth arched into his skilful hand.

'I cannot!' His lips were warm as the moistness of his tongue explored and tasted the hollows at the base of her throat. 'Do not ask something of me that I cannot give.'

Elizabeth was lost to the pleasure of those heated caresses, feeling as if liquid fire coursed through her veins now instead of blood, all of her aflame as she clung to the broad width of his shoulders. Indeed, she was so overcome from the passion of his kisses that she feared if she did not hold fast to him she might actually collapse at his feet!

'You have the most glorious hair I ever beheld.' Nathaniel's fingers became entangled in those long, ebony curls that reached the slenderness of her waist. 'I want to wrap this about me as I lie naked in your bed.' He lifted his head to gaze down in wonder at those dark silken tresses.

'Nathaniel…' Elizabeth groaned weakly at the sensual vision he portrayed.

* * *

'I must speak to you immediately, Osbourne!' A knock sounded on the door to accompany his aunt's hissed command.

Elizabeth froze in his arms, her eyes wide with alarm as she turned to look across the room.

'Now, Osbourne!'

Elizabeth half expected that at any moment Mrs Wilson might lose all patience and throw open the door to the bedchamber to see them intimately entwined…

Chapter Fifteen

'We will talk of the unsuitability of your presence in Elizabeth's bedchamber later, Nathaniel,' his aunt said primly as he accompanied her down the stairs some seconds later.

Nathaniel was sure they would—and that Aunt Gertrude would do most of the talking. But that could wait for now, as it was not the reason his aunt had come to fetch him.

'So Finch says Midnight's condition has worsened rather than improved as we had hoped?' Nathaniel asked.

His aunt's expression softened somewhat. 'I am so sorry, Nathaniel.' She placed a comforting hand upon his arm. 'Finch seems of a mind that—he believes that your beautiful stallion is likely to die.'

And as the other man had worked amongst

horses all his life, his father having been head groom here before him, Nathaniel had no doubt Finch knew what he was talking about.

It seemed incredible that Midnight had become so ill so quickly. He had seemed perfectly well when they rode out yesterday. What could he possibly have found to eat during the intervening hours that might have made him so ill?

Finch kept his stables meticulously clean and the horses expertly tended; indeed, he was so good at his job that Nathaniel had several times in the past tried to poach the head groom away from his aunt's household! No neglect there, then. So what—?

'I am so sorry, my lord.' A white-faced Finch looked up at him from the hallway, one of the young grooms at his side. 'Jim here has just informed me that Midnight died a few minutes ago...'

Despite Mrs Wilson not having spoken a reproving word to her, Elizabeth had still been left in little doubt as to the older woman's disapproval at finding her nephew in Elizabeth's bedchamber.

In truth, she wished that she might never have

to face that dear, kind lady again, yet at the same time she knew it to be a foolish hope. Mrs Wilson was probably even now thinking of how she would tell Elizabeth she was dispensing with her services forthwith. Without reference, of course—how could she possibly give a favourable reference to a young lady she had found in private company with her nephew, dressed only in a thin robe and nightgown?

Despite her shame, she had hastily dressed and followed Nathaniel and his aunt. He had looked positively ill after Mrs Wilson had quickly explained that his stallion had taken a turn for the worse, and that his presence was required immediately in the stables.

It took only one look at the white and shocked faces of the four people now standing below in the hallway for Elizabeth to realise that the summons had come too late. Midnight must already be dead.

'You must try to eat something, Nathaniel,' Mrs Wilson advised gently.

'Must I?' Nathaniel knew that his aunt meant well, that she was only concerned for him, but still he could not bring himself to join her and the other ladies enjoying their afternoon tea, feeling too raw still from the sudden and inexplicable death of his favourite stallion.

He had owned the horse since its birth, having bred him out of one of the prime mares on his estate in Kent from a prize-winning stallion. Midnight had been a likely-looking colt and had matured into a stallion of spirit and loyalty, with the sweetest mouth of any horse Nathaniel had ever possessed.

He had spent what was left of the morning in the stables with Finch and his grooms, seeing to the disposal of Midnight's body, before searching the stables from top to bottom in an effort to find what might have afflicted the stallion. They had found nothing of any relevance.

Nathaniel felt utterly heartsick and suddenly required his own company. 'I believe I will leave you ladies to enjoy your tea together and return to the library.'

Elizabeth's heart went out to him as she watched him exit his aunt's parlour, aware of his obvious suffering; his face was pale and haggard, those dark eyes for once not filled with laughing mockery or arrogant disdain, but a profound mourning. She had offered Nathaniel her sympathy on the loss of his horse earlier today, of course, but politely, even stiltedly, aware as she was of Mrs Wilson's avid attention to any exchange that took place between Elizabeth and her nephew.

At least the sudden death of Nathaniel's horse had postponed that lady's reprimands about their earlier impropriety.

'Poor boy,' Letitia Grant clucked her sympathy.

'He was ever fond of his animals.' Mrs Wilson sighed even as she cast an affectionate glance at Hector lying snug and comfortable in his basket asleep before the fire lit for that very purpose.

Elizabeth found it somewhat endearing when these two ladies referred to Nathaniel as if he were no more than a young boy, which no doubt he must seem to them. Not so Elizabeth, who would never see Nathaniel as being less than a man—a brooding and handsome man who made her heart pound loudly just thinking of the passionate heat of his kisses and caresses.

That was not all she had found to like about him, of course. She had long since realised that his air of cynical charm and studied boredom was a shield for much softer emotions. He might not have any stronger feelings for Elizabeth than the desire he had shown her on several occasions, but his affection for his aunt was genuine, he had an easy tolerance of the sometimes irritating and over-effusive Letitia and was never anything but polite to the servants and guests of his aunt.

It seemed that only she and Sir Rufus Tennant were exceptions to the latter rule…

'Perhaps we should all think of returning to London when Nathaniel leaves tomorrow.' Mrs Wilson obviously required no input from either Letitia or Elizabeth as she made her words a statement rather than a question.

It was so exactly what Elizabeth now wished to do herself that she had to bite her tongue in order to stop from saying so, sure that her opinion would count for nought in her now-precarious position within Mrs Wilson's household.

Instead she stood up. 'If you will both excuse me?'

'Where are you going?' Mrs Wilson asked suspiciously.

As well she might, considering it had been Elizabeth's intention to seek out Nathaniel in the library and offer him her private condolences. Had Mrs Wilson guessed? 'I had thought that I might take this opportunity to…rest for a while before dinner.'

'I believe that—' Mrs Wilson broke off whatever she had been about to say as Sewell quietly entered the parlour.

'Sir Rufus Tennant is here to see you, madam,' he informed his mistress evenly.

Elizabeth's heart sank at the news as she recalled those roses sent to her earlier today. She hadn't wanted to respond to the gesture, but surely it could not be ignored any longer when Sir Rufus was now here in person?

How much she wished that she had made her excuses earlier. Instead she was not yet excused by her employer and so was forced to remain here for at least the next few minutes.

Moreover, she wondered what the earl would say or do, in his present state of mind, if he were to realise Sir Rufus had dared to call after being categorically told not to come here until after Nathaniel had left.

'Show him in, Sewell.' Mrs Wilson's impatience with the inconvenience of the visit was barely contained, although she bestowed a gracious enough smile upon her guest as he was shown into the room. 'You must excuse the informality of my parlour, Sir Rufus.' She acknowledged his formal bow. 'We are all out of sorts today, I am afraid.'

'So I have heard,' he said. 'This is the country, Mrs Wilson; news always travels at greater speed here than in London,' he added as that lady raised her brows.

'So it would seem...' Mrs Wilson frowned her displeasure at finding the doings of her household the subject of such idle tittle-tattle.

Sir Rufus's pale blue gaze flickered in Elizabeth's direction as he gave another bow. 'Ladies.'

'Sir Rufus.' She gave him a cool nod as Letitia simpered a greeting.

He made himself comfortable in one of the low armchairs when invited to do so. 'Osbourne has lost one of his horses, I believe?'

There was such a lack of sympathy in his voice that Elizabeth instantly bristled with furious indignation on behalf of the earl.

An indignation Mrs Wilson shared if the angry colour that rose in her cheeks was any indication. 'We are a family with a close affinity with our animals,' she stated, her previous gratitude towards this man obviously forgotten in the face of his rudeness.

'So I have noted,' Sir Rufus replied, casting a scathing glance in the pampered Hector's direction. The little dog immediately responded by once more growling deep in his throat.

Mrs Wilson offered no apology for her pet's behaviour today. 'You speak as if you do not approve, Sir Rufus?'

He shrugged broad shoulders. 'I have to admit to a lack of understanding with regard to an Englishman's—or woman's…' he gave his hostess a wryly acknowledging nod '…obvious affection for anything with four legs.'

Elizabeth found herself holding her breath as a strained silence fell over the gathering. She waited for the explosion that seemed to be about to circumvent Mrs Wilson's usual politeness towards a guest in her home.

'Perhaps that is because you have little in the way of affection to give anyone, Tennant, four-legged or otherwise!' the cold voice of Nathaniel Thorne bit out contemptuously.

Elizabeth gasped as she turned towards the

doorway where the earl stood, his glittering gaze fixed upon the man seated across the room.

The older man rose slowly to his feet to return that gaze disdainfully. 'I will excuse your rudeness to me, Osbourne, on the basis that you are obviously overset by the loss of your valuable horseflesh.'

'Midnight's value to me did not equate into pounds, shillings and pence,' Nathaniel ground out. 'Nor am I so overset that I do not know exactly to whom I am speaking!'

'Nathaniel—'

'What are you doing here, Tennant?' Nathaniel demanded, ignoring his aunt's attempt to intercede between the combatants.

'I called to see Mrs Wilson, of course.'

'Why?'

Sir Rufus looked slightly flustered and then his normal pomposity returned. 'I called initially to offer my condolences on the loss of your horse—'

'Considering the content of the sympathies I overheard just now, you would have done better not to have bothered!' Nathaniel said cuttingly. 'And what about afterwards?' he prompted softly.

Tennant drew his breath in noisily. 'I do not believe I need explain myself to you, Osbourne.'

'As the only male in this household I have to disagree.' Nathaniel knew that there could be no argument against such a claim.

Sir Rufus once again looked less sure of himself. 'I had thought, with Mrs Wilson's permission, to invite Miss Thompson to come on a small walk with me.'

Nathaniel snorted. 'It is my understanding that after yesterday Miss Thompson has no wish to go anywhere with you ever again. Is that not so, Miss Thompson?' He turned to Elizabeth, his brows raised in arrogant query.

Elizabeth was aghast by the level of tension that now filled the room; Mrs Wilson's eyes were wide at her nephew's rudeness, Letitia actually open-mouthed with astonishment, Sir Rufus's redness of face giving every appearance that he might actually leap forwards at any moment and administer a fist to Nathaniel's chin. As for Nathaniel himself...

She had never seen him so chillingly, dangerously angry as this before, not even yesterday when he had discovered her in Sir Rufus's arms.

Indeed, he looked as if he would welcome an attack from the other man, just so that he had an excuse to retaliate. If he actually needed an excuse, of course…

Elizabeth turned to look coolly at the red-faced Sir Rufus. 'Lord Thorne is perfectly correct in his claim, sir. I am suffering from a slight cold today.'

'So there you have the refusal straight from Miss Thompson's lips, Tennant,' the earl said.

The other man's mouth thinned with displeasure. 'I am sorry to hear that you are feeling unwell, Elizabeth,' he bit out. 'Perhaps I might call upon you again tomorrow?'

'I—'

'That will not be possible, I am afraid, Sir Rufus,' Mrs Wilson put in smoothly. 'In view of my nephew's return to health, and the sad associations here at present, I have decided that all of my London household shall return to town tomorrow.'

'Tomorrow?' Sir Rufus spluttered in protest. 'But—Miss Thompson, too?'

'Well, of course Elizabeth shall come too.' Mrs Wilson, obviously now as tired as her nephew was of Sir Rufus's boorish company, was less than patient in her reply. 'She is a part of my London household, after all.'

For the moment, Elizabeth added silently, knowing that situation could not continue for long after they had all returned to town. Indeed, given the circumstances, she considered it generous of Mrs Wilson to allow her to return to London with her at all; many employers in the same situation would have cast her out without thought for how she was to find the means or money to travel back to London.

Sir Rufus scowled. 'Then perhaps I could be allowed a few moments in which I might talk alone with Miss Thompson?'

Elizabeth felt her heart sink even further as the cold, contemptuous expression on Nathaniel's face turned to a look of utter violence. 'I—'

'No, I am afraid Elizabeth cannot be spared even for a few moments if we are all to be in readiness to leave tomorrow,' Mrs Wilson took it upon herself to answer the man swiftly. 'I am sure you understand, Sir Rufus?' The steely edge to her polite tone said that he had better.

He made no answer for several long moments, as his good sense obviously warred with his dislike of being denied that which he wanted. Thankfully good sense finally won out. 'In that case I will take my leave of you, madam.' He bowed awkwardly to his hostess, blatantly ignoring every other person in the room—including Elizabeth—before sweeping from the parlour. Only seconds later the front door was heard to slam with some force behind him.

An uncomfortable silence settled over the inhabitants of Mrs Wilson's parlour, Elizabeth barely able to breathe as she waited for someone to speak, feeling unable to do so herself after what had just happened.

'Well!' Mrs Wilson was predictably the one to break that silence—although her next comment was not the one Elizabeth had been expecting. 'What a perfectly obnoxious man Sir Rufus is!' She repressed a shudder of revulsion. 'Indeed, I always had my suspicions that as a boy he was the type to enjoy pulling the legs from spiders and wings off flies!'

'Aunt Gertrude!' Nathaniel's shocked laughter was completely spontaneous as some of his tension eased.

His aunt patted the already-perfect neatness of

her hair, completely unabashed at having criti-
cised a guest in her home so roundly. 'You did not
know Rufus Tennant as a boy, Nathaniel. He was
only eight or nine years old when I first came here
with my darling Bastian and he was a stocky, un-
attractive lad even then. He was absolutely hateful
in his behaviour towards that brother of his, who
was so much younger than he.'

'Giles,' Nathaniel put in.

'Just so,' his aunt said. 'He was jealous, of
course, having been an only child for the first six
years of his life. Of course, it cannot have helped
that Giles was of such a sweet and good-natured
temperament that he succeeded in charming all
who came into contact with him. Or that he grew
up to be such a golden-haired, attractive rogue.'

Nathaniel frowned. 'I had always believed the
two brothers were close?'

'Publicly, yes. Here in the privacy of Gifford
House? Another story completely,' Mrs Wilson
revealed. 'And then, of course, Giles succeeded in
captivating the admiration and love of the woman
every man of the *ton* panted after.' She gave an
inelegant snort.

'Harriet Copeland...' Nathaniel murmured ruefully; even now, ten years after the event, he recalled that married lady's legendary beauty. He had been considered far too young at the time to be acquainted with that lady himself, of course, but he had occasionally caught glimpses of her as she'd glittered and sparkled at society balls, a dark-haired, sea-green-eyed beauty who had captured the attention of every man who so much as looked at her.

That had been before society was shaken by the scandal of Harriet Copeland leaving her husband and young family to set up home with Giles Tennant, resulting in it turning its backs and closing its doors upon both of them.

His aunt nodded. 'They were so very much in love with each other. But obviously the…oddness that characterises Sir Rufus's personality must have existed inside Giles too, otherwise how else could he have behaved so abhorrently in the end?'

Elizabeth had become very still at the first mention of her mother's name. Indeed, she could not move, barely breathed, and there was also a tightness across her chest at finally hearing that Giles Tennant had, after all, been the young lover of Elizabeth's mother ten years previously.

'I trust that you will forgive me for ever encouraging you to enjoy the attentions of a such a man, my dear.' Mrs Wilson turned to gently squeeze Elizabeth's arm in apology. 'I had believed that the years might have improved his temperament, but you were obviously far more astute than I where his true nature was concerned!'

Elizabeth had been in the right of it in deciding she did not like the man very much, perhaps, but that astuteness counted for nought now that she knew about the past connection of Sir Rufus's family to her mother. As she was left wondering why Sir Rufus would ever have wished to name a rose after the woman who was responsible for bringing such disgrace upon the Tennant family...

'I—yes, of course. Would—am I really to return to London with you tomorrow, Mrs Wilson?' She frowned, wondering what, if anything, she should do about the information she now held.

'Yes, Aunt Gertrude, what was all that about?' Nathaniel asked. 'I had thought it was your intention to remain in Devon for several more weeks?'

She gave an airy wave of her hand. 'I have not found being in the country as pleasant as I had hoped; as your health was our main reason for coming here at all in the middle of the Season, there seems little reason for any of us to remain when you are to leave tomorrow. Especially when one of our closest neighbours has proved himself to be so unpleasant,' she added indignantly.

Those reasons were all well and good, but at the same time they totally negated Nathaniel's own reason for leaving Hepworth Manor—namely to put a distance between himself and the temptation Elizabeth represented.

The pallor he could now see in her cheeks would seem to indicate she was as shaken by this sudden decision to return to London by her employer as Nathaniel was himself.

Chapter Sixteen

'You did not seem particularly overjoyed earlier by the news you were to return to London with my aunt tomorrow?'

Elizabeth had excused herself from Mrs Wilson's parlour earlier on the pretext of packing her few belongings in preparation for the journey back to London in the morning, but instead of that she had collapsed down weakly onto her bed as soon as she had closed the bedchamber door behind her, still uncertain as to what she should do now that she knew for certain that Giles Tennant had been her mother's lover. She also still pondered the strangeness of Sir Rufus's previous intention of naming his rose in honour of Harriet Copeland, when he should have positively loathed her.

To return to London, without so much as speaking with Sir Rufus again, meant Elizabeth would be leaving behind the one man who might be able to answer some of those questions. But contrarily she had no idea, after the awkwardness of Sir Rufus's departure earlier, how she was even to go about meeting him again, let alone bringing the conversation round to such a delicate subject as his brother's tragic death.

For Nathaniel to now intrude upon such confused thoughts was far from welcome. 'Your aunt would be most displeased if she were to find you in my bedchamber for a second time today,' she pointed out firmly.

'Then we must ensure she does not.' He stepped further into the room and closed the door quietly behind him. 'I thought you came upstairs with the intention of packing?' His pointed glance took in the fact that the bedchamber remained much as it had when he had been in here this morning; a brush-and-comb set sat on the dressing-table, Elizabeth's nightrail and robe were draped across the chair and the open door of the wardrobe revealed that her few gowns remained hanging there, several pairs of slippers placed neatly side by side in the bottom. The fact that she had been sitting on the bed when he entered was further evidence that she had made no effort as yet to begin packing anything.

She stood up abruptly. 'I felt a little unwell again once I had arrived here, so I sat down to rest for several minutes.'

Nathaniel studied her between narrowed lids; there was no mistaking that her cheeks were still very pale, or that her eyes were a dark and pained blue. 'You do still look far from well.'

Elizabeth turned away from his probing gaze. 'It is merely a cold accompanied by a slight fever.' She pushed the tendrils of hair from a forehead that had become damp as she gazed out of the window and realised that she could actually see the smoke curling from the chimney tops of Gifford House, visible across the hillside in the next valley. So near and yet at the same time still so very far away…

'Perhaps you should, after all, allow my aunt to call on the services of a physician?'

'No, I am sure that will not be necessary.' Elizabeth turned away from that tantalising glimpse of Sir Rufus Tennant's home. 'May I say once again how sorry I was to hear of Midnight's passing,' she added gently.

The earl's face closed. 'Would that it had been as peaceful as you make it sound, but I am afraid it was not an easy or pleasant death.'

Elizabeth winced. 'Do you have any idea what might have been the cause of it?'

'Nothing has been confirmed as yet, no,' Nathaniel replied.

She blinked. 'But you have your suspicions?'

'Perhaps,' he said evasively. 'Finch will continue to look into the matter after I am gone.'

'Can it be you suspect one of the grooms of some misdemeanour?' she pressed.

'If that's the case, then Finch will have his head on a pike.' And Nathaniel would have the rest of him, preferably sliced and diced on the end of his sword, for daring to cause such a magnificent stallion even one moment of pain.

Elizabeth looked sad. 'I really am so very sorry.'

He gave a tight smile. 'You are not to blame, Elizabeth.'

'Well. No. Of course I am not.' She frowned. 'But I am sorry for it, none the less.'

Nathaniel had no doubts about the kindness of Elizabeth's heart; he had seen that kindness time and time again during their time together. Indeed, it was one of the reasons he found it doubly difficult to resist her dark and arresting beauty.

If she had been less kind, less intelligent, less beautiful, then Nathaniel knew he would not have found himself constantly drawn to be wherever she was. As it was, even now, sick at heart as he was over Midnight's death, aware his aunt was already suspicious of his interest in Elizabeth, he had not been able to stop himself from coming up to her bedchamber to be alone with her one last time.

He sighed. 'I doubt we shall see much of each other once we are returned to London. I will be going to Osbourne House and you will be in my aunt's home.'

'No,' Elizabeth confirmed huskily, having realised as much after Mrs Wilson's announcement earlier.

Much as it pained her to think of not seeing and being with Nathaniel again, she couldn't help feeling it was perhaps for the best. There could be no future in such an attraction. Nathaniel was the wealthy and eligible Earl of Osbourne; while Elizabeth realised that, as he was friends with her new guardian, they were destined to meet again one day, the fact that she was really the impoverished daughter of the deceased Earl of Westbourne and the notoriously scandalous Harriet Copeland would make her no more acceptable as a match for Nathaniel than she had been as the young companion of his aunt.

'Although I believe you may be being over-optimistic in assuming that I shall accompany your aunt to her home there,' she said now. She smiled wanly. 'I am afraid that Mrs Wilson has been far from pleased with my behaviour today.'

'Your behaviour?' The earl scowled. 'I am the one who has come to your bedchamber. Twice!'

Elizabeth nodded. 'And, as a mere servant rather than a close family member, I am the one who will be dismissed.'

'If you truly believe that to be the case—'

'I do,' Elizabeth interjected.

'Then I will speak with my aunt.'

'I wish you would not! Please do not,' she repeated less forcefully. 'It is unnecessary to involve yourself when I have already told you that being a lady's companion does not suit me.' Elizabeth had, in fact, decided that it was time she returned to her home in Hampshire.

Running away from Shoreley Park and from

the offer of marriage from Lord Faulkner, to seek her freedom and possibly romantic adventure in London, had not turned out at all as she had expected; there could be no freedom when she had little money with which to support herself, and the only romantic adventure she had encountered was to be pursued by one man she did not care for and another whom she found she cared for far too much.

No, she could not think about her tangled feelings for Nathaniel now if she were to conduct this conversation with any degree of decorum. 'I have decided it is time to return to my home.'

The earl looked intrigued. 'Which is where?'

Elizabeth gave a slight smile. 'Not in London, certainly.'

Nathaniel found he was not in the least pleased that Elizabeth might leave and disappear off to God—or he—knew where. Which, he realised, was probably the whole point…

He crossed the room to stand before her, looking down into the delicate beauty of her face. 'I do not like the thought of not seeing you again.'

A flush entered the previous paleness of her cheeks as she avoided meeting his gaze, instead concentrating on the buttons of his waistcoat. 'I

am sure, once returned to London and your…
friends there, that you will quickly forget Elizabeth Thompson ever existed.'

It had certainly been Nathaniel's intention to do
as much. To enjoy the uncomplicated charms of
a willing woman and satisfy his physical needs,
before seeking out his friends Westbourne and
Blackstone. Neither of those activities held the
same appeal when they would be done in the
knowledge that Elizabeth was no longer resident
at the home of his aunt.

'Perhaps—' Nathaniel broke off with a frustrated growl.

'Yes…?' Elizabeth looked up at him shyly.

He was grappling with the dilemma of allowing Elizabeth to leave his life against the equally
unacceptable alternative of offering her the role of
his mistress. The first option he found painful to
contemplate, the second was just utterly distasteful to him… He was damned whichever course
he took.

And so he would do neither. 'I believe I shall
miss you,' he said instead.

Elizabeth smiled sadly. 'My sharp tongue, perhaps.'

Remembering the things this young lady had

done with her tongue only yesterday was reckless on Nathaniel's part. As soon as he did so the heat that coursed through him caused his shaft to harden and throb uncomfortably…

Madness. Utter and complete madness to even think about when he and Elizabeth had made love together!

He stepped away. 'Perhaps,' he conceded. 'As no doubt you will notice the absence of my own tendency to tease you at every turn.'

Elizabeth knew she would miss so much more than his teasing once she had departed Mrs Wilson's household. That she would long for so much more! But there was nothing else to be done. Elizabeth must return to Shoreley Park, to the company of her sisters, and as soon as was possible, so that she might share with them all she had learnt concerning her mother's involvement with the Tennant family.

'No doubt,' she answered Nathaniel softly. 'And who knows, perhaps we will meet again someday?'

He could not see how, when the two of them occupied completely different spheres in society.

'Now, if you would not mind, I believe it is time I began my packing?'

As dismissals went he acknowledged that Elizabeth's was suitably polite, if all the more final because of it.

'So it is,' he agreed with a small smile. 'If at any time in the future, you are in need of help or assistance—'

'No, that simply will not do, Nathaniel,' she cut in with a firmness of purpose.

'Then if you are ever in need of a reference, perhaps—'

'That would be even less acceptable than your previous offer!' she said drily. 'Any female employer would look askance at my holding a personal reference from the Earl of Osbourne and the assumptions a male employer might make holds even less appeal for me.'

She was right, of course, Nathaniel acknowledged, and felt no less frustrated because of it. 'So this truly is goodbye, then?' he said gruffly.

Her smile was wan. 'I am sure, as it will take several days for us to travel to London, that we will have the occasion to speak together again during that time.'

But not privately, Nathaniel knew. Not like this. Alone. Completely unencumbered by the presence of either his forceful aunt or the well-meaning Letitia.

He privately cursed the distance that already yawned between them. 'Perhaps, once you are settled back home, you might write to me and let me know. No, I realise that will "not do" either,' he answered his own question before she could.

It was something of a balm to Elizabeth's bruised emotions that Nathaniel seemed to find their parting almost as painful as she did. Almost. For the Earl of Osbourne could have no true softness of feelings towards a young woman apparently so below him in station. 'It really is past time that you left my bedchamber, my lord.'

'But—'

'If you please, my lord!' Elizabeth added with a firmness she was far from feeling.

His mouth tightened at her repeated formality. 'As usual, you are correct.' He immediately became the Earl of Osbourne: shoulders straightening, a look of cool hauteur on his handsome face as he strode over to the door. 'I will wish you good luck with your packing.'

'My lord.' Elizabeth gave a polite curtsy, maintaining her own air of distance until the door closed softly behind him, when she was at last able to give in to the tears that had been threatening to fall these past few minutes, to give in to the heartache she suffered just at the thought of parting from the man she loved so dearly.

'Where are you going?'

'Is that not obvious, my lord?' Elizabeth looked down pointedly at the leashed and panting Hector standing beside her in the hallway in readiness for their walk.

Nathaniel had been feeling decidedly out of humour since his return downstairs and was certainly in no mood now to suffer her sarcasm. 'I am sure that Hector could forgo his walk for one evening if you are still feeling unwell.' Elizabeth's eyes were red-rimmed, her cheeks were flushed and her voice was unusually husky.

Her dark curls were covered by a straw bonnet in preparation for going outside into the early-evening sunlight. 'I have completed my packing and believe a little fresh air now might clear my head before dinner.'

She was probably right, but even so… 'Perhaps I might accompany you?'

A shadow passed over the fineness of her features as she shook her head. 'That will—'

'—not do,' Nathaniel finished harshly, hands clenched at his sides. 'I am growing a little weary of hearing what will or will not do concerning the two of us, Elizabeth.'

She gave a rueful smile. 'I was about to say that will not be necessary, my lord. I am perfectly capable of taking Hector for his evening walk alone,' she continued as he would have protested.

He was behaving as ridiculously as Elizabeth's dryness of tone implied that he was, Nathaniel accepted self-disgustedly. Moreover, several letters of correspondence had arrived for him a short time ago and been placed in the library; they were in need of his attention before his departure tomorrow. 'I will not delay you any further, then.'

Elizabeth only allowed herself to breathe again once Nathaniel had disappeared in the direction of the library, the composure she had pulled about her like a cloak before coming down the stairs having been shaken the moment she saw him again. Her interest, the feelings she had for

Nathaniel, were the things that definitely would 'not do'!

Elizabeth was afraid of examining those feelings too closely; no doubt she would have plenty of time—days, months, years—in which to do so, once she was safely removed from his presence and returned to Shoreley Park.

In the meantime, it was her intention to keep herself as busy as possible so as not to allow herself the time to dwell on those feelings, starting with a long and hopefully pleasant walk with Hector.

However, within minutes of leaving Hepworth Manor, she unfortunately happened upon Sir Rufus strolling purposefully along the pathway towards her.

A look of satisfaction settled upon his homely features, his first words confirming that this was no idle encounter. 'I have been walking here for some time in the hopes that I might meet with you again.'

'Sir Rufus.' Elizabeth's own greeting was less fulsome as she eyed him warily. She was very aware of Mrs Wilson's comments earlier about an oddness in this man's true nature, but at the same time she could not help but wonder if this meeting was not fated to be. An answer, in fact, to her earlier uncertainties as to what, if anything, she should do about her new-found knowledge.

'I have not had the opportunity to thank you for the roses, which you had delivered to me earlier today, Sir Rufus,' she murmured as he fell into step beside her.

His face lit up with pleasure beneath his tall hat. 'I am pleased you appreciated them.'

Elizabeth had not actually said that. 'They are very beautiful,' she acknowledged noncommittally.

He gazed down at her admiringly. 'Nowhere near as beautiful as their namesake,' he said.

Actually, Elizabeth knew herself to be nowhere near as beautiful as their original namesake, nor was she any nearer to answering why Sir Rufus would ever have considered naming his treasured rose after the woman who had been his younger brother's scandalous lover. 'You do me great honour, sir.'

'Not at all.' He came to a halt to turn and take her free hand in his much larger one. 'Elizabeth, you must be aware by now of the esteem in which

I hold you—' He broke off abruptly as Hector chose that moment to announce his feelings about this encounter by growling fiercely as he sank his teeth into one of that gentleman's boot-clad ankles. 'Infuriating little beast!' Sir Rufus's face darkened angrily as he kicked out at the little dog, the force of it wrenching the leash from Elizabeth's hand as Hector literally flew through the air to whine in pain as he landed several feet away on the dry and dusty pathway.

'Sir Rufus!' Elizabeth gasped her shocked dismay as she pulled her hand free to run to the little dog's side. 'How could you!' She turned to glare accusingly at the man even as she aided a slightly dazed Hector to stagger awkwardly to his feet.

His expression remained dark with anger. 'I am sick of the constant interruptions caused by the presence of that animal.' Sir Rufus strode forwards to take a firm grasp of Elizabeth's arm to pull her up beside him. 'We will go to Gifford House where I might converse with you in uninterrupted privacy.'

Elizabeth's eyes opened wide in alarm, both at this suggestion and Sir Rufus's strange and wild behaviour. 'I have no wish to go to Gifford House with you, sir.'

'Of course you do.'

'No—'

'Yes, Elizabeth!' He began to drag her along the pathway at his side.

'Sir Rufus, I really must insist that you release me this instant!' Elizabeth's own efforts to free herself were met with resistance as the curl of his fingers became painful about her arm and would no doubt result in leaving bruises on the tenderness of her flesh.

Hector, seemingly recovered from the vicious kick, chose that moment for another attack on Sir Rufus's booted ankle, his growls low in his throat.

Sir Rufus, his face twisted into a look of cruelty, did not hesitate to deliver another kick to the little animal's side with the booted foot not held captive by sharp little teeth. A kick that Hector did not get up from this time, instead lying unconscious upon his side some distance away. 'With any luck, the brute is dead!' his attacker announced with satisfaction.

Elizabeth turned fiercely on the man standing

beside her. 'How can you even say such a thing?' She tried once again to release herself from the steely grip of his fingers, uncaring of the pain to herself in her desperation to return to Hector's side. 'Let me go this instant!' Her cheeks burned with fury.

'You must know I cannot—'

'I know of no such thing!' Temper glittered in Elizabeth's eyes. 'You are a monster!' She turned and began to pummel her fists upon Sir Rufus's chest. 'A cruel and unfeeling monster!' Elizabeth was beyond reason, pushed well beyond all need to restrain the disgust and abhorrence she felt for this man. So much so that it took several minutes for her to realise that he was offering no resistance considering he had a fiercely angry woman beating her fists upon his chest!

But it slowly crept into her consciousness that he was unmoving against that heated onslaught. That he had, in fact, become unnaturally still.

Elizabeth stopped her pounding to look up at him, all the colour draining from her cheeks as she saw that he was looking down at her with such an odd expression in those pale and glittering blue eyes that it sent a shiver of apprehension down the length of her spine.

A nerve pulsed in his grimly set jaw. 'Why do you continue to talk to me in this way when you know I only acted as I did so that we might finally be together?'

Elizabeth swallowed hard before speaking. 'Sir Rufus—'

'I will suffer no more of your squeamishness over something that needed to be done, Harriet!' he thundered.

'Harriet?' Elizabeth's eyes had now widened with more than alarm—was this man so lost to all sense that he actually believed her to be her mother?

His expression softened slightly as he looked down at her. 'My darling Harriet.' His hands moved to cradle each side of her face. 'I am fully aware of your softness of heart. Indeed, I am sure I would not love you half as much if I did not know of your consideration for the feelings of others.' His expression tightened. 'For my brother's feelings especially. But it is time for us to stop all the pretence, my darling. Time for us to be together, as we were always meant to be.'

There was such a look of unholy madness in his face now that Elizabeth realised at this moment that Sir Rufus truly did believe her to be Harriet Copeland returned to him.

Chapter Seventeen

'You must come at once, Nathaniel! At once, do you hear?'

Nathaniel frowned as he looked up from reading the correspondence he had received from Gabriel Faulkner only that afternoon, to see his pale, dishevelled and obviously distraught aunt standing in the doorway of the library, those things alone enough to tell him that something was seriously amiss; his Aunt Gertrude prided herself on being both calm and practical on all occasions.

He stood up quickly from behind the desk. 'What has occurred?'

Tears glistened in his aunt's eyes as her hand moved to the agitation of her rapidly rising and falling chest. 'Hector has returned terribly injured and without Elizabeth!'

Nathaniel frowned darkly as he stepped into the

centre of the book-lined room. 'Without Eliza-beth?' he repeated.

Mrs Wilson nodded. 'Oh, Nathaniel, I fear she may have fallen over the cliff-top! Might even now lay dead and broken upon the rocks below—'

'You must calm yourself, Aunt,' he cut in sharply, her hysteria only succeeding in sharpening the keen edge of his own concern. 'Hector has returned injured, you say?'

His aunt nodded quickly. 'He is limping badly on his right front leg and his ribs appear to be either bruised or broken.'

'Show me.' He crossed the room in two long strides to join his aunt as she turned to lead the way to her private parlour where Hector lay un-naturally still and quiet in his basket beside the fireplace.

The little dog looked up with soulful eyes as Nathaniel went down on his haunches beside the basket, his hands gentle on the soft rise and fall of Hector's ribs before he inspected the injured leg.

He turned to look at his hovering Aunt Ger-trude. 'His leash was still in place when he re-turned?'

'Yes.'

Nathaniel straightened. 'I do not believe anything is broken…'

'Oh, thank goodness!' Mrs Wilson breathed her relief before her expression once again clouded with concern. 'But what of Elizabeth? Where can she be? You must go out and look for her immediately, Nathaniel!' She wrung her hands together in her anxiety.

He had every intention of looking for Elizabeth. Indeed, he had only delayed that search long enough to examine the little dog first, in an effort to gain any information from Hector's appearance as to where she might be. 'Hector does not appear to have fallen down the cliff, Aunt, otherwise I am sure he would have sustained other cuts and injuries.'

Mrs Wilson frowned. 'But surely Elizabeth would have returned by now if she had only lost hold of his leash?'

Nathaniel, knowing it would have taken some time for Hector, with his injured leg and bruised ribs, to have made his way back to Hepworth Manor, had already reached that same conclusion. Which meant that she was either lying injured on the cliff path somewhere or had been prevented from returning by some other means.

Means in the shape of Sir Rufus Tennant, perhaps?

Nathaniel scowled, knowing he had absolutely no basis for that conclusion. Except, of course, for the other man's almost fanatical interest in Elizabeth these past few days.

His mouth was tight at the thought of Tennant being anywhere near her. 'You will instruct Sewell to organise a search party at once, Aunt.'

'But where will you be?' His aunt turned to stare as him as he walked purposefully towards the doorway.

Nathaniel looked at her with eyes that were dark and stormy. 'I am going to pay a visit upon a neighbour before joining in the search, dear Aunt.'

Mrs Wilson's eyes widened. 'You do not think Tennant has something to do with this?'

'At this moment I am trying not to think, but to act, Aunt,' Nathaniel rasped.

Her knuckles showed white as she clutched her hands together all the tighter. 'He has seemed rather obsessed with Elizabeth recently...'

An obsession, knowing of her intended departure on the morrow, that he might just have decided to act upon before it became too late to do so, perhaps?

Nathaniel should never have allowed Elizabeth to go walking alone. He should have insisted on accompanying her earlier. Should have—

Damn it, never mind what he should have done! The most important thing now was to find her and reassure himself, and everyone else, as to her welfare.

Elizabeth had never felt so frightened in her life as she stood in the eerie silence of Sir Rufus's hothouse, as unnerved by his belief that she was her mother as she was by the sharp pruning knife he held distractedly in one hand.

She had not come willingly to Gifford House with him, but he had been so fired by the intensity of his emotions that it was as if she weighed nothing at all as he dragged and pulled her along beside him, knocking her bonnet askew and forcing her to remove it completely when she could no longer see where he was taking her.

It had taken barely any time at all to reach Gifford House, where any hopes of Elizabeth being able to ask for assistance from one of Sir Rufus's servants had instantly been dashed, as he had ignored entering the house by the front door and instead circled straight round to the back of the house, where he had entered the hothouse to shut and lock the door firmly behind them.

His earlier comments about her mother were enough to have persuaded her into holding her usually wayward tongue, most especially his comments as to Harriet's 'squeamishness over something that had needed to be done', so that 'the two of them might finally be together', as they had 'always been meant to be'.

Elizabeth was frantically wondering exactly what Sir Rufus had done in the past in order to ensure that he and Harriet might be together…

Nathaniel had left Hepworth Manor so hastily that he had not even paused to collect his hat and gloves as he hurried to the stable to help Finch saddle a brown gelding. He rode out onto the cliffs as if the devil were at his heels, all the time keeping a lookout for Elizabeth in case she had, after all, accidentally slipped over the side of the cliff. The nearest Nathaniel came to finding any sign of her was a particular part of the dusty pathway where he could see the scuffle of tiny footprints and Hector's paw prints intertwined with a pair of men's boots.

Tennant's boots?

Nathaniel had no proof of that, of course, but, considering those two pairs of footprints led in the direction of Gifford House, he turned his horse firmly in that direction, his expression grimmer than ever.

'Please, sir—'

'My darling Harriet, I believe we may stop all pretence now and call each other by our given names!' Sir Rufus assured indulgently as he looked down at Elizabeth with warmly glowing eyes.

She feared he had completely lost all reason; perhaps it was safest to indulge him in his fantasy? 'Rufus,' she complied softly, 'would we not both be more comfortable if we were to go into the house and talk? Over dinner, perhaps?' Elizabeth knew she would certainly feel more reassured if there were servants within screaming distance.

He gave a puzzled frown. 'But you always said how much you longed to see my roses…'

'And I am very happy to have seen them now,' she hastened to reassure with a sideways glance at the knife in his hand. 'I—I thought only of your comfort when I suggested we might go into the house for dinner.'

His expression softened again. 'As usual, Harriet, you are ever considerate of others.'

Elizabeth did not remember her mother very well, having been but nine years old when Harriet departed Shoreley Park for the last time, but she did have memory of her mother's warmth, and the laughter that had always filled the house whenever she was at home; it had become more than obvious these past few minutes that it was not only Giles Tennant who had fallen in love with Harriet Copeland, but that Sir Rufus Tennant had, too.

Had her death at the hands of Giles Tennant completely unhinged him?

Or was it something else, something much darker, something so much more terrible that was responsible for Sir Rufus's present deranged state of mind?

Elizabeth moistened dry lips, very aware that his state of mind was so mercurial that he might turn violent again at any moment, most especially if she were to challenge his belief that she was Harriet. 'I have to admit to welcoming the idea of partaking of a light supper myself.' She would do or say anything in order to persuade him to go into the house and away from the complete isolation of this secluded hothouse.

He chuckled softly, giving her a brief glimpse of the younger man he must once have been. He was still not an especially handsome or dashing man, as his younger brother was reputed to have been, but he'd certainly had his own homely appeal. 'You know that I have never been able to deny you anything.'

'Then we may go into the house and eat supper?' Much as she tried, Elizabeth could not keep the eagerness to escape being alone with him from her tone. 'You might show me around the rest of the house then, too,' she added encouragingly as he frowned slightly.

'Of course; my beloved Harriet, you must be eager to view what is to become your new home.'

Sir Rufus gave one of her hands a reassuring squeeze.

'Very eager.' Elizabeth resisted a shudder at the mere thought of any woman having to live with him, let alone with those glassy-eyed hunting trophies that adorned the gloomy entrance hall of Gifford House; her mother had certainly been a woman who had surrounded herself with light and laughter and beautiful things.

'Would you not like to see the rest of the roses first?'

'Perhaps later.' It took every effort of will on Elizabeth's part to slip one of her gloved hands companionably into the crook of his arm as she smiled up at him. 'Let us go to the house for a warming drink, at least.' She gave a delicate shiver to accompany this statement.

In truth, she felt so inwardly cold it was as if ice ran in her veins, caused by her fear of this man—and the knife he still carried—rather than the temperature of the hothouse. But it was the lengths Sir Rufus might have gone to in order to ensure that Harriet Copeland became his own that Elizabeth feared knowing more than anything else.

* * *

'You must have some idea where Sir Rufus is!' Nathaniel glowered at the butler who had opened the door to Gifford House in answer to the remorseless pummelling of his fist.

'I have told you, my lord, Sir Rufus is not at home,' the elderly man repeated patiently.

Nathaniel looked about him wildly, wondering where the other man could have gone. Where he could have taken Elizabeth. If, indeed, she was with him at all...

The butler flinched slightly as he once again became the focus of Nathaniel's steely-eyed gaze. 'You might perhaps try the hothouse at the back of the house? Sir Rufus is there often and—'

Nathaniel did not linger to listen to any further explanations but ran down the steps and round to the back of the house to where the hothouse glinted in the late-evening sunlight.

Only to come to an abrupt halt beneath the shade of an oak tree as he saw Elizabeth and Sir Rufus just emerging from inside the glass hothouse, giving every appearance of taking an evening stroll together. Elizabeth's arm was linked with that of Sir Rufus's as she smiled up at him, chatting happily as they walked towards him.

Until Nathaniel saw her eyes…

Elizabeth had the most expressive eyes he had ever beheld, a startlingly clear and beautiful sky-blue, more often than not filled with either warmth or the light of battle that was so much a part of her feisty personality.

At the moment those lovely eyes showed neither warmth nor anger, but were instead dark and un-naturally wide, and filled with such an expression of fear and apprehension that Nathaniel felt a lurching jolt in his chest.

His concern deepened as he noticed other things about her appearance that did not sit well with her outward show of charming loveliness: her straw bonnet was gone completely, her dark curls in disarray, several ringlets falling onto the creaminess of her shoulders, and dusty smears upon her pale gown and gloves. As if she might have fallen—or been pulled along against her will?

Nathaniel deliberately stepped out from beneath the sheltering oak. 'Good evening, Tennant.'

Elizabeth's heart began to pound loudly at the first sound of Nathaniel's voice, her relief immense as she turned to see him standing only feet away. Until, that is, she became as aware of the tension of the man at her side; Sir Rufus's arm had become rigid beneath the soft touch of her gloved fingers, his whole body seemingly coiled as if he might spring forwards and attack the younger man at any moment.

Under any other circumstances Elizabeth knew that Nathaniel, ten years younger and having been a soldier, was more than capable of besting the other man, but at this moment Sir Rufus was filled with a strength and purpose fuelled by insanity— and he was still carrying that pruning knife in his other hand!

All things which Nathaniel must be made aware of if he were to fully understand the danger of the situation. 'How lovely, Rufus; Lord Thorne has come to join us for dinner.' She ignored Nathaniel's start of surprise in favour of turning to smile warmly up into Sir Rufus's demented features.

For several tension-filled seconds she feared he had not even heard her, so intense was his expression of dislike as he glared his fury at Nathaniel's intrusion into this time with his 'beloved Harriet'.

But he finally appeared to become aware of

the encouraging warmth of Elizabeth's smile, the tension easing slightly in his arm, his expression softening as he turned to look down at her. 'I had thought we might spend our first evening here together alone, my dear.'

Elizabeth forced herself to continue to smile up into those wild pale blue eyes. 'We must not be selfish, Rufus. We must be prepared to share our good fortune and happiness with our friends and neighbours.'

'Of course.' He returned her smile approvingly. 'You are gracious as always, my dear Harriet.'

Elizabeth did not see Nathaniel's start of surprise this time, but she felt it in his sudden tension and saw it in the dark scowl that marred his brow when she turned to look across at him with pleading eyes. 'I trust you are free to join us for dinner, Lord Thorne?'

Nathaniel's initial anger at finding Elizabeth in company with Sir Rufus had first turned to puzzlement, quickly followed by utter confusion. It now turned to uneasy concern—after Tennant referred to Elizabeth as Harriet. Harriet Copeland? Giles's lover?

Elizabeth, hoping and praying that Nathaniel

would at last understand Sir Rufus's state of derangement, instead became aware of the surprised widening of his eyes as he looked at her searchingly. As if he were seeing her for the first time...

Which perhaps he was?

Nathaniel would have been a very young man when Lady Harriet Copeland had run off with Giles Tennant, but not so young he would not have at least seen the notorious countess. Now the final piece of the puzzle had been put in place by Sir Rufus, did Nathaniel finally see Elizabeth's physical resemblance to that lady?

The same resemblance which had, no doubt, instigated Sir Rufus Tennant's present madness...

Elizabeth's throat was so dry that she had difficulty swallowing before she said again, 'Oh, please do say that you can stay for dinner, Lord Thorne.'

There was no chance Nathaniel was not totally aware of the slight edge of hysteria to Elizabeth's urging, or of the silent pleading in those troubled blue eyes that looked at him so intently.

Or, indeed, the air of barely leashed madness that surrounded Sir Rufus Tennant!

'Yes,' Nathaniel answered calmly. 'Yes, of

course I would be happy to join the two of you. If Sir Rufus is sure I will not be intruding?' He turned to look enquiringly at the older man, eyes narrowing as he took note of the slightly unfocused wildness of Tennant's eyes, the unnatural flush to his cheeks. The knife that he held in his left hand, of which he did not even seem to be aware…

Had he used it to threaten Elizabeth with? God, this madman had mistaken Elizabeth for Harriet Copeland!

There was a surface resemblance, of course. The same dark curls. The same delicacy of features. Admittedly Lady Copeland had been much older than Elizabeth when she died, and her eyes had been green rather than blue, but the slender elegance of her figure was the same. Could Elizabeth actually be in some way related to the beautiful Countess of Westbourne?

Tennant mistaking Elizabeth for Lady Copeland was all too much of a coincidence in view of the letter Nathaniel had finally received from Gabriel Faulkner earlier today. His friend had announced his betrothal to Lady Diana Copeland—a love match, apparently, rather than the businesslike affair the other man had originally intended it should be—the eldest sister of the three. He had also written that their other best friend Dominic Vaughn was to marry Lady Diana's younger sister, Caroline.

Both those weddings would take place as soon as they had found and returned the youngest Copeland sister, Lady Elizabeth, to her sisters' anxiously awaiting arms.

Lady Elizabeth Copeland.

Elizabeth.

Could it possibly be the very same woman whom Nathaniel had found so irresistible this past few days? The same Elizabeth he had made love to so passionately? It was rather a large assumption for him to make, and yet the similarity between Harriet Copeland and Elizabeth was obvious, as were several other clues if one knew of them.

Elizabeth's sudden appearance in his aunt's London home almost three weeks ago after the two had met at the park… Gabriel had stated in his letter that Lady Elizabeth Copeland had been missing for almost four weeks now. Elizabeth's assurance of manner during Mrs Wilson's dinner party on Saturday and her innate elegance and refinement—all indications she had been brought up as a lady of quality rather than a subservient companion.

Nathaniel had believed Elizabeth was perhaps a young lady from an impoverished if genteel family, but they could all just as easily be attributed to the fact that she was, in fact, Lady Elizabeth Copeland, an earl's daughter.

Tennant seemed convinced of the fact that Elizabeth's second name, at least, was indeed Copeland!

Chapter Eighteen

Elizabeth had absolutely no idea as to Nathaniel's thoughts during these past few minutes of silence, but the look that glittered in the darkness of his eyes as he spotted the knife in Sir Rufus's hand indicated that he was at least aware of the other man's instability of temperament, as well as the precariousness of Elizabeth's position as she stood beside him.

'Rufus?' she turned to prompt lightly.

He smiled down at her. 'Of course Osbourne must stay to dinner, if that is what you wish, Harriet.'

Elizabeth swallowed down the nausea she felt each time this man called her by her mother's name instead of her own. She couldn't help shuddering inwardly when she contemplated what events could have led to his decline into madness.

Of course, it could simply be that Giles Tennant, having killed first Harriet and then himself, had initiated Sir Rufus's mental decline, in that he had lost in one day both his younger brother and the woman he himself had so obviously loved. Yet Elizabeth was inclined to think there was more to it than that, especially as Mrs Wilson had revealed earlier today that Sir Rufus had not cared for his brother as much as people had believed that he did, and that he'd been jealous of him from the moment of his birth.

How deep would that jealousy have been towards his much more handsome brother for having captivated the woman that he himself loved? Enough, perhaps, for Sir Rufus to have wished to destroy them both?

Elizabeth felt another cold shiver of apprehension down the length of her spine even as she suggested, 'Then shall we all go into the house?'

'An excellent idea.' Nathaniel stepped forwards to offer Elizabeth his arm, his gaze compelling on the paleness of her face until she had come to his side. He was instantly able to feel the trembling of her hand she placed it on his sleeve. 'Perhaps you should return that knife to the hothouse first, Tennant?' Nathaniel prompted.

'What? Oh.' Sir Rufus looked down at the knife in his hand as if seeing it for the first time. 'Of course,' he said and turned back into the hothouse.

It was exactly the opening that Nathaniel needed and he wasted no time in placing Elizabeth firmly to one side before stepping forwards to pull the door tightly closed behind Rufus Tennant and holding it there. 'Go, Elizabeth,' he instructed fiercely. 'Go now!' He wanted her in a place of safety before he opened the door and dealt with Tennant.

'But—'

'I am unsure how long I will be able to contain him!' Even now the older man had realised Nathaniel's intent and was trying to force the door open from the inside and the nine-glass windows that made up the top of the door would not withstand the force of a fist should Sir Rufus decide to use that method of escape.

'I will get help—'

'I do not care what you do—as long as you leave here immediately!' Even now Tennant had increased his efforts to free himself, tugging on the door with all the strength of his derangement, the knife still in his hand.

Tears flooded those beautiful blue eyes as Elizabeth seemed unable to move. 'Oh Nathaniel, he—he—'

'I know.' He winced as he imagined her terror during these past few minutes of being completely alone with a madman. And the danger was not yet over. 'We can talk of this later!' he said as the window beside the door handle was smashed outwards, quickly followed by Tennant's hand reaching through the jagged remains of glass to grasp Nathaniel's arm in a clawlike grip. 'Go, Elizabeth!' Nathaniel grated as he managed to keep the door closed.

Elizabeth had no intention of leaving Nathaniel to deal with this situation alone, instead looking frantically about her for something to help him in his efforts to contain the other man. She finally spotted some small decorative rocks in the garden bed a few feet away, dashing over to wrench one of them from the soil before running back and bringing it down painfully on Sir Rufus's clutching hand.

'Harriet!' Sir Rufus looked at her soulfully

through the glass-topped door, but made no effort to release his hold on Nathaniel's arm.

'Elizabeth,' she breathed raggedly, wincing as she brought the rock down on that grasping hand a second time. 'My name is Elizabeth, not Harriet!'

'That is a lie!' Sir Rufus's expression darkened furiously. 'A nasty vicious lie! Did Osbourne put you up to this?'

Elizabeth blinked. 'Nathaniel is but an innocent bystander—'

'Not so innocent!' Sir Rufus turned his vicious blue gaze on the younger man. 'Was the death of your horse not enough of a warning to keep your filthy hands and thoughts off Harriet? Do you wish me to teach you another lesson in manners—?'

'You killed Midnight?' Elizabeth gasped in shock as she stumbled back a step.

Sir Rufus looked pleased with himself. 'A little poison from one of the compounds I use for growing my roses mixed into his water bucket soon took care of him, yes.'

Not soon at all—Midnight's death had been slow

and agonising. And this man—this monster, was responsible for that death and Nathaniel's pain.

'And Hector?' Elizabeth glared at him. 'Did you have something to do with his disappearance?' Remembering Hector's recent growls every time this man came anywhere near him, and the unexplained abrasion on the dog's front paw, Elizabeth was sure that he had.

Sir Rufus smiled. 'He is such a trusting little animal that it was an easy thing to tie him up for an hour or so before then returning him to his grateful mistress.'

Elizabeth saw red at the pain and suffering this man had deliberately inflicted on innocent animals. 'You—truly—are—a—monster!' With each word Elizabeth brought her rock down on the back of the man's hand, who refused to release his grip despite the skin now being broken and blood running freely. Elizabeth felt sick at the sight of all that blood. But she felt sicker still at the thought of Sir Rufus escaping the hothouse!

'Harriet—'

'I am not Harriet!' Her voice rose angrily. 'Do you understand?' Her eyes flashed through the window at him. 'You have mistaken me for some-one else. Do you hear me? I am not Harriet!'

Nathaniel instantly felt concerned at the look of utter fury that possessed the other man's face. 'Elizabeth, do not incite him—'

'He is mad, Nathaniel!' Elizabeth cut angrily through his reasoning tone. 'Completely and utterly mad. Worse than his treatment of Midnight and Hector, I believe he might actually be a—a murderer!' she choked emotionally, the tears starting to fall hotly down her cheeks.

'Harriet—'

'Harriet is dead!' Elizabeth turned fiercely on Sir Rufus. 'Dead, do you hear? She has been dead these nine years or more!'

'No!' A look of horror washed over his face and Nathaniel felt the grip on his arm fall away as the other man staggered backwards, his face deathly pale, his gaze unfocused.

'Did you kill her?' Elizabeth stepped forwards to press against the broken hothouse window. 'Did you kill both my mother and your brother?' she demanded angrily.

If Nathaniel had needed any further confirmation as to Elizabeth's real identity, then he now had it. For his callous treatment of Midnight and Hector alone, this man deserved to be horse-whipped, but if Sir Rufus had actually killed Harriet Copeland and Giles Tennant all those years ago, as Elizabeth suspected, then he must be captured and presented to the law to be dealt with accordingly.

'Answer me!' she demanded coldly as Tennant continued to stare at her blankly. 'Did you kill my mother and your brother?'

Tennant blinked, a faint glimmer of awareness returning to those pale blue eyes. 'I loved her. And she loved me. We had to be together. But Giles stood in the way. So I killed him. But then Harriet became hysterical, accusing me of terrible things, and so I—I had no choice but to kill her too. Do you not see—?'

'I see perfectly,' Elizabeth said flatly, backing away, the bloodstained rock falling from her hand as she allowed the full horror of the past to wash over her.

Her mother had been wrong to leave her family ten years ago for the arms and love of a younger man, but Harriet would still have hoped one day to be able to resume some sort of relationship with her three daughters, if she had not fallen victim to Sir Rufus Tennant's warped and twisted sort of love. If he had not ended Harriet's and Giles's lives so prematurely.

'You really are a monster,' Elizabeth repeated dully. 'A cruel and heartless monster.' She turned away, only to find herself facing a shocked Mrs Wilson, as well as several gentlemen wearing livery that Elizabeth did not recognise. She could tell from the paleness of their faces that they had obviously witnessed part of Sir Rufus's conversation at least.

Waves of darkness began to wash over her and she swayed weakly.

'Nathaniel!' Mrs Wilson had time to warn sharply as he moved forwards just in time to catch her up in his arms as she fainted.

'It is incredible! Unbelievable!' Nathaniel's aunt gave a horrified shudder as she later sat in her parlour at Hepworth Manor. 'That Sir Rufus should have allowed us all to believe for so many years that Giles was responsible for killing Harriet Copeland, and then himself.' She shook her head vehemently. 'I am sure I shall never recover from the shock of it!'

Nathaniel was just as convinced that, once the immediacy of the scandal had passed, his aunt would recover well enough to discuss the story of Sir Rufus's guilt with her cronies once she returned to London. Nathaniel was less convinced that Elizabeth would make such a full recovery.

It had been fortunate that his aunt had come to Gifford House in her carriage in her own search for Elizabeth. She had remained in a faint in Mrs Wilson's carriage for the time it had taken to bring Viscount Rutledge, as local magistrate, to Gifford House to take charge of the captured Sir Rufus, that elderly gentleman sternly assuring them that the insane man would be dealt with as the full measure of the law allowed in such cases.

Elizabeth had only returned to consciousness as Mrs Wilson's carriage came to a halt in the grounds of Hepworth Manor, her face still deathly pale. She had entered the house and informed them distantly that she wished to be alone in her bedchamber. A wish Mrs Wilson had instantly protested, but which Nathaniel knew she very much needed if she were to be allowed to regain some of her usual composure; he could not begin to imagine how she must feel after learning that her mother had not been killed by her young lover at all, but by a man whose jealousy of his younger brother had in the end driven him completely mad.

For there could be no further doubt that Elizabeth was indeed one of the daughters of the late Countess of Westbourne.

It placed Nathaniel in something of a dilemma as to how he should proceed, or if it was possible for him to proceed at all…

He had played fast and loose with Elizabeth Thompson these past few days, both physically and emotionally, stealing kisses and making love to her. Except she was not Elizabeth Thompson, humble lady's companion, but Lady Elizabeth Copeland, daughter of an earl, and ward of the present Earl of Westbourne, Nathaniel's own good friend; Gabe would be honour bound to demand marriage or call Nathaniel out if he were to ever learn of his reprehensible behaviour towards one of his wards. Just as Nathaniel was surely now honour bound to reveal his behaviour to Gabriel…

Which was no way for any two people to begin a marriage, especially when Nathaniel knew Elizabeth would never believe now that he had any true or enduring feelings for her.

'I apologise for having deceived you, Mrs Wilson.' Elizabeth came to stand awkwardly in that lady's parlour where Mrs Wilson and Letitia now sat together following a dinner from which Elizabeth had excused herself; she could not even bear the thought of food after the shocking events of earlier today.

Any more than she could have sat down at the dinner table and suffered Nathaniel's coldly accusing gaze…

Midnight would never have died if it had not been for Sir Rufus's obsession with Elizabeth's resemblance to her mother and his desire to hurt any other man who came near her. Hector would not have suffered as he had, either.

Nor could Nathaniel, or indeed anyone else in the area, be unaware of her real identity, just as they must all be wondering about the reason for her duplicity.

She had not seen Nathaniel since going to her bedchamber earlier, so she wasn't certain about his feelings, but it was not too difficult to guess at his disgust. Not only had his horse died unnecessarily, but she was a liar and an imposter; she could only imagine how he must now despise her.

'Not at all, my dear. I am sure that you had your reasons.' Mrs Wilson smiled as she patted the cushion on the sofa beside her encouragingly.

Oh, yes, Elizabeth had had her reasons. To escape the offer of marriage from Lord Faulkner and at the same time seek adventure in London. Both of which now seemed rather ridiculous in light of recent events, although without her presence here at Hepworth Manor none of them would ever have discovered the truth concerning the tragic deaths so many years ago…

Elizabeth still trembled to think of what had happened earlier. Her fear when she realised Sir Rufus was not in his right mind. Her terror when she puzzled as to how she was to escape his clutches. Her shock when he revealed he had poisoned Midnight and held Hector captive. Her fury once he had confirmed killing her mother.

She sat down beside Mrs Wilson, her hands trembling as she clasped them tightly together. 'I behaved both foolishly and naïvely,' she said dully.

'And in doing so I have lied to you and—and to your family.' Elizabeth could not even bring herself to say Nathaniel's name, so deep was her distress at knowing how he must now hold her in contempt and distrust.

'I should have guessed who you were, of course.' Mrs Wilson tutted to herself. 'Now that I know of the connection I can clearly see that you have a definite look of your mother,' she added gently as Elizabeth looked up questioningly. 'Oh, yes, I knew your mother. Quite well, as it happens. She was the most beautiful of women, both inside as well as out.'

'Then I cannot resemble her in the slightest!' Elizabeth protested.

'But of course you can,' Mrs Wilson said reprovingly. 'I knew from the very first, when you succeeded in rescuing that scamp Hector from the wheels of a passing carriage, that you possessed a good and kind heart.'

Elizabeth smiled wanly as she shook her head. 'I believe you are the one who is now being kind.'

Mrs Wilson placed her hand reassuringly on Elizabeth's. 'Not at all, my dear,' she said briskly.

'And perhaps you should not think too badly of your mother...'

Elizabeth had never really known what to think of her mother's behaviour. To leave one's husband and children was shocking indeed. And yet... There had always been an element of doubt—of hope—in Elizabeth's thoughts concerning her mother's abandonment of her family.

She blinked back the tears. 'Did she ever love any of us, do you suppose?'

'I am sure that she loved her daughters very much.' Mrs Wilson looked most concerned. 'I cannot speak from experience, you understand, having spent almost twenty wonderful years married to the man that I loved, but Harriet's marriage was an arrangement between her parents and your father. He was much older than her, you realise, already over forty to Harriet's eighteen years when they were married. Totally besotted with her, too, of course.' Mrs Wilson smiled ruefully. 'And I am certain that Harriet respected and liked Marcus Copeland.'

'Except respect and liking are not always enough to sustain a marriage, are they?' Elizabeth now knew that only too well herself. In fact, she very much doubted, in light of her feelings for Nathaniel, that she would ever marry at all; it would be unfair to any man to always be comparing him to Nathaniel. And finding him wanting.

'No, they are not.' Mrs Wilson sighed sadly. 'I am sure, if your mother had been allowed the time in which to do so, that she would have tried to broker some sort of arrangement with your father so that she might see her daughters again, at least.'

It was what Elizabeth had always wanted to believe. What she had to believe now that she knew it was Rufus Tennant who had ended Harriet's life rather than the young man her mother had fallen in love with.

'And now I believe it is time we saw to returning you to your sisters,' Mrs Wilson prompted gently.

'Yes,' Elizabeth confirmed huskily, knowing she wished for nothing more than to be encircled within Diana's and Caroline's arms as she sobbed the truth of the past to them.

Except, perhaps, to be held in Nathaniel's arms… which would not happen. Not now. Not ever.

Elizabeth stood up. 'I believe, with your permission, that I will return to my bedchamber and try to rest until we leave for London in the morning.'

The older woman chuckled softly. 'I do not believe that Lady Elizabeth Copeland requires the permission of one such as I to do exactly as she pleases.'

Perhaps not, but at this moment she did not feel very much like Lady Elizabeth Copeland. What she truly felt was battered and bruised, inside as well as out. She—

'Ah, here you are, Nathaniel.' Mrs Wilson turned to greet her nephew warmly as he came through to the parlour after having enjoyed his brandy and cigar alone in the dining room. 'Lady Elizabeth and I were just discussing leaving here tomorrow for London, and then returning her to her family in Hampshire soon after.'

Hooded lids hid the expression in his eyes as he looked across at Elizabeth. He noted the drawn pallor of her cheeks. The bruised darkness beneath her eyes. The slight trembling of her body as she stood up. He also recognised that rather than look at him, she preferred instead to stare down at her daintily slippered feet.

His mouth tightened as he recognised the distance that now yawned between them. 'The latter will not be necessary, Aunt.' He stepped further into the room to stand in front of the fireplace. 'I happen to know that both of Lady Elizabeth's sisters are at this moment in residence at Westbourne House in town.'

Elizabeth looked up at him sharply. 'How do you know that?'

'I finally received a correspondence from Gabriel Faulkner earlier today. In it he related to me that our friend Lord Dominic Vaughn, the Earl of Blackstone, is to marry Lady Caroline, and that he is to marry Lady Diana—'

'No!' Elizabeth gasped, her cheeks taking on a grey tinge. 'I know absolutely nothing of Caroline's involvement with the Earl of Blackstone— how could I?' Indeed, Elizabeth had never even met the gentleman. 'But I cannot allow Diana to sacrifice herself in marriage to Lord Faulkner! She—'

'Not even if it is a love match?' Nathaniel asked gently.

'But it is not!' She gave a pained groan. 'Diana is to marry Malcolm Castle. She does not even know Lord Faulkner; she can only have agreed to marry him now because of his threat to cast us all out of our home unless one of us agreed to marry him!'

'Does that sound like the sort of thing Westbourne would do, Nathaniel?' Mrs Wilson frowned.

'No, it does not,' he confirmed. 'I assure you that you are mistaken in the matter, Elizabeth,' he said definitely as he turned to her. 'Westbourne may have started out feeling obligated to marry one of his wards, but I assure you he is now completely smitten with Diana. And she is equally smitten with him.'

'No—'

'Yes,' Nathaniel insisted firmly. 'They all await your return before both marriages will take place.'

It made no sense to Elizabeth. Not Caroline's involvement with the unknown Earl of Blackstone, and certainly not Diana's agreement to marry the Earl of Westbourne.

There had been an understanding for years between Diana and Malcolm Castle, the only son of the local squire; indeed, it was the existence of that understanding which had allowed Caroline and Elizabeth to run away from Hampshire in the first place, safe in the knowledge that Lord

Faulkner would not be able to force Diana into marriage with him.

What pressure could he possibly have brought to bear on Diana for her to have abandoned Malcolm in favour of marrying the earl, after all?

'I do not understand…' Elizabeth allowed the letter Nathaniel had received from Lord Faulkner to flutter down onto the desktop in the library where he had brought her a few minutes ago so that she might read it for herself.

Nathaniel leant back against his desk, arms folded across his chest. 'It seems perfectly clear to me, Elizabeth, that Diana's previous understanding has come to an end and that she and Gabriel have now fallen in love.'

'But—' she gave a dazed shake of her head '—Diana has intended marrying Malcolm since childhood.'

He looked rueful. 'I believe you saw Gabe when he visited me at my aunt's house a week or so ago?'

Elizabeth blinked up at him. 'Yes.'

'Handsome, is he not?'

Delicate colour warmed her cheeks. 'Very.'

Nathaniel's smile faded. 'And how would this Malcolm's looks measure against such handsomeness?'

Her eyes widened indignantly. 'You make my sister sound the most fickle sort of woman—'

'Merely a discerning one,' he corrected harshly.

'But—but what of Lord Faulkner's past scandal?'

His mouth tightened. 'As to that, I can only assume that Gabe has told your sister the truth of it and that she has, quite rightly so, believed him.'

'The truth of it...?'

'It is not my secret to share, Elizabeth,' he said. 'I have only allowed you to read Gabriel's letter at all so that you might stop these feelings of guilt concerning his marriage to your sister—'

'But of course I feel guilty!' Elizabeth's cheeks were flushed with temper. 'Thank goodness the marriage has not already taken place. I must return to London immediately.'

He frowned. 'You will return to town in the morning with my aunt and me as arranged—'

Her eyes flashed. 'You are no longer in a position to tell me what I can or cannot do, Nathaniel!'

He eyed her wryly. 'Was I ever?'

Elizabeth frowned. So much had happened today, so many awful things, that hearing Diana was betrothed to their guardian was just too much for her to take in. Admittedly she and Caroline had never seen Diana's attraction to the slightly shallow and pompous Malcolm Castle, but they had accepted it. To now learn that her always calm, no-nonsense sister was to marry a man of Lord Gabriel Faulkner's dangerous good looks and reputation seemed incredible to her.

'No, you weren't,' she declared. 'Now, if you will excuse me, I really should go upstairs and finish my packing.'

'By all means,' Nathaniel drawled drily. 'But if I know anything of Gabriel—and I do—your objections to the marriage will count for nought.'

Her eyes sparkled a deep and angry blue. 'And if I know anything of Diana—and I do,' she added derisively, 'then Caroline and I will have no trouble whatsoever in persuading her to rethink her decision to marry Lord Faulkner!' She whirled on one heel and swept from the room, her chin held defiantly high.

Nathaniel's humour faded as soon as Elizabeth

had gone. She had looked every inch the daughter of an earl just now. A young and singularly beautiful lady of quality now placed far beyond his reach by his own actions.

Chapter Nineteen

'——And I repeat, this situation of Elizabeth retiring to her bedchamber whenever it is known Lord Thorne is due to visit Westbourne House simply cannot continue!'

'But we cannot force Elizabeth to leave her bedchamber.'

'It is not my intention to use force, as such.'

'Then what do you intend to use?'

Elizabeth, sitting inside her bedchamber listening to her two sisters arguing in loud whispers outside the hallway on the other side of the closed door, was most interested to hear the answer to that question too.

Although the fact that it was the normally calm and no-nonsense Diana who was arguing heatedly for ejecting her from the bedchamber, and the impetuous and forceful Caroline reasoning against it, was a cause for bemusement.

Elizabeth had found many changes to her two sisters since her arrival at Westbourne House three days ago...

The hurried two-day journey up from Devon had been arduous but uneventful, Elizabeth's time spent secluded in the carriage with Mrs Wilson and Letitia, whilst Nathaniel travelled separately in his own carriage. The two met only when they stopped for luncheon or to stay at an inn for the night, times when it was not too difficult for them to continue to avoid each other's company.

It was enough that she now fully understood her feelings for a man whom she knew could never love her in return, without having to witness the disillusionment with which Nathaniel must view her now that he knew of the lie she had lived in order to enter his aunt's household.

Elizabeth's arrival at Westbourne House had been tearful as well as eliciting many surprises. Tearful, because she was as glad to see her sisters again as they were to see her, the three of them crying together once Elizabeth had related the true sequence of events concerning their mother's death. Surprising, because all of Nathaniel's claims concerning her sisters had proved to be true. Including Diana's very real love for Gabriel Faulkner...

Being introduced to Lord Dominic Vaughn, a tall, dark and dangerous-looking man, with a livid scar running the length of the left side of his face, and the man Caroline had fallen in love with, had instantly filled Elizabeth with a feeling she had seen him before.

It was a feeling she had initially dismissed as being ridiculous; if she had ever met the broodingly handsome Dominic Vaughn before then she would certainly have remembered him!

Until she recalled that day in the park a few weeks ago when she had rescued Hector from beneath the wheels of a passing carriage... A carriage driven by a handsome dark-haired man with a scar running down the left side of his face and with a young and beautiful woman seated beside him who had so reminded her of Caroline.

A discussion of their movements had confirmed that it had, indeed, been Caroline and Dominic, after all! Indeed, Caroline's adventures since arriving in London were more shocking than surprising. Not least because it had been revealed that Nathaniel had received the cuts and bruises to his face and his broken ribs in defence of Caroline during a drunken brawl at a gentlemen's gambling club owned by Dominic!

Even more astonishing was the way in which her normally headstrong sister now consulted Lord Vaughn on everything, from the gown she was to wear for dinner that evening to the arrangements for their wedding due to take place the following week. A deferment the arrogant and authoritative Earl of Blackstone did not exploit, but instead chose to indulge by being equally as lovingly accommodating to Caroline's every need.

The two were obviously so much in love with each other that it was almost painful for Elizabeth, deep in the throes of her unrequited feelings for Nathaniel, to be in their company.

Most startling of all to Elizabeth were the changes she found in Diana. Always dutiful, ever putting others before her own wants or needs, these few short weeks apart, and Diana's unmistakable love for Gabriel, had turned her into a self-confident young woman who knew her own mind and was no longer afraid or reluctant to speak it and had needs that Gabriel was only too happy to comply with, the love he felt for the serenely confident Diana glittering in the approving midnight-blue eyes with which he constantly watched her.

Indeed, it was, as Nathaniel had already stated in Devon, and which, out of ignorance of her sister's feelings, Elizabeth had at the time disputed, clearly another love match.

It seemed that only she was miserable in the midst of this strange turn of events. Oh, not because she in the least begrudged her sisters their obvious happiness, or the handsome men with whom they were in love, but because for the first time in her life Elizabeth felt truly alone. The closeness to her sisters was still there, but tempered by the other emotional demands with which Diana and Caroline were obviously so happily engrossed.

It was because Elizabeth was in such despair over Nathaniel that she felt herself alone even when surrounded by the people who loved her. She often chose to retire to her bedchamber rather than sit as a silent witness to those love affairs.

And she always chose to go there whenever Nathaniel was to visit Westbourne House.

However, as Diana had already stated so firmly, and Elizabeth had decided for herself this past few minutes, this situation could not be allowed to continue. Especially as Elizabeth and Nathaniel were to be the two witnesses to the Copeland ladies' marriages the following week.

Elizabeth drew in a deep breath before standing up and throwing open the door, instantly silencing her sisters' heated conversation as the two turned to look at her guiltily. 'I believe it is Diana's intention to use the argument of good manners in order to attain my agreement to leave my bedchamber, is that not so?' she murmured drily.

Indeed, Diana was the first to recover as she turned to Elizabeth, her flushed face partly obscured by the bouquet of red carnations which she carried. 'These are for you.' She thrust the bouquet into Elizabeth's surprised hands.

Elizabeth gave a wobbly laugh. 'Having already decided to join you all downstairs for dinner, after all, I assure you it was not necessary for you to bring me flowers in order to persuade me.' Nevertheless, she could not resist drawing in the deep and gratifying perfume of the beautiful blossoms.

Diana shook her head, blonde curls dancing at her temples. 'The flowers did not come from me.'

Elizabeth frowned slightly as she looked up at her eldest sister. 'Then from whom?'

'Lord Thorne,' Caroline was the one to announce with satisfaction.

Elizabeth felt the colour drain from her cheeks even as her arms tightened possessively about the beautiful blooms. 'From Nathaniel?' she breathed disbelievingly.

'Ah ha!' Caroline pounced knowingly. 'I knew it! I told Dominic only last night—'

'Caroline.' Diana's rebuke, although softly made, was nevertheless heeded as Diana now looked at Elizabeth searchingly. 'Elizabeth, Lord Thorne has been in Gabriel's study with him this past half an hour, and is now awaiting you there so that you might talk privately together,' she explained gently.

For three days Elizabeth had kept her own counsel concerning her feelings for Nathaniel, determinedly hiding her heartache in light of Diana's and Caroline's obvious happiness, but she saw now that her silence had only succeeded in becoming a cause for speculation.

Although she was at a loss to know quite what Nathaniel wished to talk to her about, just as she had no idea why he should have brought her red carnations.

Nathaniel paced Westbourne's candlelit study, his impatience barely contained as he waited to see if Elizabeth would agree to speak with him. Although he believed not; she had succeeded in avoiding his company completely since their return to London and he saw no reason why that aversion to his company should have changed.

It had seemed like a good idea at the time, but perhaps, after Tennant's madness that day in the hothouse, he should not have brought her flowers? Although he had deliberately chosen blooms as unlike Tennant's roses as he could find at this time of year.

Damn it, he did not even remember the last time he had brought flowers for a woman—if indeed he ever had—and now he had bungled—

He turned suddenly towards the door as it quietly opened, his breath catching in his throat as Elizabeth stood framed in the doorway. She looked both pale and fragile against the darkness of the hallway behind her, her lashes resting on shadows above hollow cheeks, her mouth—those beautiful kissable lips—unsmiling above the tilt of her chin.

'You wished to speak with me, Lord Thorne?' Even her voice was different, low and husky, and totally lacking in the challenge he had come to expect from her.

Nathaniel's heart sank, in recognition of the changes in her and the fact that she once again addressed him so formally. 'Would you come inside and close the door, please?'

The heavy weight of her lashes rose as she looked across at him, the expression in those deep blue eyes guarded. 'If you feel it is completely necessary?'

Nathaniel's mouth tightened. 'I do.'

Elizabeth swallowed hard as she turned to close the door behind her before stepping further into the austereness of the room Gabriel had chosen to make his study. 'I believe I owe you an apology, my lord,'

A frown appeared on his face. 'I can think of no reason—'

'I have been less than polite these past three

days.' Having made her decision to cease avoiding Nathaniel's company, she did not intend to indulge in any half measures. 'Which was particularly ungrateful of me considering that I owe you my very life.'

'Come now, you are being melodramatic—'

'Not in the least.' Elizabeth stepped further into the candlelight, a slender figure in a gown of pale cream, a matching ribbon arranged in the darkness of her curls. 'Sir Rufus was truly mad, and his emotional instability was as like to turn murderous once he realised I truly was not my mother.'

A nerve pulsed in his tightly clenched jaw. 'And I should have known from the first that you were not what you seemed.'

Elizabeth gave a rueful smile. 'But I believe that you did realise there was something amiss with my role as lady's companion.'

'Perhaps,' he admitted. 'Unfortunately, that re-alisation did not prevent me from…taking certain liberties.'

Elizabeth felt the warmth in her cheeks as she recalled the intimacies she had shared with this man. 'I believe I am guilty of taking the same liberties where you are concerned.'

Nathaniel almost groaned aloud as he felt himself swelling, hardening—physically aching inside his pantaloons at the mere thought of the delicate touch of Elizabeth's hands and mouth upon his rigid shaft.

He turned away to stare down into the crackling fire in the hearth so that she should not see the evidence of his physical reaction to those memories. 'I am attempting to apologise to you for my previous behaviour, Elizabeth—'

'I would rather you did not!' she protested sharply.

Nathaniel turned back to her. 'In the circumstances, it is the least that I owe you.'

'You owe me nothing!' Elizabeth gave an agitated shake of her head, dark curls bouncing.

He drew in a harsh breath. 'I have spoken privately to Westbourne this evening concerning my behaviour in Devon.'

'What?' Elizabeth gasped in obvious dismay.

'My earlier behaviour towards Lady Elizabeth Copeland was reprehensible. Unforgivable. As such, it required that I either offer marriage or give Westbourne, as your guardian, the satisfaction of a duel—'

'That is preposterous!' Elizabeth protested desperately.

'—and as such I have agreed to meet Gabriel at a time and place of his choosing,' Nathaniel finished gravely.

Elizabeth stilled, chilled to the bone. Indeed, she felt as if ice had entered her veins. Rather than even contemplate the idea of marriage to her, Nathaniel had chosen to risk his life in a duel with a man who Diana had already confided was adept with both the sword and pistol. Not only that, but if both men survived such a duel, Nathaniel would surely have irrevocably destroyed his friendship with Gabriel. A fate he obviously preferred rather than suffer a lifetime of unhappiness with her as his wife.

Elizabeth felt ill. Utterly sickened. Indeed, she was not sure if she could even stand on her own two feet for much longer.

'I have not told you any of this in order to hurt you, Elizabeth…'

Hurt her? She was beyond being hurt by his

admission. Indeed, it felt as if he'd reached inside her chest and ripped her very heart from her.

'Elizabeth…?'

She gave a choked laugh. 'I am not hurt, Nathaniel! I am—you would rather risk being killed in a duel than offer marriage to me? An offer you have no idea I would even accept?' Her face was ashen as she looked across at him.

'Of course not,' he exclaimed.

'Then—'

'Elizabeth, I have chosen the latter option as the only way in which I might prove to you that—damn it!' he grated harshly, crossing the room in two strides to stand in front of her as he reached out to take her hands in his, alarmed as he felt the chill of her skin through the lace of her gloves. 'Elizabeth.' He dropped down onto one knee in front of her. 'My darling, beautiful Elizabeth, will you do me the honour of agreeing to consider becoming my wife?'

She stared down at him as if he were the one who had gone mad rather than Rufus Tennant. 'But you have just said—'

'I have attempted to explain to you—to prove to you—that I am not making this offer under duress, but because it is what I most dearly wish to do.'

Elizabeth looked utterly confused. 'I do not understand.'

Nathaniel looked up at her earnestly. 'I love you, Elizabeth. I have loved you from the first, I believe. Certainly I could not stand to have Tennant anywhere near you. And even Viscount Rutledge was in danger of incurring my wrath with his attentiveness to you at my aunt's dinner party,' he acknowledged bitterly. 'I love you deeply, Elizabeth. With every part of me.' His hands tightened about hers. 'And if I have to fight one of my closest friends in a duel in order to prove that to you, then that is what I shall do.'

The only part of this muddled explanation that mattered to her was that he claimed to love her! 'You are truly in love with me?'

'So much so that these past three days of having you avoid me have been a tortuous hell for me,' he groaned, his face pale, his eyes glittering darkly in the firelight. 'Darling Elizabeth, can you not see I am attempting—clumsily, I admit it—to woo you?'

'That is why you brought me flowers?'

He scowled. 'Tennant's behaviour ruled out red roses, but—will you not please give me a second chance? At least the opportunity to show you how much I love and adore you? The chance to persuade you into learning to love me in return? I will do anything, be anything, if you will only allow me to do that, my dearest Elizabeth!'

That sudden chill inside her melted with the suddenness of a tidal wave as her own love for him threatened to overwhelm her. She looked down at the emotion shining in the clear depths of his eyes and knew it to be love for her. Nathaniel loved her. Loved her so much he was willing to fight a duel with one of his best friends in order to prove it to her.

She moistened dry lips. 'And if I refuse your offer?'

He flinched. 'Then I am afraid you will give me no choice but to follow you about as slavishly as Hector. To become such a nuisance you might eventually take pity upon me and throw me some scraps of your affection.'

Elizabeth gave a choked laugh at the very thought of this arrogantly assured man ever behaving in such a manner. 'After you have fought a duel with my guardian over my honour, of course!'

Nathaniel eyed her warily. 'Are you laughing at me?'

'Never that.' She shook her head as she dropped down onto her knees in front of him before releasing her hands to cradle each side of his dearly beloved face. 'Nathaniel, the offer I am refusing is the one of you persuading me into loving you. I already love you,' she told him huskily. 'I love you so much that—' she gave an emotional laugh '—even to have seen you this past three days would have been an agony of emotions for me! To have looked upon you and known that you now saw me only as the daughter of Harriet Copeland, a woman who—'

'Whose only sin was to love more deeply than was perhaps wise,' Nathaniel finished firmly. 'I am not proud of this admission, Elizabeth, but if by some mischance you had been married to another when we met, then I am afraid I would have behaved no differently than Giles Tennant did ten years ago and attempted to beguile you from your husband and family.'

Elizabeth gazed at him wonderingly. 'You would?'

'I would have had no choice,' he said honestly. 'You really love me?' he added incredulously.

'Really. Truly. Eternally,' she confirmed huskily, that love shining in the deep blue of her eyes as she looked up at him adoringly, no longer having any need to hide it from him or anyone else. 'Do you suppose—is it possible that the two of us might be married at the same time as my sisters?'

Nathaniel took her into the warmth of his arms. 'I will make it so,' he vowed fiercely. 'Now, for heaven's sake, kiss me, Elizabeth!'

Something which she was only too happy, indeed eager, to do.

And so it was that five days later the Ladies Elizabeth, Caroline and Diana Copeland were joined in marriage to the Earls of Osbourne, Blackstone and Westbourne respectively.

* * * * *

HISTORICAL

Large Print

MARRIED TO A STRANGER
Louise Allen

When Sophia Langley learns of her estranged fiancé's death, the last thing she expects is a shock proposal from his twin brother! A marriage of convenience it may be, but Sophie cannot fight the desire she feels for her reluctant husband...

A DARK AND BROODING GENTLEMAN
Margaret McPhee

Sebastian Hunter's nights, once spent carousing, are now spent in the shadows of Blackloch Hall—that is until Phoebe Allardyce interrupts his brooding. After catching her thieving, Sebastian resolves to keep an eye on this provocative little temptress!

SEDUCING MISS LOCKWOOD
Helen Dickson

Against all advice, Juliet Lockwood begins working for the notorious Lord Dominic Lansdowne. Juliet's addition to his staff is pure temptation for Dominic, but honour binds him from seduction...*unless, of course, he makes her his wife!*

THE HIGHLANDER'S RETURN
Marguerite Kaye

Alasdhair Ross was banished for courting the laird's daughter, Ailsa. Six years later, toils and troubles have shaped him into a man set on returning to claim what's rightfully his. When Ailsa sees him, she knows a reckoning is irresistibly inevitable...

MILLS &
BOON